POPLAR HILL

Book design by Industrial Myth & Magic

Hardback ISBN 978-0-9827115-9-0
Paperrback ISBN 978-1-960082-01-5
e-book ISBN 978-1386935292

Wilderness House Press
145 Foster Street
Littleton MA 01460
www.wildernesshousepress.com

PAPERBACK EDITION

Introduction

On Writing this Novel

POPLAR HILL IS A REAL PLACE. Kitty Stevenson was a real person. Barb and Vince are real as are Joe, Cozzi, Sam, Betty, and Herman the Vermin. I borrowed their souls for this novel. Mandy Betts is an amalgam of real and imagined Pentecostal preachers I've met over the years. Little Sophie and her family are just made up stories of ordinary Jewish folk caught up in the Holocaust. Growing up in New York City in the 1950's I got to know many Holocaust survivors. I hope I have done their collective stories justice. That said, this is fiction. All the dialog is fiction. Most of the stories that make up this novel are based very loosely on stories I heard growing up. Where memories recalled one thing but history recorded another, I chose to use the more dramatic of the two stories.

SRG
March 3 2019

POPLAR HILL

a novel

Stephen Ramey Glines

Wilderness House Press

PAPERBACK EDITION

Prologue

Kitty's Wake — July 1, 1994

"CAN YOU COME UP FOR ME WAKE?" she said in her mock Scottish accent.

"Gee Mom, I didn't know you were dead," said Jimmy, laughing.

"Well James, I'm not ... yet," said Kitty, "But I am on that slippery slope. Besides, a wake is the best party a person can have but the guest of honor rarely gets to enjoy it. I plan on enjoying mine!"

By the time Jimmy arrived in Poplar Hill, word had gotten out that Kitty was having a wake, a living wake and it was going to be an event. Everyone in Pictou county knew about it.

"How many people are you expecting?" Jimmy asked.

"Oh, a few hundred, I suppose," was the answer.

Jimmy didn't believe it. Twenty or thirty people, he thought, so he set out all the chairs he could find in the house, about fifteen, at the top of a natural amphitheater in the back yard.

The first hint that he was wrong came around five the next morning when he woke to the *beep, beep, beep* of a truck backing up.

"Go down and make them coffee," his mother yelled from her bedroom. "That would be the CBC crew from Halifax, up to film me wake."

This was followed almost immediately by a crash at the back door.

"Hello Kit," boomed a voice from the kitchen below. It was Earl, the dairy farmer down the road. "The people from the home are here and want to move their kitchen into your garage. I'm going to cut the field for the cars. Now, I'm only going to cut about ten acres since it's not really ready for haying yet, but you should have room for a few hundred cars if I calculate right."

A few minutes later Jimmy was dressed, and Kitty was standing in the doorway of her bedroom looking completely disheveled. "I'll make my grand entrance in about an hour, after I put myself together," she said with the biggest grin Jimmy had ever seen on her.

By the time Jimmy got downstairs, he could hear Earl on his tractor out in the field mowing. Someone from the Odd Fellows Retirement Home had started a big percolator of coffee in the kitchen, and a coffee-filled thermos was on the kitchen table for early comers. It wasn't even 6 a.m. but there were already several dozen cars and a large truck in the field. Two cars from local radio stations were parked on the front lawn, and two TV remote trucks were blocking the front of the driveway. A harried producer was yelling instructions to a grip about cabling.

The garage was now filled with industrial-grade restaurant equipment borrowed from the Odd Fellows in Pictou and the smell of bacon grease soon rose into the air as the four cooks and six servers prepared to cook breakfast and lunch for ... hundreds.

About eight a.m., Kitty was ready to make her grand entrance. The diamonds were real, the emeralds and jade necklace were real, but to anyone who inquired she would say, "Oh heavens no, they're paste. The real ones are in the vault in New York." Kitty loved saying that to people. It left everyone from farmer to "Socially Registered snoot" scratching their heads, wondering. Jimmy loved it. About the only

4

thing Kitty wore that wasn't insured for thousands of dollars was the green cotton dress she had bought in Halifax for $30 because it matched her jade necklace.

When Kitty was sure she looked the part of "the grand dame" (with the word "grand" pronounced with a rolled "r"), she carefully snuck down the stairs making sure no one was in the kitchen so that she could perform her morning rituals in private. These included taking a dozen pills chugged with a cup of coffee. She preferred doing all that in private. When she was ready she stood up from the kitchen table, threw her shoulders back, thrust her chin forward and marched into the sunlight.

By now there were thirty or forty people milling around in the yard. Kitty made the rounds, inspecting preparations like a general before a battle. She made little suggestions that were swiftly acted upon with a big smile and a "Yes Chef."

She was the boss, or rather, had been. The twenty or so people from the Odd Fellows Home had mostly worked for her as either cooks or as part of the dining room staff. For over twenty years Kitty had been the undisputed queen of the Odd Fellows kitchen.

She was, after all, the only internationally licensed and certified "Master Chef" in all of Pictou County, and one of less than a half dozen in the entire country. Of all the places in Nova Scotia Kitty could have cooked, she chose to make the Odd Fellows Retirement Home her kitchen.

While Kitty and her staff boiled dozens of pounds of peas, mashed potatoes, and roasted meat for the fifty or so residents of the home, she conducted gourmet cooking classes for the farmers wives and laid-off machinists that constituted her crew. They loved her for it. They had their very own Julia Child in the kitchen. Kitty not only looked like Julia Child, big, tall and buxom, but she had the same demeanor, and high pitched squeaky voice. They were cut from the same cloth, doppelgangers.

The lawn sloped gently away from the house so Jimmy

thought that anyone attending his mother's wake could sit in the chairs up by the house or on the grass, while anyone who wanted to speak could stand at the bottom of the natural amphitheater, bordered by brambles.

When Kitty saw the arrangement, she thought it might work better if the chairs were at the bottom of the incline. She enlisted the help of some children who were scurrying about to move a plastic lawn chair to a position more to her liking. She dropped into the chair and immediately fell over backwards, doing a full somersault, into the brambles.

She lay on her back in astonishment. Her first thought was, *Did I break anything?* She wiggled her legs, arms and neck and finally her nose and concluded that all but her dignity was intact. Next she carefully checked her necklace and earrings and concluded that they too were intact. Finally, she looked up and said to the gathering crowd, "I could use a hand here." A TV cameraman put down his camera and waded into the brambles to help. Kitty promised him some extra cookies to take home as he pulled her to her feet. Dusting herself off, she bowed to the assembled, but speechless, crowd and announced that she thought that James was better at arranging chairs than she was. The laughter broke the tension when Kitty announced to the multitudes that the arrangements were, "Splendid altogether."

As noon approached, the smell of cooking hamburgers and chicken filled the air, and the crowd had swelled to more than two hundred. The reporters, there were now about a dozen, TV, print and radio, were having a field day taking pictures and interviewing everyone willing to be interviewed. Some were interviewed multiple times.

Anyone who appeared to be a local dignitary — and that included anyone dressed better than the average farmer — was made to run the gauntlet of reporters, giving their name and having their pictures taken as they walked from the road to the back yard. For many, it was extreme flattery and more peacocks and peahens emerged from the gauntlet than entered it. Some of the dignitaries were real, as real as there are such things in Poplar Hill and the rest imagined themselves to be. Kitty was pleased.

There was the retired politician, a respected member of parliament in his day whose motto was "No soft soap with Harvey A., vote him in election day." Kitty had a full collection of soap dishes that Harvey had given her over the years. He had always made it a point of visiting Kitty when he was running for re-election because she listened to what he had to say and, even when she vehemently disagreed with him, she would draw him out as few others could; besides, she always fed him well and sent him on his way with a glass of sherry. Harvey always gave a great interview and the reporters loved it. He played the Grand Old Man to Kitty's Grand Dame image.

Not to be outdone were the two gentlemen in full kilt, men Kitty had called her "Gentlemen Callers." One, Wendell MacEamailinn, had spent his life in the Canadian Air Force. He had never been married and had retired as a brigadier. He always showed up unexpectedly at her door wearing a kilt, with a military jacket bedecked with colorful ribbons. Kitty had asked him several times what the ribbons were for and had always gotten something that sounded to her like "brahump bump bump" in return. Everyone whispered that he was important and famous but Kitty had never heard of him and his name never came up in the Canadian media so Kitty really didn't know what he might be famous for. Of course, Kitty would feed him whenever he showed up and send him on his way with a glass of sherry or two. She often wondered if he was trying to get up the nerve to ask her on a date, but it had never come to that.

The other gentleman, in a rather more traditional kilt, was said to be the chief of a minor branch of an obscure clan. His clan had, apparently, been encouraged to leave Scotland for one reason or another and had settled on Cape Breton Island in Nova Scotia. Daniel MacDaniel was his name and a thicker brogue could not be found this side of Newfoundland. Daniel had come in handy whenever Kitty needed an escort to some function or another. He was always obliging and would drop whatever he was doing to escort Kitty to things like the annual Hector Society fundraiser. He once gave up a vacation to Bermuda to escort Kitty to an event in Halifax.

Jimmy had learned from Barb, Kitty's one time neighbor and friend, that Kitty and Daniel had had a minor romantic fling when she was in her fifties but it had never developed beyond an occasional night in a Halifax hotel. Their picture had been in the Halifax paper, and that made him a petty celebrity to Kitty's minor celebrity status. Kitty thought Daniel could swagger in his kilt better than anyone she knew, better than the brigadier who always slumped a little in public.

After running the gauntlet of reporters, Daniel bowed to Kitty and kissed her hand slowly making sure all the TV cameramen and press photographers got a good shot. Kitty just laughed and curtsied in return, she loved it.

By one o'clock the field was filled with cars as were the ditches on both sides of the road for half a mile in all directions. Jimmy overheard one radio reporter estimating "well over 400 people in attendance." Almost everyone had been fed and Vince, Barb's husband, had already made an "emergency" trip into Pictou for more beer.

Lined up at the top of the hill were Kitty and her "dignitaries." The radio, TV, and print reporters took their turn interviewing Kitty and the others. Jimmy overheard Kitty answer one TV reporter's questions with, "I'm far from dead but I do have a number of life threatening conditions so I thought I'd enjoy my wake while I still could." When she spoke to her local friends, Kitty often feigned a Scottish brogue but whenever she was "on stage" her voice was far more the-atrical and reminiscent of the voice of a 1930s Hollywood starlet. It sounded almost English, a mid-Atlantic accent.

After all the reporters were satisfied, Kitty rose to her feet and clapped everyone to attention. In her mock Scottish accent and with a flourish of her arms she said, "I want to thank you all for coming to me wake. Any good wake re-quires a eulogy, and my son James has been kind enough, and brave enough, to have written one. I had asked a profes-sional, our new Reverend MacDonald, to deliver one but he has declined, preferring to wait for a more auspicious occa-sion. I am sure he will be rewarded for his patience ... in due time."

Reverend MacDonald bowed deeply to Kitty while grin-ning from ear to ear.

The moment Jimmy finished reading his eulogy, the loud high-pitched squawk of a truck's air brakes broke the si-lence. Everyone looked in the direction of the road. A big yellow school bus had stopped in the middle of the intersec-tion with a plastic banner tied to the side that read, "Heath-erbells (all girl) Bagpipe Band."

A middle-aged woman in a Heatherbells uniform came running up to Kitty panting, "Today was the girls' annual picnic, and the girls voted to come serenade you at your wake. What would the deceased like to hear?" she asked.

A look of consternation clouded Kitty's face for a moment then she lit up, "Dirges, nothing but dirges," she replied with a smile.

Jimmy leaned over to his mother and asked, "I didn't know you liked bagpipes?"

"Oh, I can't stand them," Kitty replied, "but under the circumstances they are appropriate. Don't ya think?" She winked at Jimmy as she turned her hearing aids off.

Jimmy gave his mother a quizzical look, then they both burst into uncontrollable laughter as several dozen young girls in kilts, plaid shirts, and bonnets, came slowly marching into their midst playing "Amazing Grace" on their bagpipes and muffled drums. By the time the song was over there was not a dry eye at the wake, all from laughter.

After a half dozen dirges, Kitty stood up and thanked the Heatherbells for coming and told the girls to go get something to eat. The twenty young girls quickly scattered, running for the makeshift kitchen in the barn. The band director let them eat then arranged for groups of three pipers to play while wandering among the guests in the field.

By five o'clock Kitty realized that no one was leaving. The food was gone, the beer was gone, and the press was packing up — if they hadn't already left — and the kitchen had been packed up and was heading back to the Odd Fellows Home in time to cook dinner. Kitty called the Heatherbells band director over and asked her to summon the girls and have them form up in the driveway *en masse*, and play some martial music. After a few tunes Kitty hobbled over to the drum major, grabbed the baton with one hand while steadying herself on her cane with the other and started marching. The band followed.

After marching the girls up and down the street several times, Kitty marched them down the street to their bus, stopped and put down the baton, which the girls rightly interpreted as an order to stop playing.

Kitty climbed up on the steps of the bus and said in her theatrical voice, "I want to thank you all for serenading me at my wake. I now understand why the Scots went into battle with bagpipes blaring. On the one hand, the sound of a bagpipe should rightly terrify anyone not familiar with it, man and beast alike. On the other hand, the sound of a bagpipe has clearly been crafted to wake the dead should there be any after a battle. I want to thank you all for waking the dead today. It's been a battle getting this far, and victory is just over the horizon. Again, thank you all for coming, and I trust I shall offer you just one more opportunity to play on my behalf."

The girls were giggling with delight, and the crowd of adults that had followed the pipers were still doubled over in laughter. With a serious nod Kitty handed the baton back to the drum major, waved, turned and walked slowly back to the house. Like a good politician, she shook hands with everyone she met on the way and thanked them for coming. The party was over and in less than 10 minutes Kitty had cleared the yard of visitors after thanking each one profusely.

"Quick, what time is it?" she asked Jimmy.

"Ten of six," he replied, "why?"

"The news will be on and I want to catch my fifteen seconds of fame."

They settled in front of the TV and turned to the Halifax news. Kitty's wake was the "human interest" story of the day. The reporter described the food service while the video panned the makeshift kitchen in the garage then played about fifteen seconds of the interview with Kitty where she described having "a number of life threatening ailments" and ended by panning the "dignitaries," while bagpipe music played. It was nearly a minute of air time.

"Not bad at all," exclaimed Kitty. "Let's see if I get another minute on The National."

Jimmy timed it with the second hand of his watch, Kitty's story got exactly thirty seconds.

Satisfied, Kitty announced that she could now, "r-r-r-rest in peace."

Jimmy saw his mother wince as the pain of a mild angina attack pierced her chest. Kitty sighed, "Yes, rest in peace," she said to herself quietly, "rest in peace."

1

The Ice Storm - January 9th 1998

Another branch snapped on the tree outside as a sense of doom overcame her. It was not panic exactly but, rather, the sudden realization that she might not live through the night. The angina had not receded as it should have by now, and Kitty came to the surprising conclusion that she must be having a heart attack. It was so ... unexpected. "Well, that's one hell of a how-do-you-do," she exclaimed to no one in the room. Have I fallen and can't get up? Harrumph, she could still amuse herself. Well, no, let's think about it. What would Stan do? She had been a widow for over thirty years but she could still remember the voice of her late husband, it always calmed her at times like this. She thought for a moment, with the storm outside those poor boys might kill themselves trying to rescue me, and I'm not that bad ... yet.

Just the same, she picked up the telephone handset and listened for the dial tone. Its presence was reassuring. If the power went out the phones might, too. She thought she should let someone know about her heart attack even if it was mild. She could explain the weather conditions and perhaps someone smarter than she could decide what she should do.

"Hello, James." Kitty always called her son James rather than Jimmy as everyone else did.

"What's up Mom?" he asked.

"Well, you've heard about the great ice storm we're having up here in Canada!" she exclaimed more than asked.

"Yes."

"Well, it began here about noon today. The roads are so slick that there is already a truck in the ditch across the street."

There was a pregnant pause.

"And ...?" Jimmy asked.

"And, I think I may be having a mild heart attack. I've had angina all afternoon and it hasn't let up"

"Well," said Jimmy, suppressing a feeling of panic, "I think you should stop talking to me, hang up, and press your button. Would you prefer I call the RCMP?"

"No, no, it would be far too dangerous. I'd hate to have those cute boys kill themselves trying to rescue me. They would try you know."

"I'm sure they would, Mom, that's their job."

"Tell ya what, as soon as a sander comes by I'll call the RCMP. Is that a fair compromise?"

"Who are you trying to bargain with?"

Kitty laughed.

"Look Mom, I can't judge your situation, but I'd press the button and let the medics decide if it was worth it. Hell, they'll probably send a sander with the ambulance."

"No, I don't want you to call the RCMP now. It's just too dangerous, and I'm not that bad. It's just angina. I did want someone to know my situation in case this is it. I don't want to stink up the house," she laughed. Kitty was amazed that she could actually laugh in the face of death ... but what else could you do?

"Have you called Barb and Vince?" Jimmy asked.

For some reason, Kitty had not even thought of calling them. She had a complicated relationship with Barb and Vince that had begun almost as soon as she moved to Nova Scotia.

The deed to her farm had said, "100 acres, more or less" but being a native New Yorker, "more or less" was not the kind of precision Kitty was used to, so she hired a surveyor to mark the irregular boundaries of her property. It was then that she discovered that Vince had built his house on her property. Not a house exactly, but rather just the cement foundation with a tar-paper-covered plywood roof for shelter and a wood stove for heat. Not the best environment in which to raise two small children, Kitty thought, so she had loaned Vince enough money to finish the house and promised to reconcile the land problem later when Vince was ready to sell, even if it took years, and it had. And over those years Barb and Vince had become her closest friends but Kitty didn't like to impose.

"No, Barb would make Vince kill himself trying to get me to the hospital. I thought it was better to call you."

"Thanks, you called me because I can't do anything about your situation besides calling the RCMP."

"Well, I suppose there is that," Kitty replied. "I just wanted your advice."

"All right, I won't call the RCMP if you promise to call Barb. If I don't hear from Barb or you in the next half hour I'm calling the RCMP anyway. Okay?"

"Okay, I'll call her. If you don't mind, I'd like to call you periodically just to keep the line open."

"Of course," said Jimmy feeling anxious but relieved.

Kitty called Barb and explained her situation, omitting the "heart attack" part and admitting only to severe angina. Barb, of course, offered to send Vince right over as soon as he cleared the fallen trees from their lane but Kitty persuaded her not to let Vince out of the house until the roads were clear. Barb agreed to call Jimmy and calm him down and to keep up contact throughout the weekend.

Kitty had been on the phone for almost an hour by now, and the angina had still not subsided. She found herself breathing harder than she had been and wondered if it was the result of the fear she felt or a result of her decaying heart. She was feeling hot and sweaty too, another sign of a heart attack she told herself. No, she remembered, being hot and sweaty was the result of two extra sweaters and a thermostat being set at 68F, a good thirteen degrees warmer than she normally kept the house. She had turned the thermostat up when the lights first flickered. Better change that, she thought, but when she tried to lift herself from the chair she didn't have the strength. That surprised her.

The phone rang, it was James. "Hi Mom," he said. "I called Maggie and told her about your problem then I called the RCMP in Pictou and asked about road conditions. It's all iced up, and they don't think anything is going to be able to move for a day or so. Do you think you can hold out for the weekend? Do you have enough food?" He knew the answer to that question. Kitty was a canned goods pack-rat. During the Cuban missile crisis, she carefully packed a three month's supply of food and water in the basement of their Connecticut home in anticipation of nuclear near-apocalypse. It took years to eat the stock of canned soup and even then when Kitty abruptly packed up and left for Nova Scotia in the summer of 1968, she had to throw out hundreds of cans whose expiration dates had long since passed.

"I'm glad you called your sister, I didn't want to hear her lecture about living in the woods again. Anyway, I'll be fine," said Kitty, trying not to show the pain that tore through her chest. "I have plenty of canned soups ..., and a nice loaf of crusty bread," she added almost as an afterthought. She could hear Jimmy laugh at the other end of the phone line.

"I've never worried about you starving to death in Poplar Hill."

There was a pause, then Kitty said apologetically, "I'm not afraid of dying of malnutrition either. I'm more afraid of the power going out; it could get very cold."

Both felt the weight of the unspoken elephant entering the conversation.

During the long pause, Kitty could hear her labored breathing amplified by the telephone receiver. She decided to acknowledge the elephant and keep the conversation from becoming maudlin.

"Well," she said finally and with as much energy as she could muster, "If I kick the bucket tonight, it's indeed been a pleasure knowing you."

Jimmy laughed. He knew there wasn't anything he could do about his mother's situation but, mercifully, the thought of her imminent death was something very abstract at the moment. It was a shame that it would happen sooner or later, and he knew there would come a time where he would cry his heart out ... but this wasn't it. His mother was right there on the phone, a living, breathing sentient human being. He could talk to her and say ... what?

"I love you, Mom," he said finally. "Stay warm."

"I love you too, James. Call me in the morning. If the ice storm doesn't bring the phone lines down I'll answer. Okay? Call Barb otherwise."

There was a long pause, and Kitty felt she had to end the call politely.

"So long," she said as upbeat as she could muster and, without waiting for Jimmy to say anything back that might prolong the conversation that had grown very awkward, she hung up.

Almost before she had put the phone back in its cradle, it rang. It was Barb.

"I hope you were talking to your doctor or the RCMP for the last hour."

"James actually, We had a great chat."

"Does Jimmy know you're having a heart attack?" Barb asked getting right to the point.

"Well," said Kitty, starting off slowly, "I don't really know

17

if I'm having a heart attack or not. It could be a combination of angina and the pip." She knew better of course, but she didn't want to worry Barb.

"It's a heart attack, Kit," Barb said with authority. "I called Dr. MacKenzie and described the symptoms. He says you're having a heart attack, a classic heart attack, and you really need to get to hospital."

"Oh, okay. I didn't want to worry anyone, besides I don't think the ambulance is running tonight. They couldn't make it up Scotch Hill."

"Humph. The good news is that if the heart attack hasn't killed you yet, it may not but every hour you're not in hospital the worse it's going to get. Dr. MacKenzie told me to tell you to take aspirin."

Kitty interrupted, "I've been taking aspirin all afternoon, and it's helped a bit, so have the nitro pills, but I can't get out of my seat."

"I'm calling Earl," insisted Barb.

"No don't call Earl; his truck's already in the ditch across the street. I'll be fine."

"I'm calling him anyway."

"Okay," said Kitty weakly as she hung up the phone. She hadn't thought of calling her other neighbors either.

Kitty's relationship with her neighbors was complex. On the one hand, they were rural neighbors and, as such, were expected to look out for each other. On the other hand, Kitty wasn't a local, she wasn't a working farmer, and she had some money, or so everyone thought, and she didn't like imposing.

She always felt that everyone in the neighborhood treated her with the kind of respect due the "Lord of the Manor." If they invited her to an intimate event or even "lunch," they always gave her the seat of honor. It seemed to her that everyone had a deal up their sleeve and wanted her to participate, which she often did, one way or another. Kitty never quite understood why they thought of her that way, but she enjoyed the attention. It was a far cry from New York Society. Still, the only locals she considered herself to be on intimate terms with were Barb and Vince. In fact, it was Vince who had negotiated all of the deals for Kitty.

Earl, for example, cut the hay on about 40 acres of Kitty's land for his cows in exchange for milk, cheese, and bales of hay to bank her house within the winter, and plowed out her driveway whenever it needed it. Earl had a dour Scotsman's disposition, and to Kitty, left the impression that he felt he had gotten the worst of every deal. He hadn't, and Vince often had to quietly remind Earl of the good deal he had whenever he balked at performing an agreed upon duty, or parting with a pound of farmers cheese, or a bale of hay.

Kitty wasn't sure how many bales of hay or pounds of cheese it would cost her if Earl came down to look in on her, and she wasn't sure if Earl's attention would aggravate or help her condition. She wasn't sure Earl could do anything about her situation anyway since his pickup truck was stuck in the ditch across the street from her.

That thought was put on hold as another spasm of pain exploded from her chest and radiated down her left arm and out through her fingertips. It registered as extremely painful but she was becoming numb to it. Shock, she said to herself, I must be going into shock, she thought, like a deer after it's been shot. Oh, happy days, she mumbled.

An hour passed, then another. Kitty realized that the pain had indeed subsided but that she had lost all her strength. The angina was still there but the sharp stabbing pains had given way to a generalized ache all over her upper body. She could put up with that, she told herself as she fell asleep exhausted.

It was the cold that woke her up. The lights were out and it took a few moments for Kitty to wake. Her sleep had not been very deep or particularly satisfying and she still felt exhausted as she became conscious of her situation. The power had gone out and with it the furnace. It was pitch black outside.

Power outages were not unknown in rural Canada and Kitty was as prepared as anyone. She kept a hoard of candles in the kitchen and in the chest of drawers upstairs as well as a flashlight by her bed and another one on the floor next to her chair. That was smart, she thought to herself as she fumbled in the dark looking for it.

The filament in the tiny bulb gave only the barest orange glow. It was enough for Kitty to see her breath. She laughed to herself, the batteries in the flashlight had to be 10 years old but they worked when they had to, she thought. She had replacement batteries in the drawer in the table next to her chair. They were at least five years old. She would reluctantly replace the almost dead batteries in her flashlight once she got a candle lit. Well, I got my money's worth out of them, she thought, as she poked around the drawer for matches.

Kitty's house was filled with inherited antiques. The mercury mirrored wall sconces and the sterling silver candlesticks dated from the 1820s and were meant for use rather than decoration. Kitty had placed them where they could be used during a power failure. There had been enough of those over the years so that each of the candle holders held a half burned candle. The candlestick on the table next to her chair had been used more than most, so the wax had overflowed and dripped down to almost cover the tarnished sterling silver.

It took Kitty a great deal of effort to find a book of matches and light the candle. The pain in her chest reminded her that her heart was dying, and she was completely winded by the exertion.

One thing at a time. The candle was lit, so she could see well enough to replace the batteries in the flashlight. She leaned back in her chair and managed to replace the batteries without too much fuss. This time when she turned the flashlight on, it projected a brilliant white beam across the room. She aimed it at the battery powered clock she kept on top of the television. It was 4:45 AM, Saturday. In an hour and a half, there would be light. Earl would already be up milking his cows and would come by in a couple of hours to get his truck out of the ditch. If Barb got in touch with him, he might poke his head in to see if there was a corpse.

She laughed at that last thought. She could picture Earl, a big stocky man's man, creeping quietly into her kitchen expecting to find her stiff on the kitchen floor. Maybe she should call Earl to assure him that she was indeed alive. She remembered the ice storm as she picked up the telephone receiver. To Kitty's surprise, she heard a dial tone. As she was about to dial Earl's phone number, she heard the pounding, thud, thud, thud, on her back door.

"Hello Missy," roared the voice. It was Earl, crashing through the door.

"Hello yourself. Barb got a hold of you I see."

"Oh yes, Missy, she said you were feeling poorly, and that I should check on you. Are you all right? It's still icing out, must be an inch or three all over everything; probably lost most of me orchard. The roads are bad enough, and me truck's in the ditch so I can't take you no place but I see you have plenty of food. That's good. I brought you some milk, Missy. I'll put it right here. You shouldn't open the refrigerator when the power is out ya know. The lights should be back on in a bit. It's cold in here. It's a pity you sold off that beautiful wood stove. How much did you sell her for, Missy? Would you like your quilt?"

Earl took the quilt that was lying on the sofa and covered her with it. Kitty was shivering and for a moment the quilt made her feel even colder. Both of them could see their breath in the feeble glow of the candle. Earl stopped for a moment and stood up straight.

"I think we have a problem, Missy," he said looking around, "Your pipes could freeze."

Kitty knew Earl well enough to know he meant that Kitty could freeze to death but he didn't want to say it. She had noticed that he had said, "We have a problem." She smiled, Earl would normally have said *you* have a problem and for whatever small amount of money he needed that day, he would fix it. But this was the "law of the rural neighbor" at play, she told herself, but there comes a point where commerce ends and survival begins. Kitty's survival might very well depend on what Earl was able to do for her. Earl was more businesslike.

He owed her, Earl was thinking, Missy was important. She knew people; she had money. "Missy, the roads are closed."

"I know," she said. "I don't want you to kill yourself trying to get me to the hospital."

"Oh, I wasn't planning on that Missy. My truck's in the ditch with a foot of ice on her. I was thinking I could put the old sled on the back of the tractor and haul you down to the house. It's warm. Betsy's already cooking breakfast, and the teapot's hot."

Kitty was about to tell Earl that she'd be all right when the power came back on. A second or two after the lights came on she heard the rumble of the furnace firing up.

"Well there you go, Missy," said Earl straightening up. He was back to business. "The heat should be coming back up, and the sander is probably up to the top of Scotch Hill by now. I guess I can get back to feeding me cows, so goodbye. I'll call on you later." Earl turned and opened the back door, and was out in an instant.

She was glad to see him go but.... Kitty tried to speak but a blast of dry, icy air came rolling into the room like a breaking ocean wave and slapped her in the face. She gasped involuntarily and shuddered under the quilt. "Okay, goodbye," she said weakly as the stabbing pain of angina returned and

Earl pulled the door shut tight behind him.

I guess our problem has gone away, she said to herself as she blew out the candle.

Several hours passed as Kitty tried to sleep in the recliner. It was very uncomfortable. If she lay back, her angina left her panting for breath. If she sat up, she could breathe but she couldn't sleep. By Noon on Saturday, Kitty was thirsty and a bit hungry. She'd not had lunch or dinner the day before and the last liquid she'd had was the drop of acidic tea she had squeezed from the teabag in her cup. She was a diabetic, who knows what a heart attack does to blood glucose levels? I must get moving, she thought.

But moving wasn't easy. As soon as she sat upright and tried to get out of her chair the stabbing pain in her chest sent her flying back like an electric shock. "Oh!" she exclaimed out loud. She was out of breath from the exertion. "This will never do," she exclaimed between gasps for air.

As she sat back in her chair trying to catch her breath, Kitty was thinking, well, the heart attack hasn't killed me yet and I haven't frozen to death ... I could die of dehydration I suppose. Something's going to kill me, but I don't think I'm ready yet. Is anyone ever ready?

Kitty was mad at herself, win or lose, she wasn't going to just sit there if she could help it. In her youth, she had walked 20 miles on a lark through the Adirondack Mountains in high heels and survived. She'd gotten herself out of Nazi Germany when it counted, more than once she remembered. The small valise at her feet was there to remind her of that. And she'd raised two children all by herself. She could get to the kitchen and feed herself if she had to crawl on the floor.

It took her well over an hour to get to the kitchen but it wasn't as hard as she thought it might be. It was just a matter of patience, of not exerting herself too much and then resting between each step. First, she sat up, then kicked the small valise under the table to get it out of her way, and pulled the chair sitting at the far end of the table closer with her cane. She edged herself onto the chair and took a rest. The pain in her chest almost overwhelmed her, but she clenched her jaw and fought it. She repeated this operation until she was finally sitting at the kitchen table.

The phone began to ring. There was nothing she could do but let it ring. I'm going to give James and Barb heart attacks, she thought, but I can eat or I can talk on the phone. Right now I'm going to eat.

The bags of food she had bought in town the day before were still on her kitchen table. It's a good thing I didn't buy anything perishable, she thought, but that was the point. She'd been through ice storms before. She bought a half dozen cans of soup that would still be tasty cold, a loaf of French bread that she could nibble with butter, a jug of Gatorade and two bottles of fizzy water.

Kitty had convinced herself that Gatorade tasted sweet when her electrolytes were "out of kilter," salty otherwise. Today it tasted sweet, so she took a long guzzle and smacked her lips. "Ah," she exclaimed, "as good as tea."

The power went out again just as Kitty was pulling cans out of her shopping bag. "Nuts!" she exclaimed. Her kitchen was not as well organized as the universe around her chair; it was far more spread out. There was a small silver candelabrum that held three candles standing on her kitchen table, but the old box of wooden strike-anywhere matches was on the shelf above the sink. There was plenty of light to see in the gloom of the mid-winter afternoon, but within an hour or two, it would be too dark to easily navigate back to her chair. Kitty had some choices to make in case the power didn't come back on.

I guess I'd better eat quickly, she thought. She was grateful for the easy-open cans of soup. In the old days, opening cans required serious manual dexterity and strength that had long since left her hands. Kitty was not big on saying grace but she liked the formality of a meal even when she was alone and she laughed at the thought of formally entertaining ... herself. Who else would appreciate it, she smiled. Food should be placed on plates and soup in bowls, and, while a paper towel can serve as a napkin, the proper utensils should be used, when possible, like the sterling silver flatware she kept in an old pickle jar on the table. The paper towels were over the sink and without thinking she stood up to pull a sheet off the roll. A dull throb in her chest reminded her of her situation, but she was on her feet, perhaps a bit unstable but on her feet nevertheless.

She took down the roll of paper towels, and the box of matches and threw them on the table. She thought carefully about what else she might do while she was standing up. Moving was painful but standing as she was, was exhausting. She realized that she was panting again from the exertion and thought she had better sit before she passed out. She just caught herself in time and wheeled about and sat down with a discernible thud. For a moment she wondered if she had broken the chair when she fell onto it, but it held, and she breathed a sigh, which only gave her momentary relief. She was out of breath again.

Adrenalin! Adrenalin kept Kitty's heart pumping fast, faster, faster still. She could tell her blood pressure was very high from the headache she had and the pain in her chest, shoulder, and arm told her that her heart attack wasn't over yet. There was a bottle of aspirin and nitroglycerin pills on the kitchen table. The pain in her left arm made her hand shake but she forced herself to calm down and concentrate. Rotate the cap to the left until the arrows line up and pop the top. Two aspirins with a gulp of Gatorade, it still tasted sweet, and two more nitroglycerin tablets under her tongue. Her nitro patches were on the kitchen table too, and Kitty realized that she had not changed her patch in almost two days. She wasn't sure what would happen if she got an over-dose of nitroglycerin, two pills plus a nitro patch but it prob-ably wouldn't kill her, she thought and laughed to herself at the possible irony.

Kitty sat at her kitchen table trying to calm herself down. She could feel the pain subsiding in her chest and her blood pressure coming back down to more or less normal. That's better, she thought, as she watched her pulse throb on the back of her hands.

The light of the receding day cast a gray pall over the room. There were no shadows, just the gray of approaching night. Kitty's breathing had gotten almost back to normal and she made an effort to keep her movements to a minimum, just like the Hindu priest or Buddhist monks in prayer, she thought. This is one hell of a path to nirvana, she laughed to herself. I suppose I might as well make my last supper. You're full of gallows humor, she thought to herself; only James would sit here laughing, Barb would be horrified.

She found the strike-anywhere matches and lit the cande-labrum on the kitchen table. It's got to be a couple of years, she thought, I should have dusted the wax dripping off the candles. Satisfied, she set her table from the pickle jar that held her grandmother's college silverware.

Her grandmother was in the fifth class at Vassar College and had been sent to school with a full service suitable for entertaining a dozen as well as a maid fully trained in Soci-ety etiquette. Kitty always preferred her grandmother's sil-verware for the serviceability and beauty of the set over the set her mother had given her as a wedding present, which was much heavier and robust.

Given the circumstances I wonder what the proper setting should be, she thought; Larousse would insist on a full set-ting even if not all the utensils were used. That settled, she placed all the utensils in their proper place and smiled.

The silverware was perfect but the plate in front of her, a

stoneware "second" made by a local craftsman, was not. She couldn't reach for a bowl. She laughed, nothing will ever be perfect ... and who would know the difference anyway, she thought. She pulled an easy-open can of Vichyssoise from the supermarket bag and placed it in the center of the plate, and used a fork to pry it open. Next, she placed the loaf of now day-old crusty French bread on the table in front of her and ripped off a good sized piece. My last meal, I suppose I should say grace, she thought. She sat there for a moment staring into the gloom with a blank thought. "Humph," she said at last.

The Vichyssoise tasted better than she expected and while the silver soup spoon proved difficult to use in the narrow opening of the soup can, the stale French bread did a marvelous job soaking up the remaining soup. Kitty, satisfied, sat back in her chair and finished off the rest of her Gatorade which had by now begun to taste salty.

Kitty suddenly realized that she had to pee. "Curses," she said to herself. She wondered if getting to the bathroom would bring back the heart attack or angina. Sliding her chair across the floor towards the bathroom only got her halfway before the chair became stuck in a rip in the linoleum where the old wood stove had been. Kitty pulled herself up and stood leaning on the electric stove. She felt better and took a hesitant step towards the bathroom, then a second. By leaning on the stove, a cabinet and finally a shelf she managed to get to the bathroom. Getting back seemed a little easier....

Kitty could hear the telephone ringing in the distance. I wonder who that is, she thought; I better answer it. It seemed like a dream. Kitty could hear the insistent ringing of the phone but was unable to move. The ringing was waking her up. She realized that she was back in her chair in the living room. The last place she remembered being was in the bathroom. The phone rang again. She picked up the receiver and weakly said, "Hello." She could hear the weakness in her voice so she cleared her throat and said as forcefully as she could, "Hello!"

"Hello, Kit," said the voice on the phone. It was Barb. "Are you hanging in there?" she asked.

"I ... I must still be here," said Kitty weakly. "I made myself some dinner."

"That's good. Jimmy called, said you didn't answer your phone this morning."

"What?"

"Kit, It's Sunday morning. Hang in there," said a nervous Barb.

"I was in the kitchen. I couldn't run to the other room to pick up the phone. The best I can do right now is crawl around."

Then Kitty remembered that she had fallen getting out of the bathroom and had crawled back to her chair. It seemed like a dream, she thought. Too much nitroglycerin I guess, she thought.

"What's the weather like outside now?" asked Kitty. She couldn't see anything beyond the ice-glazed window.

"Well, the freezing rain has stopped but the power is still out here. They say it's some main line near Truro that's down – should be up any time now, according to the radio."

Kitty made a mental note to find her emergency radio. She had fresh batteries for that too, just in case.

"Call James for me and tell him I'm still alive and to call his sister, so I don't have to. Do they know when the roads will be clear?"

"The ambulance is in New Glasgow, is the answer to your question," said Barb. "The causeway is still closed but the RCMP said it might be open later this afternoon. You are first on their list."

"I'll be here," said Kitty weakly.

"Take care of yourself then," said Barb.

"I will. Bye for now," said Kitty as she dropped the receiver on its cradle.

She was fully awake now, conscious of her surroundings. It was late morning, Sunday, the skies were still gray but lighter than they had been, or so it seemed; it was impossible to tell the time, everything was so gray. Kitty realized that she must have been unconscious for 12 or more hours. The power was out again and she was covered in an unfinished hooked rug. She could see her breath. She was very, very cold, and her breathing was very, very difficult, she was very, very tired. Still, she was as snug as a bug in a rug, she was thinking as the world dissolved into white.

2

Saving Kitty - January 10-12 1998

The ice storm began in Western Quebec on Monday, January 5th, 1998. The slow-moving storm finally reached the northern coast of Nova Scotia by mid-day on Friday. The only news on the radio was how bad the ice storm was becoming: trees and power lines were falling from the weight of the growing ice. That was enough for the management of the Trenton Locomotive Works to send everyone home for the weekend at noon. As Vince was leaving the shop, the foreman handed him an envelope. It wasn't pink inside, but it looked official. He put it in his pocket.

Vince stopped at the Super Sobey's to pick up the list of items Barb had requested the night before and a loaf of French bread for Kitty. Vince knew that if he brought Kitty a loaf of fresh French bread he'd get fed or a shot of something strong and warming — sometimes both — and a good story or advice. He thought about the envelope in his pocket and wondered if he needed advice from Kitty this time.

On a good day it took almost an hour and a half to drive each way from Trenton to River John. Today, though, the sleet had already started, so Kitty was going to be his only other stop on his way home. It wasn't out of his way; she lived on the River John Road.

By the time Vince reached the top of Scotch Hill, the sleet was freezing on the windshield, and the road was beginning to get slippery. Vince began to wonder if he should stop or not, but he didn't want to wait until the following week.

Vince couldn't read. It was one of those quiet secrets everyone kept. It wasn't that Vince was dumb, he wasn't, but growing up on a farm and not particularly enjoying school, learning to read just didn't seem to be worthwhile at the time. He'd regretted it, of course, and occasionally Barb had signed him up for adult literacy classes but, for one reason or another, learning to read just wasn't in him. Barb would read letters and such to Vince, but she grew impatient and would just badger him to try to learn to read one more time. That's where Kitty came in. She never judged him on his illiteracy, she knew more about his capabilities than almost anyone, and she appreciated them, too. Whenever Vince brought something for Kitty to read to him, they would sit down, and after reading the document would chat about what it meant and how to respond to it. Occasionally, Kitty would write a letter for him.

Vince wanted Kitty to read the letter his foreman had handed him. He knew it wasn't a layoff notice, but he suspected it might be a reprimand for not following some written directions. It wasn't a big deal — whenever new instructions came down, the foreman was pretty good about explaining everything Vince needed to know, but every once in a while there was a gotcha, and Vince was caught in the middle. He might need Kitty's advice.

The truck shimmied noticeably after hitting a small patch of ice and, for a moment, Vince wondered if he was in control as he gingerly turned into the skid. The truck righted itself, but Vince backed off the accelerator and breathed a sigh of relief.

Kitty's house was in sight. She was home, he could see her car. As he approached her driveway, he gently applied the pick-up truck's brakes. Nothing! By now there was a sheen of ice on everything and Vince and his truck silently spun

360 degrees right through the Poplar Hill intersection. He was finally able to bring his truck to a stop nearly a half mile down the road. He took a deep breath and decided that he better just head home and not visit Kitty today. It took another full hour to drive the remaining ten miles. By the time Vince made it to the end of the quarter-mile dirt lane leading up to his house, his truck was encrusted in ice.

Driving up the dirt lane was easier than driving home on paved roads. The weight of his truck fell through the crusted ice into the soft, rutted mud below, allowing the rubber teeth of his tires to grip as they dug in. As Vince drove up the lane, he could hear the firecracker snaps of tree limbs breaking all around him, and as he approached the house he heard, no felt, the thunderous report of a 150-year-old maple tree crack open and fall across the lane behind him. Vince parked as close to the house as he could, kicked open the door, and ran towards the house. He slipped and fell twice from his truck to the open back door.

Barb had been stacking wood in the kitchen and living room all afternoon, enough, she thought, to keep the house warm all night and the next day, too. She expected the power to go out and was ready with food, fuel, and kerosene lamps. This was nothing new, just another winter storm and she was ready. She even kept her tall workmen's boots and an extra thick plaid flannel shirt on in case she had to go out again for some reason. She still had on the fluffy down jacket Kit had given her, when she heard Vince's truck in the driveway. She opened the door as he stumbled in.

Vince sat down hard at the kitchen table and Barb handed him a beer as the phone rang. It was Kit.

As soon she hung up, Barb turned and said, "I think Kit's having a heart attack. I'm going to call Dr. MacKenzie."

"Jesus, I just went by Kit's house. Is she all right?"

Barb shrugged as she dialed Dr. MacKenzie in New Glasgow. Vince drank his beer slowly as Barb got more and more frantic on the phone. "Dr. MacKenzie says that Kit's symptoms are a heart attack. She's got that angina, and she's out of breath, and it's been going on for hours."

"Why don't she call Saint John's Ambulance?"

"Why don't I call St. John's myself?" Barb asked, dialing the number. The ambulance was stuck in Halifax. Barb was annoyed. "Why don't they have a Snow Cat or put a litter on the back of a Skidoo like they do at ski resorts?" she groused. "They have every other kind of machine."

Barb picked up the phone again, this time to call Kit. "You're having a heart attack," she started.

Vince was sitting at the kitchen table sipping his beer and heard the conversation getting more and more animated. Barb hung up with a frown. Vince was sure Kit would be complaining of her high blood pressure the next time he saw her. "I guess I better go clear the lane if I'm going to take Kit to hospital. That big old maple split in two just behind me and fell over the lane as I came in. It's going to take some doing to clear it."

Vince threw on his overcoat and walked out of the house towards the barn. The crackle and snap of breaking tree limbs was loud and continuous and, as Vince opened the side door to the barn, a medium sized branch snapped above him and showered him in a hail of ice chips, pine needles, and sharp stinging twigs.

"Damn," Vince cursed to himself as he pulled the door shut, turned, and fumbled for the light switch. Nothing! The branch that had just fallen over the barn door had taken the power line with it. In the dark, Vince fumbled for the flashlight he kept on the shelf near his tools, knocked it to the ground, bent over, and found it. The batteries were old but threw enough light for Vince to find his chainsaw. Luckily, there was more than enough fuel in the tank. Vince engaged the choke, turned the switch on, and pulled the rope. Two more pulls and the chainsaw sputtered to life. Satisfied, he turned and went back into the cold.

The freezing rain had turned heavy again. It would splash and freeze leaving an added sheen on whatever it touched. Vince struggled over to his truck with the idea of using the beams of his headlights to illuminate the fallen trees, but the truck was covered in so much ice the doors were iced shut.

Barb called from the house, "I called Earl. Told him to look in on Kit. So come in and get supper."

Vince shook his head but listened to Barb. He wouldn't get far cutting wood in the dark, and it could get dangerous. He threw the envelope from his jacket pocket on the table.

"What's that?" asked Barb.

"Tommy gave it to me when I was leaving work today. I was going to get Kit to read it to me."

Barb grabbed the envelope from the table and tore it open. She put on her half-frame reading glasses and said with a grin, "Well, Vince, you just got a merit raise. Your welds have been perfect for over a year."

Vince grinned.

The "crack, whoosh" of trees cracking and falling went on all night. Vince was up well before dawn. The fire in both wood stoves had almost gone out and needed stoking and new wood. It only took a few minutes for the stoves to throw out enough heat to noticeably warm the house, and the kettle sitting on the stove in the kitchen was whistling in less than ten minutes.

Barb picked up the telephone receiver. There was a dial tone. It was too early to call Kit but not Earl. Alice, Earl's wife, answered and said that Earl had been up to look in on Kit and that she was warm and okay. Barb hung up with a "harrumph." Kitty was not all right. She was having a heart attack.

Barb went out into the gray freezing mist to help Vince clear the lane. There was an inch or more of ice on everything, and Vince was having trouble cutting through the massive tree with his chainsaw. It was slow work, but by noon, Barb and Vince had cleared the lane of the first tree.

Barb counted nine more, that is, nine that she could see.

When they went in for lunch, Barb called Kit, no answer. Kit's phone might be out, she thought. She called again three hours later when they had cleared another tree from the lane, still no answer. Barb could fear the worst but chose not to. Still, she had an uneasy feeling in the pit of her stomach.

By late Saturday afternoon, the freezing drizzle had stopped, the power had come back on, and Vince had cleared most of the lane. The phones still worked, and Vince had arranged for a cousin who worked for the highway department to meet him at the end of the lane with a sander early Sunday morning.

Rescuing Kitty Stevenson had become a county-wide effort. Barb had been calling the RCMP and St. John's all weekend. The ambulance had made it back to Stellarton by Saturday afternoon. The Pictou causeway was still closed as was the roundabout way through Scotsburn.

The highway department was going to get the causeway open by midnight, then start on Scotch Hill about 6:00 a.m. Sunday with two plows and five salt trucks.

John MacNamara, like Vince, a tall, lanky, muscular fellow more at home with a hammer than a book, and one of Vince's cousins, was waiting at the end of the lane. It was 4:50 a.m. Sunday. When Vince didn't appear immediately, John let loose a long echoing blast from his air horn. Vince was there in his pickup seconds later.

John, with 20,000 pounds of a sand-salt mixture in the back of his truck, started slowly down the hill towards River John, spreading his salt/sand mixture as he went. Vince was right behind him.

At the Highway Department garage in Lyons Brook, a convoy was assembling. It had been determined that the easiest way to Poplar Hill was right up and over Scotch Hill. The longer route by Toney River would require as many as five more sand trucks and could take hours more to accomplish, so straight up the hill it was going to be. Tommy Patriquin, whose grandmother had sold the house to Kitty, would take the lead with his big ten-ton truck.

Tommy put the truck in second gear as he pulled out of the lot. He wanted to hit the hill as fast as he could go. If he made it to the top of the hill, it would be an easy day. But he wasn't sure he could make it without ending up in the ditch. The hill started out as a slight incline, then rapidly became steep enough to force most cars and trucks to downshift. The grade wasn't too bad but it was long, almost a mile and a half to the top. The trick was to find just the right speed so that the engine would apply just enough torque to the tires without slipping, to keep the truck moving up the hill at a steady or increasing pace. Tommy thought he knew that sweet spot, and he held the truck steady for almost a mile.

Just before the top of the hill came into sight, the grade sharply increased but only for a few hundred yards. When the truck began to strain as it hit the steeper grade, Tommy instinctively pressed the accelerator. Almost immediately, the truck spun sideways, a tire caught the shoulder, and the truck spun slowly into the ditch.

A minute later the convoy reached Tommy's truck, which was now firmly stuck in the ditch but with most of its sand gone. Tommy's brother-in-law, Ian, took his smaller truck and very slowly backed up the remaining half mile to the top of Scotch Hill. He, too, had used up his sand in the ascent. A conference was called at the summit. They would pull the ten-ton truck from the ditch first, and reload it with sand before finishing the mission. The smaller trucks ran back and forth along the plateau that fell gently away from the top of Scotch Hill, emptying their sand, as the Highway Department winched the big ten-tonner out of the ditch.

Vince and John had a lot less distance to go, and they were on the far side of Scotch Hill, so Vince figured on an hour, maybe an hour and a half. But they only had one sand truck, which would get them to Poplar Hill but no further. Vince decided that he'd worry about that later.

It took them almost three hours to get to Poplar Hill. Tommy sanded past the intersection, then, carefully parked on the shoulder, being careful not to drive into the ditch. Vince pulled into Kitty's driveway.

Vince had to give Kitty's door a solid kick to free it from the accumulated ice. "That should wake the dead," he thought to himself. He immediately felt remorse for thinking of a joke at a time like this. He hesitated, and a small pang of guilt caught him in the chest.

"Hello, Kit. Are you okay? This is Vince, Barb sent me," he said hoping to hear the familiar "come on in." There was silence. Vince stretched his head into the kitchen a little further. "Kit, are you all right?" he said as he closed the door behind him.

A loud, raucous snore came from the direction of the dining room. Vince immediately poked his head in to look. Kit was there all right, and sound asleep in her overstuffed chair covered in a hooked rug. Vince laughed.

"What?" said Kitty as she woke up to the noise.

"Kit," yelled Vince, assuming Kit did not have her hearing aids in. "Barb sent me to take you to hospital."

"Oh, hello, Vince," said Kitty, "Let me put on a pot of tea." She pushed against the arms of the chair to get herself to her feet but nothing happened; she was too weak. "Oh, yes," she said. "I do need to get to the hospital." Kitty was still a New Yorker who could never understand why Canadians took people "to hospital" rather than "to the hospital" as an American would say. It was one of the few Americanisms she had steadfastly refused to give up voluntarily. American grammar simply made more sense to her.

Vince was grinning at her again. Yup, Kit was alive. "Don't worry about making tea," said Vince. "We have to figure out how to get you to New Glasgow and hospital." Just as Vince was beginning to worry about the second half of the problem, he heard the low throbbing staccato of a big diesel engine downshifting to a halt.

"The cavalry has arrived," said Kitty with a little more gusto than she felt.

A moment later a big burly EMT came crashing through the door followed by his partner and two RCMP officers.

"Take me away," said Kitty with a grin and a dramatic sweep of her arm. Damn that was tiring, she thought.

"Are you Catherine Stevenson?" yelled the burly EMT at Kitty. "We were told you had a problem."

"I have my hearing aids in so there is no need to yell," said Kitty. "I'm Catherine and I believe I need to go to ... hospital." There she'd said it. She was Canadian now.

3

Retirement - January 12-29 1998

The gurney wouldn't fit through the door so Kitty was brought to the waiting ambulance sitting upright in a kitchen chair.

"I'll close up the house and keep an eye on her for you," said Vince.

Kitty gave him the thumbs up as she was being strapped onto the gurney in the ambulance and an oxygen mask placed over her nose and mouth.

Kitty made no effort to move. It was warm and comfortable and the slight jostle of the ambulance, as it moved, was reassuring. Kitty felt drowsy again.

"Are you still with us," the attending EMT asked shaking Kitty slightly.

"Sure am," said Kitty, "just taking a nap. Not much else I can do at the moment." And so she drifted off to sleep.

She woke up with a headache. She thought she was in a private room; no, it was intensive care. There was more noise here. She turned her head. There were five patients in the room all with tubes and machines beeping and gurgling every few seconds. Time for an assessment, she thought.

Above her was an intravenous drip with three different bags hanging loosely on one hook. She wiggled her nose and discovered an oxygen tube around her ears and blowing into her nostrils. She wiggled her right arm. Yep, there was an IV in that arm. She wiggled her left arm, Humph. There was an IV in that arm too, she thought. She rolled her left leg. Good, nothing there. Then she rolled her right leg. Damn, another big IV there.

She knew what that meant. She had had an angioplasty performed a few years before and they went through her leg for that. That had left her leg aching and bruised for months. Damn, she thought, I hate that.

I wonder if they are managing my diabetes? What's my blood sugar? I'm hungry. She looked around to find the button that would summon a nurse. When she lifted her right arm to grab the button, she discovered that there were not one but two IVs stuck in her arm with enough tape to prevent her arm from moving more than a few inches. Humph, she thought again. Her left arm was free, and the weight she had felt was an oxygen sensor attached to her fingertip with a spring.

To Kitty, it seemed like a very long time, but when the nurse finally came in, she was breathless having obviously run to Kitty's side. Right behind her was a pantheon of medical personnel with all sorts of equipment in tow.

Kitty was surprised by the commotion. "I'm fine," she said. "I was wondering if I could have some tea or water or something like that and perhaps a bit to eat. Crackers or something?" Kitty suspected the answer would be 'no,' but she felt the need to ask anyway.

The attending physician pushed his way through the crowd.

"Let us take a look," he said with a noticeably East Indian accent. "You have had a very serious heart attack," he continued without making eye contact with Kitty.

"I know," she interrupted. "I was wondering if I might have something to drink. My mouth feels like cotton." Kitty was looking straight at the attending and was determined not to let him squirm away without making eye contact. It was, she determined, the only way to keep doctors honest. The attending looked up and caught her eye. She smiled, and so did the attending who was obviously uncomfortable with the situation. "Well, what is the immediate prognosis?" Kitty asked.

The attending physician had moved up and out of Kitty's line of sight. "Well," he said, "you have had a very serious heart attack, and frankly we are very surprised at your recovery. You came to hospital in very poor shape and hypothermic. I am very, very surprised."

Kitty could see the shadow of the attending physician shaking his head.

Oh, thought Kitty, he's surprised I'm alive. She was terribly weak, but everything still worked, but then the thought came to her: Is this is the beginning of the slippery, slippery slope? Well, that would be interesting. Something all of us eventually get to.... Kitty shook her head. "Where is Dr. MacKenzie?" She asked.

"He's making rounds," said a nurse. "He's been paged."

"I will order a light meal for you," said the attending as he turned and left the room.

The gaggle of nurses that had come running when Kitty pressed the red button slowly filtered out of the room. A nurse raised Kitty's upper body by pressing a foot pedal on the electrically operated bed. Kitty could now see the room around her. It was full of electronic gadgetry, only some of which she recognized. Heart monitor: looked reasonable to her. Oxygen levels, 88 percent, a little low. A nurse had once told her that the Oxygen level should be above 95%.

Dr. MacKenzie, a short swarthy man of obviously south Asian descent, came into the room at a brisk pace. "Good afternoon Miss Stevenson," he said in a vaguely British accent. "You gave us all quite a scare and I understand you hesitated to call an ambulance. You are quite lucky you are still with us."

"So I understand, but the ice storm was very bad when this started and the ambulance was in Halifax apparently," said

Kitty. She knew Dr. MacKenzie would stop lecturing her if she could jump ahead of him with logic. "What is the prognosis and what are we going to do next?" she asked.

"You had a heart attack that should have killed you," he said softly with a warming smile. "I am very glad to see that you are conscious and feeling better but you are very, very weak. I don't know yet if you will ever be able to return home. We may need to consider a nursing home for you. In any case, you must consider yourself retired. No more driving an automobile and no 'more late-night carousing."

That brought a smile to Kitty's face. "What is the plan for my convalescence and rehabilitation?" Kitty asked, knowing that if Dr. MacKenzie had a plan it would involve eating sawdust and unmercifully torturous exercise.

"Short of making you young again only time will kill you or cure you. Time has brought you out of a coma and into a fighting mood so I expect progress to be rapid and sure, now that you are back among us."

"How long was I out?"

"Would you like to guess what day it is?"

"Wednesday?"

"Monday."

"I've been out a week?"

"Kitty Stevenson is back among the living and spoiling for a fight," said Dr. MacKenzie with a theatrical flourish. "Yes, We kept you sedated."

Some hesitation came into Kitty's voice. "How soon do you think I will be up and about?" she asked.

Dr. MacKenzie shook his head, "I think we can get you into a wheelchair in a few days, but I think it will be several weeks before you can use a walker. This incident did a lot of damage to your heart. Try lifting your head."

Kitty lifted her head and held it for a second then let it fall back onto the pillow. The exertion left her breathless. "Oh, I see."

Catching her breath was difficult, she realized. "We need to talk seriously about donating the remains to science," she said rolling her Rs on the word "remains" and with as much authority as she could muster continued, "I don't think I'll have many more opportunities to persuade you."

MacKenzie smiled. Among the elderly and widowed it had become popular to donate their body to science because it promised a free burial. Donations had become so common and problematic that a law had been passed requiring a doctor's approval. Kitty had broached the subject at least a decade before, and he had simply smiled and said "no." But Kitty persisted; her father and mother had donated their bodies to science, and she wanted to do so as well. "Okay, I'll treat this as your last wish and approve your donation. I'll come back with the paperwork."

A few minutes later, Dr. MacKenzie reappeared with a clipboard. "Well," he said pausing, "I believe you have a case that would be of interest to the faculty at 'Dal,' so I'm going to approve your request to donate your mortal r-r-remains to Dalhousie Medical School." He rolled his Rs too but only for Kitty's benefit. He, too, could affect a Scottish accent.

He had said it with such finality it startled Kitty, "Well, thank you, but the remains are not quite ready to be enlisted in the services of science, at least not just yet."

Dr. MacKenzie smiled, "They'll be ready whenever you are. Anytime after you and I sign this release that is."

They both signed the document, and a broad smile grew on Kitty's face. "Excellent, splendid altogether," she said with satisfaction.

"Now, Catherine," Dr. MacKenzie sternly asked, "tell me honestly, are you donating your remains to science out of generosity or are you being Scotch?"

Kitty looked at him a bit surprised then smiled, "A little bit of both I guess."

Dr. MacKenzie left the room with a smile and his clipboard, leaving Kitty alone to think about her condition. She was adaptable, and she could adapt to this. She kept telling herself that, but it wasn't particularly comforting. She had found herself in tough situations, and by remaining calm, she had planned her way out of trouble. This was different. There wasn't much she could do to affect the situation besides following doctor's orders, and they were beginning to lose their certainty when giving those orders. Kitty laughed at that.

Doctors were always serious, but she could tell when they were bluffing. Keeping a professional face on was getting harder and harder for the doctors around her and Kitty would insist on eye contact. Dr. MacKenzie was about the only doctor she knew who would be honest with her. "If I eat enough vegetables to keep me gut filled, will you promise I'll live to 100?" she had asked him once. He had babbled incoherently until Kitty had caught his eye and gave him a disapproving look. He stopped babbling and said, "I can't promise anything. All I can do is pass on advice from those more expert than I." That was an answer Kitty could live with.

Daydreaming was the only way to pass the time in a hospital, and Kitty was well into a dream about picking the grapes that covered her chicken coop when she smelled food. She wondered if the daydream about picking and eating grapes had started with the first wisps of food in the air or if the two were unrelated. In either case, she was hungry.

None of the other patients in the room were conscious, so when the orderly came into the room with the food cart, he left it there and walked off to check with the nurses. Kitty could identify all the ingredients from the smell: chicken, cooked to death no doubt, with a lemon tarragon sauce, some unrecognizable boiled vegetables, probably peas and carrots and some form of potato with margarine. It didn't strike her as appetizing, but then she hadn't eaten solid food in a week. This was going to taste good, she told herself.

The orderly and a nurse came into the room and raised Kitty to an almost sitting position. "Can you raise your arms," asked the nurse, "or would you like someone to feed you?"

Kitty discovered that she did have the strength to lift a fork and thanked both the nurse and the orderly for such a delightful meal. The orderly blushed at the compliment, and the nurse just smiled and said, "Dr. MacKenzie has asked that you be moved to a private room. It would be more convenient for us, given all the people wanting to see you."

"Who wants to see me?" asked Kitty with a limp carrot string hanging out of her mouth.

"Well," said the nurse trying to remember, "a bunch of ministers has been dropping by every day, as have a family named Betts. They said they weren't related, so we didn't let them in to see you."

Kitty could feel her blood pressure rising. "Thank you for that," she said emphatically.

"Hmmm," said the nurse, "Shall I keep them out?"

"Yes, if you could, but be polite."

"Of course," said the nurse. "What about the ministers?"

"Ministers?"

The nurse nodded with a smile.

Well," said Kitty slowly, "They are largely harmless but please don't let them stay very long, maybe 15 minutes tops, then come in and tell them they have to leave because you need me for some sort of test."

Satisfied, the nurse and orderly left Kitty to her meal. It was a rather meager meal, but surprisingly delicious Kitty thought, more than the light meal the attending physician had promised. When she finished, Kitty looked around, and seeing no one, picked up the plate and licked it. That's when she noticed an envelope had been left under the plate. She opened it. It read:

Kit – We're glad to hear that you are up and about. To the

staff here you are an inspiration and a legend. For those of us lucky enough to have worked with you, we thank you for having given us an honorable profession. We can't promise that each meal we serve you will be Chateaubriand and truffled potatoes but, without you, we wouldn't have known what they were.

Kitty smiled, it was signed by 25 or 30 people — none of whom Kitty recognized.

Kitty was the only "Master Chef" in all of Pictou County and one of only six in all of Canada. Of all the places she could have cooked she chose the Oddfellows Retirement Home in Pictou. Over the years the flow of cooks had blended into a constant stream at the Oddfellows Home. Cooking for 40 people required a half-dozen full-time cooks and Kitty was always short of help because as soon as someone learned institutional cooking, they left for better-paying jobs like the ones at the hospital. It made Kitty smile, Chateaubriand indeed, and with a vintage Burgundy, she thought.

The next day Kitty was moved to a private room filled with flowers. Her first reaction was to sneeze, then laugh. "Who died in here?" she asked the nurse pushing the gurney into place.

"They are all yours, dear. They have been coming in all week."

Kitty was very patient, but after weeks in the hospital she still couldn't walk, even with a walker, and she hated being in a wheelchair.

Barb came to visit almost every day after lunch and would push Kitty around the hospital in a wheelchair with bottles and bags hanging from a pole, a portable heart monitor in Kitty's lap, and an oxygen bottle sitting in a small pouch behind the seat. It was an effort getting into the wheelchair, but Kitty thought it was worth it. "Stay active," Kitty kept telling herself, "and nature will take care of the rest."

To her surprise, Kitty had become a minor celebrity. The

kitchen staff regularly made gourmet meals for her. She reciprocated by having Barb wheel her down to the industrial kitchen where she'd make a breathless speech about some arcane aspect of cooking to the gathered chefs. This almost always happened on Tuesday and Thursday afternoons. Kitty would ask the charge nurse to call down to the kitchen and formally ask permission for a visit. After the third or fourth visit, the kitchen staff came to expect it and would prepare a meal or dish expressly for Kitty's enjoyment and comment.

Kitty loved the attention. "I've rarely met a dish I didn't enjoy," Kitty would tell anyone within earshot. It wasn't true, of course. Kitty had eaten and prepared some truly awful dishes, but she had found over the years that cooks, like everyone else, would rather be complimented than castigated. If a dish needed "adjustment" she'd make a suggestion but only after profuse compliments. The kitchen staff loved her for it, and over the weeks Kitty's visits attracted a larger and larger audience, made up mostly of the cooks, immigrant orderlies, janitors, and other "non-professionals" in the hospital. After the sixth week, the gathering was moved to the staff cafeteria. Kitty was satisfied but exhausted, and after each of her forays Dr. MacKenzie had threatened to curtail her visits, but she brushed him off.

To the medical staff, Kitty had become a celebrity too; not because she had a famous disease, which she didn't, but simply because she was, well, the famous Kitty Stevenson. It seemed that everyone in the hospital knew her.

Dr. MacKenzie would try to be at Kitty's bedside during visiting hours. He was there, he said, as much to bask in her glory as to make sure the visitors didn't tire her out too much, and to assure everyone that Kitty was making great progress in her recovery. Kitty suspected otherwise. She didn't feel quite right.

One day, after everyone had left, Dr. Mackenzie cleared

his throat and said in a very casual voice, "I've arranged for a minor procedure in Halifax to clear out some of the debris from around your heart. Then we need to talk about nursing care."

"Do you mean a nursing home?" asked Kitty without emotion.

MacKenzie cleared his throat again and said, "Yes. I'll need to put you on the list. Would you like to go to the Oddfellows home or Shiretown?"

Kitty thought for a minute then said with a smile, "Shiretown, I think. The food must be better there, and I won't have to listen to everyone I know cackle like starlings."

Dr. MacKenzie gave her a soft pat on the shoulder before he left.

The ambulance ride to Halifax was uneventful, and Kitty slept the whole way. Once there it only took a few minutes for Kitty to be settled in a private room.

An hour later the bedside phone rang, surprising Kitty. She picked it up. "Hello," she said softly, stretching out the "O." It was Jimmy. "Oh, hello James, what's the occasion?"

"Mom," said Jimmy with a bit of anger in his voice, "Why didn't you tell somebody that you were having angioplasty done on you?"

"I am?" said Kitty with mild surprise.

"Mom, are you all right?"

"Oh, I'm fine," said Kitty, "I didn't ask what the procedure they were going to perform. After a while, they are all the same, and all are painful. I was sure Dr. MacKenzie would tell you if I forgot."

"Forgot?" screamed Jimmy. "Mom, we want to know."

Kitty thought for a moment then slowly said in a soft voice, "Well I didn't want to bother you. I mean, my slippery slope is no reason for you to stop your life. I'm in no imminent danger. There is no need for a vigil ... yet."

"Oh, Okay, Mom, but I want to know what's happening. Okay?"

There was silence on both ends of the phone line. It was awkward.

"Jimmy," said Kitty slowly and with some pain in her voice, "remember when I told you not to put me in a nursing home until I said, 'when'?"

"Yes Mom," said Jimmy with surprise. It was the first time his mother had called him Jimmy since he was a small boy.

"When!" Kitty said softly with a tear in her voice. She let a long pause hang in the air, "Dr. MacKenzie is going to put me on the list for Shiretown."

"What's Shiretown? You're not going to the Oddfellows Hall?"

"Hell no," said Kitty with a laugh, as she began singing softly, "I'll never forget that night you can bet, I went down to Oddfellows Hall.

"Besides, the food has got to be better where Hobbits live. You know, in the shire."

This time they both laughed but Kitty had to suppress a coughing fit.

"Okay Mom," said Jimmy with a sigh, "Next time, please leave a forwarding address."

"Oh, I will," said Kitty emphatically, "if I know where I'm going." Kitty was grinning at her own wit which she assumed was utterly lost on her son.

"By the way as soon as you can I want you to come up and take my valise, the one I keep under the table near my chair. It has all my Nazi contraband. I'll let you decide if it should go to a museum or be destroyed. The simple possession of some of my things are highly illegal in Germany. I'm not sure about Canada."

"OK, Mom. I remember you showed me some of that stuff a few years ago, interesting. I'll come up as soon as I can. In a couple of weeks. Can you hold on?"

"Sure can. I have to go," interrupted Kitty, "there is a nurse waiting to impale me or otherwise apply medieval torture, so goodbye." She hung up the phone before Jimmy could prolong the conversation. There was no nurse in the room. But she just didn't want to talk to Jimmy anymore. Both of them could get maudlin if she let the conversation go that way. Life is for the living she said to herself.

The night before the procedure the doctor came to explain what he was going to do, but Kitty let the details roll over her, catching only a word here and there. It was some advanced form of angioplasty (she already knew that), hers was a specially difficult case, significant risk of failure, blah, blah, blah.

The procedure would start at 7 a.m. the next morning. Kitty hated that, it meant no dinner that night and a swollen, painful leg when she woke up ... if she woke up. Well, thought Kitty, if I wake up, I'll have something to complain about which is better than the alternative. She giggled to herself. She was alone again.

"Hellooo," said a familiar voice from behind the door as it swung wildly open. It was Mandy Betts. Kitty could feel her blood pressure rising.

"Praise be to God, I've found you alive," said Mandy. "Catherine, are you ready to accept Jesus as your personal savior as you prepare yourself for the coming ordeal?" She charged into the room waving an oversized Bible wildly in the air while breathlessly trying to suck enough air to support her 350-pound body.

"Well, I've had this procedure before, and it's not likely to kill me any time soon."

"Ya never know Catherine, ya never know," Mandy continued while pushing Kitty's bed out of the way to make more room for her bulk which she promptly let drop with a thump into the only chair in the room. The industrial chair held, but Kitty heard a squeal as the wooden joints on the chair complained.

Kitty found Mandy annoying, but she had long ago decided the best policy was not to argue with Mandy but to let her sermonize as long as she wanted. Eventually, Mandy would run out of energy and leave in search of food.

Mandy was thumbing through a well-worn Bible, intently looking for something. Kitty raised her head in curiosity. Mandy's Bible was dog-eared with pages folded in at the tips and papers marking dozens of passages Mandy thought important. Gray duct tape held the binding together. Too many important items for Mandy to remember thought Kitty. "Did you lose your place?" asked Kitty with some pleasure.

"Oh dear, oh dear, oh dear," said Mandy without looking up. "I read a passage just the other day in Luke, I think, and it reminded me of you, which is why I'm here."

Kitty took a deep breath and rolled her eyes towards the ceiling.

There was a knock on the door and another, "Hellooo, Mrs. Stevenson." It was Matthew Betts. Matthew was the least offensive of all the Betts, but a Betts nonetheless, thought Kitty. "I hesitate to ask what occasioned this visitation," said Kitty, thinking she should be polite with small talk anyway.

Mandy tried talking but was out of breath after just uttering, "Well."

Matthew took over, "There is an evangelical conference in Halifax this week, and the preacher challenged us to go out into the world and bring cheer to everyone we knew personally; but everyone we knew, except you, was at the conference, so we decided to come visit you. Praise the Lord."

"Amen," Mandy echoed as she fidgeted in her oversized purse pulling out a monstrous candle.

"Don't light that thing," said Kitty. "You'll blow the place up."

"She's right, Mom," said Matthew.

"Aw, Shesh," said Mandy dismissively as she went about the business of creating a small altar on the window sill using the candle as a centerpiece. Unconsciously she lit the candle.

Kitty pressed the nurses' call button.

"MOM," yelled Matthew, "Put that out!"

"Oh," Mandy exclaimed as she smashed the lit candle with the open palm of her hand which, of course, sent the smoldering candle and hot wax flying.

Kitty squinted and closed her eyes expecting to be splattered with hot wax, but it was Mandy who got covered and started cursing loudly from the burn on her hand. Kitty chuckled under her breath.

Matthew screamed at his mother, "This is an oxygen tube." He yanked the oxygen tube right off Kitty's nose. "If you light that candle again this oxygen could burn up that candle in a few seconds. It does 'blow up' ya know."

The noise coming from Kitty's room and the fact that the nurses' call button had been pressed sent the floor into an automatic Code Blue. The attending physician was paged; the crash cart was unplugged from its standby position next to the nursing station and pushed in the direction of Kitty's room while nurses, interns, and orderlies came running from every quiet corner of the floor.

Ezekiel and Hosea Betts had just gotten off the elevator when the alarm rang and were about to ask where Kitty's room was but instead decided to join the throng running past them. Zeke yelled to his brother, "This is like chasing fire engines." His brother grinned as they ran into the room.

The nurse with the crash cart pushed into the room first, followed by two other nurses and the cardiac intern. Kitty, who had been laughing, was now in the middle of a coughing fit, Matthew was still yelling at his mother, who was busy jamming her "altar" with its still smoldering candle into her oversized purse. The door, which had swung closed, burst open again with a grinning Zeke and an out of breath Hosea. There were eight people in the room pushed up against Kitty's bed when the attending physician burst into the room pushing the crash cart into Mandy Betts who fell, spilling her bag in the process.

Kitty, who had regained her composure, pointed to Mandy and laughed, "Groucho ... Room Service?"

The attending physician was not amused and ordered everyone that wasn't in scrubs out of the room. Mandy Betts left the room muttering to herself while still trying to stuff loose items into her oversized bag. When everyone was finally out of the room the attending physician took a deep breath, turned and asked, "What do we have here?" Kitty's blood pressure was 212 over 110, way too high. The nursing staff was ordered to only allow clergy and family into the room from now on.

"Well, that should keep the wolves at bay," said Kitty as the last nurse left the room turning down the lights.

Kitty heard a soft knock on the door. "Come on in," she said with some hesitation since nurses and doctors don't knock. The door slowly opened and an unfamiliar head cautiously looked in.

"Are ya Catherine Stevenson?" said the head with a Cape Breton accent.

"I am. And who'd like to know?"

"I would," said the head cheerfully. "I'm Angus MacDougall, pastor of the New Covenant Church in Shelburne. Mandy Betts asked me to look in on you. May I come in?"

Kitty could feel her blood pressure rising at the name of Mandy Betts. Mandy was a born-again Christian who had made it her personal mission to "Christianize" Kitty. It wasn't that Kitty wasn't "Christian" — she was, after all, a member in good standing of the Scotsburn United Church of Christ — it was more that Kitty often said that she didn't know what to believe in and didn't have a personal savior as far as she knew. Kitty hated having the Betts come to call, but she had always been polite even if she made it a point of not serving them tea. Kitty laughed at that. The Betts never got it and now they were sending emissaries.

"Hello pastor. Do come in," said Kitty with some hesitation in her voice.

"I've been asked to come and pray with you," said the pastor somewhat awkwardly. Angus MacDougall always found it difficult meeting new people in settings like this. He never knew what to expect. Some were grateful for a chance to speak with a man of God. But if the subject of his visitation was a Roman Catholic, he was likely to be expelled from the room for being a heretic, sometimes politely sometimes not. Still, Angus had the calling to help people realize that Christ was their personal savior, so he was never deterred.

Kitty was annoyed by this apparition. She didn't want to be bothered by the rantings of a preacher, especially not the "born-again" kind, but she didn't particularly want to offend him either. She decided that she just wanted him to leave.

She knew she could stop him in his tracks. To a "born-again Christian" the word "humanist" almost meant "atheist" while to most Protestants it meant Unitarian or at worst a churchgoing agnostic, which is exactly what Kitty was. The United Church was a social home where Kitty went to meet her neighbors once a week, catch up on the gossip, and meet new people.

"Well, reverend," Kitty began slowly, "I've always found the Lord's Prayer to be sufficient. Any more and you're asking for special treatment, any less and you ask for calamity. I'm not a Pentecostal you know."

"How do you know Mandy Betts?" asked Pastor Angus with a reverend and serious tone.

"She has been coming to call for years.

"Being a member of the United Church of Scotsburn, in good standing, I have always felt obliged to entertain anyone with a calling loudly enough to knock on my door and if you know Mandy Betts her calling is loud enough to wake the dead."

Pastor Angus was caught flat-footed. He burst out laughing then struggled to regain his composure. Surely he had sinned just now. For if there were saints to be found in the

Pentecostal church, surely Mandy Betts was one of them and to laugh at her was a sin ... wasn't it?

Kitty saw the cloud of consternation creep over Pastor Angus's face and realized she had the upper hand; she was enjoying this. "Reverend," she began seriously, "to be able to laugh at one's self is a blessing. We should never take ourselves too seriously because if we do, we will miss the most pleasant gifts God has bestowed on mankind." Oh, shut up, she thought, don't go overboard or this poor soul will die of apoplexy. But she couldn't help herself, and she was having fun.

"You know the Greeks had a god called Bacchus," Kitty continued, the glee building. "They believed that life was hard work and extreme pain most of the time and that your only obligation was to enjoy, to its fullest, what little license the fates gave you so 'eat drink and be merry for tomorrow we die.'" Kitty was satisfied with her soliloquy and it had the desired effect. Pastor Angus was as white as a sheet. He turned and, with some mumblings which Kitty took for either an apology or an exorcism, left the hospital room in a hurry just as a nurse was entering.

"Oh dear," said the nurse. "He didn't look too happy."

"No, I suspect he wasn't," said Kitty with glee. "I do believe he thinks I'm possessed of the devil." Kitty was beaming. The nurse frowned.

"You're blood pressure 220 over 140 Miss Stevenson," said the nurse abruptly. "This isn't good for you; we may have to limit your visitations." Kitty's smile turned into a grin.

4

Pillows or Bolsters - January 30 1998 (August 1925, November 1933)

A nurse woke Kitty from a deep sleep, interrupting a vivid dream. *Kitty was sitting in the back of a speeding taxi, her valise on her lap. Beside her was a German Army officer, the letters SS shaped like lightning bolts on his lapel. They were in Munich Germany in the spring of 1939. They were traveling with some urgency and had to get someplace quickly or something dire would happen.* "Harrumph," said a startled Kitty at being woken up so early. Kitty would muse on dreams she could remember for hours, occasionally writing out a synopsis of the more interesting ones and amuse herself by thinking, "What would Freud say?"

"I'll be taking you down to the OR in a few minutes," said the nurse, taking Kitty's blood pressure. "One forty-four over ninety-two," she announced, satisfied. "This is an antibiotic," the nurse continued, hanging a little bag containing a brownish liquid on the IV rack, "and this will take the edge off," the nurse added, injecting something into the IV line.

"I wonder what edge they are planning to take off," Kitty mused as she fell into a torpor.

Kitty was sitting in the taxi with the Nazi officer. They were speaking French, when she heard, "We don't have a next-of-kin listed here. Is there anyone in the waiting room?" I must be dead, she thought. She was confused. It didn't make sense that she might be dead ... something to ponder at length ... more insight perhaps, she thought. "Is there no one that needs to know?" she heard someone say as she drifted off again.

Kitty remembered it vividly; she was six years old on her first "Grand Tour of Europe." After a whirlwind tour of London, Antwerp, Berlin, Vienna, Rome, and Paris she was standing with her parents before the convent of Sainte-Marie-d'en-Haut at the foot of the mountains in Grenoble, France, uncomprehending. You will be attending school here, her mother had told her in French. French was spoken at home among the social elite in New York City because it was the civilized thing to do in the mid-1920s and attending boarding school in France was de rigueur. *Kitty had replied in English that she would prefer to stay in New York. Her mother and father had smiled at that in that slightly condescending way that said, you'll know better when you're older.*

The Mother Superior was very friendly and quite fluent in English with only a hint of a French accent. After a long chat with Kitty's parents, of which Kitty could remember very little, the Mother Superior asked, in French, "Do you prefer pillows or bolsters?"

"Pillows, I think," Kitty had replied in English.

"We have bolsters," replied the Mother Superior with polite authority. "Do you speak French?" she continued.

"Un petite," Kitty had replied.

"Good," the nun had said in French, "we speak only French here."

Kitty began to dream in French, struggling with words she had not used for over fifty years. All her worldly possessions were in a small valise her mother had given her. She wouldn't be needing anything else. The convent supplied the required uniforms and everything else.

For eight years she had only spoken and written in French.

The biennial visits by her parents were always conducted in French with her mother far better at it than her father.

Monthly letters from her parents were always in French and Kitty's replies, also in French, were always dictated to, and later inspected by, one of the nuns. It became a game to add a phrase or deliberate misspellings to a letter that would pass the censor but convey secret meaning to her parents and siblings. She once described the Mother Superior's relationships as being like that of a donkey that eagerly shares its stall with a horse. (The inference being that the Mother Superior was a "horse's ass.") Her father had understood the reference, replying, in French, that she should always stay away from the business end of any who cohabit with horses.

Kitty had an ambivalent attitude towards the nuns and the convent. It had been mostly work, and Kitty had trouble remembering much from her elementary school days. One day had blended into the next. It was very tedious, she remembered. She had learned to love Grenoble and remembered the donkey carts delivering bread in the early morning.

Kitty felt a sharp pain in her leg and had a sudden feeling of falling and being bumped.

She fell into a dream again.

She was summoned to the Mother Superior's office, she was 14 years old, and handed a telegram from her father. Strings of letters from the telegraph ticker were glued to yellow telegraph office letterhead, which read:

NO MONEY - STOP

SEND C HOME VIA PARIS - STOP

AT AMERICAN EXPRESS - STOP

"Ouch," Kitty exclaimed. She was coming out from under the sedation and could feel the catheter in her leg which was throbbing. She expected that. She was alive, probably, yes; she could wiggle her big toe on her left foot and her right. She could get her eyelids half open. She was in a room with lots of subdued flashing lights. Intensive care, she thought, that's appropriate.

It was hard to stay conscious, and Kitty didn't try very hard but, with effort, could surface long enough to hear snippets of conversation between nurses and to grunt some kind of response when asked a question. She wasn't always sure what the doctors or nurses were saying, but she always responded, just to make sure they knew she was still with it. She was sure they had her well drugged and was equally sure that she didn't have her hearing aids in. That posed a dilemma. "What if they want to pull the plug," Kitty thought. "Better pull meself up by me bootstraps," Kitty laughed to herself as she made a conscious effort to wiggle her toes and fingers. The few moments of exercise was exhausting, and she fell back into a deep sleep.

There was a knock on the door, and the Mother Superior nodded towards the door and said, "Your valise has been packed. Here is a train ticket to Paris and your passport. Please come with me." With no further discussion or explanation, Kitty followed the Mother Superior out the door and into a waiting automobile. They drove in silence to the Grenoble train station, past a donkey cart delivering bread to the convent.

Kitty had retrieved her valise from the car and was standing on the curb ready for a prolonged goodbye. The Mother Superior simply nodded saying only, "Au revoir," before getting back into the car. Kitty replied sheepishly, "Adieu" as the car drove out of sight leaving a trail of oily white smoke belching from the aging Citroën.

The rhythmic bouncing of the railroad car was putting Kitty to sleep when she felt a pain in her leg. "She's coming out of it; put her under a bit deeper. I don't want her wiggling while I'm trying to...."

Kitty was standing in front of the American Embassy in Paris feeling the urgency to go in but not remembering why.

A marine guard in full uniform walked up to Kitty and said, in English, "May I help you?"

That startled Kitty, who said in French, "I need to go home."

The marine gave her a strange look, pointed to her and said, "Moment! Let me find a translator."

"Oh no," said Kitty struggling to find the words in English, "I need to go home ... to America." Kitty waved her passport frantically at the marine who took it and looked at it with curiosity.

A moment later he said, "Come with me." Kitty duly followed the enormous marine as he took her up a huge staircase, down a long dark corridor and into a small side room. "Wait here," he said as he disappeared into an office deeper into the building.

A moment later a smiling chargé d'affaires walked in exclaiming in French, "Welcome to Paris Miss Stevenson," adding in English, "we've been expecting you."

There was a swirl of parties, dinners, literary and artistic soirées hosted by the embassy. Kitty's host was the cultural chargé d'affaires of the embassy and his wife. According to a letter from her father that was waiting for her at the embassy, he was a failed playwright with enough swank and social connections to be appointed to this post in Paris. He knew Kitty's parents and grandparents and had promised to look out for Kitty while she was in Paris. A telegram had alerted the chargé d'affaires of Kitty's arrival and of the American Express credit for $100 to be used for her care while in Paris.

A week or so later she was on a train to the coast, then a ferry across the channel. Unwelcome in London she was off to Southhampton. First class cabin on the Olympic, sister ship to the Titanic. Dinner with the Captain.

Pulling into New York, a radio telegram: "Take train to New Canaan - STOP."

Thanksgiving day 1933. All the servants, except Bessie MacDermott, had been dismissed. The Depression: The house in New York City, sold; the house in Bar Harbor, sold; the house in Newport, sold; little food; no heat in the mansion, except in Archie's study.

"If you're cold, put on another sweater," her mother had said.

"Are you with us...?" the voice asked as a bright light forced Kitty to turn her head. "Good," said the voice. "Catherine, you came through a tricky operation with flying colors. You'll be in intensive care for a while, but we think we repaired a lot of damage."

Kitty was returning to consciousness.

"Did you make it home?" asked the nurse standing over her.

"Why, yes, of course, but how did you...?"

"We've been listening to you for the last couple of hours," the nurse said with a smile as she turned to walk away.

"Was I dreaming in French or English?" Kitty inquired.

"French mostly," said the nurse, "but you don't have a Quebecer accent, and there were a lot of words I didn't understand."

Kitty laughed as best she could with the room still spinning. "It doesn't sound French because it *is* French," she said. "I grew up in France," she continued without her usual jab at the provinciality and pronunciation of Quebecer French.

"What's the rest of the story?" asked the nurse, as she hung bottles on the IV drop poll.

"I went home on the Olympic, the sister ship of the Titanic. I had the pleasure of dining with the ship's captain every night for the entire trip. There weren't many on board at all.

Kitty took a breath, "Just before we docked in New York City on Thanksgiving afternoon 1933. I received a radio-telegram instructing me to take the train to New Canaan. That's in Connecticut."

"I've been to New York City," said the nurse.

Kitty smiled and continued, "I expected to be met at the New Canaan train station by my father and his valet. Instead, it was just my father. I assumed my father had given the staff the day off. Or they were too busy cooking dinner and preparing everything.

"It began to sink in that we were broke when I walked into a very cold house and found my mother and my old nanny, Bessie MacDermott, in the big empty kitchen, alone, trying to cook a turkey, for the first time in their lives.

The house was empty, and this was a very big house; the servant's wing alone had twelve bedrooms and the main part of the house eight more."

"That's pretty big," said the nurse. "So how did you end up in Nova Scotia?"

"Well, before the Depression my father built a sewage treatment plant for the town on some property he owned and traded it for a fifty-year tax abatement on his estate. He owned the house outright so all he had to do was earn enough money to feed, cloth and keep us warm. Keeping us warm was a problem on occasion, but we grew a lot of our own food and bartered for a lot more. It was tight, but we survived.

"Later when my husband went broke in the 1950s we moved, kids and all, into the coachman's cottage at the back of the estate. My husband died the same year the fifty-year tax abatement ended in 1963. I stayed on for a few years simply because we had no other place to go, but when the water main to the cottage burst in 1968, I just gave up."

"So is that when you moved to Nova Scotia?" asked the nurse.

"Well not quite that fast but, yes, just like that," Kitty said. "I had already bought the house in Poplar Hill the year before so what choice did I have? I couldn't afford to fix the cottage in New Canaan, I couldn't afford the taxes, and besides, I didn't want to stay there. I didn't want to be stuck in the past."

The nurse thought about what she'd heard for a moment then said slowly, "So you moved to Canada, just like that?"

Kitty thought about it for a moment, "Well," she finally said, "I did have to apply for landed immigrant status."

"How long did that take?" asked the nurse with real curiosity.

"Not long at all, they told me just to move up, and since I already owned a house, it wouldn't be a problem."

The nurse smiled, "You'll be heading back to New Glasgow tomorrow. Have a good night."

Kitty drifted off to sleep as the shift changed and the lights in the ward were dimmed.

A few minutes after Kitty arrived back in New Glasgow, Barb walked in with a small box of chocolates. "How ya feeling Kit?"

"I do feel a lot better," said Kitty, "but I don't think I'll be dancing any time soon. Did you talk to Dr. MacKenzie?"

"Yes I did," said Barb. "He says you can either 'stink up' his place or your own."

Kitty smiled. Kitty always used the phrase 'stink up the place' to refer to the presence of unwanted guests, and she'd said it once too often in front of Dr. MacKenzie, so he used it on her. Kitty thought it was the funniest thing she had heard in years and said so to Barb who beamed.

"You are definitely on the mend," said the nurse who had just walked in. "I'm supposed to see if you can walk to the bathroom. If you can, then you can go home; if not, then you'll have to wait here for a room at the Shire. We will arrange for nursing when you are home."

In three months the most Kitty had accomplished physically was to sit up and dangle her feet off the edge of her bed. That had been exhausting, but she thought she might be feeling better since the angioplasty. She thought she'd better sit up for a few minutes before waltzing around the room.

Barb helped her sit up and swing her legs off the bed. Kitty looked around expecting to be dizzy but wasn't. "I'm feeling just fine," she exclaimed.

"Take it slowly dear," said the nurse pushing a walker in front of her.

Barb helped Kitty get her feet firmly on the ground before letting go. Kitty, for her part, grabbed the walker and held on tightly, fully expecting her legs to buckle under her. They didn't, and everyone breathed a sigh of relief.

Kitty looked up at Barb and sheepishly smiled, "Well, I've got this far, now ten long feet to the bathroom." She stretched out the word "long" for more than a second and everyone burst out laughing, "and just as far to get back." It took twenty-two baby steps, she counted them, to get to the bathroom door and another five to position herself in front of the mirror. She wasn't out of breath exactly, but her breathing was labored. She waited for the image in the mirror to catch up. She didn't like what she saw looking back at her.

The skin on the face looking back at her was tallow and flaccid. Lines that had once given that face its mature character now marked points where flesh hung loosely. Hair that was once golden yellow and so long Rapunzel would have been envious, was now white and thinning. It was not the face of the young girl Kitty remembered seeing in the mirror, and not even that of the middle-aged mother determined to make it on her own terms, no, this was the face of an old woman. An old woman near the end of her rope thought Kitty. That brought a small tear to her eye, so many things still to be done. I guess not, she thought, as she took a deep breath. She shook her head to get rid of such thoughts. Happy thoughts only, she said to herself.

She had walked, with the aid of a walker, yes, but still, she had walked from her bed to the bathroom, sat down, got up and walked back to bed. It was a small victory. Kitty was happy. "So I guess we're going home," Kitty exclaimed with some pride.

"I guess we are," said Barb, nodding affirmatively.

The nurse agreed and began disassembling the IV setup. Kitty didn't need it anymore, but the oxygen was a different story. Without a constant stream of pure oxygen blowing at her face, Kitty would quickly begin to feel dizzy and start gasping for breath.

Barb frowned when Kitty began to struggle for breath after the nurse removed the oxygen tube draped under Kitty's nose. The nurse noticed too and remarked that perhaps it was too soon to be going home.

"It's all taken care of, I hope," said Barb. "Dr. MacKenzie ordered an oxygen machine for Kit a while back, and it's been delivered and installed."

"We can send you home with a 24-hour oxygen tank," said the nurse to Barb, "but don't let it run out then call for a replacement. If the machine hasn't been installed then bring her right back. Okay?"

"I'll bring her back kicking and screaming if I have to," said Barb.

Kitty was happy. "Back to me haunt," she said pointing in the direction of the door.

Kitty had once been a very large woman but now she was small and frail, and it was easy for an orderly to pick her up from a wheelchair and deposit her in the back seat of the Ford Expedition that Barb had borrowed from her cousin. Barb thought the oxygen tank weighed more than Kitty did.

"All set?" asked Barb. Kitty nodded.

Barb headed onto the highway in the direction of Poplar Hill. It was a pleasant day, and neither Barb nor Kitty felt the need to rush. As Barb turned off the highway in the direction of Scotsburn, she heard a small voice in back seat. "Did you say something, Kit?", Barb asked.

"Yes," said Kitty clearing her throat, "I think I need to put my affairs in order."

"Whatever for?" asked Barb although she fully knew why.

Kitty didn't answer. When Barb had passed through Scotsburn and was making the turn to Meadowville, Kitty said, "I have lots of historical material that needs to be handed over to Betty McConnell at the Hector Society."

"What do ya got, Kit?" asked Barb.

"I have lots of junk," said Kitty, "and you can help me get rid of that, but what might interest future generations the most is, perhaps, my stuff from Germany. It's in my little valise that's under the table."

Barb laughed at that, "Oh, that old thing. I've been wondering what's in there."

When they pulled into Kitty's driveway, Vince came running out. "Hello, Kit, Ya be feeling better are ya?" he asked as he tried to figure out how he was going to get Kitty inside. "Can you walk?"

"A little," said Kitty a bit sheepishly.

"No, she can't," said Barb, "we are going to have to carry her. Go get a chair."

Vince did what he was told and returned with one of Kitty's antique upright kitchen chairs and placed it firmly down on the ground beside Kitty.

"I think I can get that far," said Kitty, "... with a little help," she added.

Once Kitty was safely planted in her chair Barb and Vince carried her inside to a completely new world. The first thing she saw as she was carried into her kitchen was a big red sign that read, "No Smoking, Oxygen in use."

Vince was prepared for Kitty's arrival. The smell of venison stew filled the kitchen, and a loaf of french bread protruded from a shopping bag on the kitchen table.

A smiling Kitty shuffled into the living room with the new walker Barb had gotten her. The living room had been rearranged. The couch had been replaced by a bed, and Kitty's recliner and table had been moved forward to accommodate an oxygen making machine in the corner.

"No lighting candles, okay," said Vince looking at Kitty and to prove his point struck a match in front of the loose oxygen tube connected to the machine humming in the corner. The match nearly exploded in Vince's hand and he had to drop it with a not-completely silent curse onto the table where he put it out with the palm of his hand.

"Jesus, Vince!" yelled barb.

"I get the point," said Kitty.

"Well, Kit," said Vince, "here's where she stands: Earl has banked the house with hay for you since you might be here through the winter, and he and I built this here bed from scraps of wood we had. Barb brought down all the clothes she thinks you need and put it in this bureau here."

"We put your silver from the bureau in the front room," said Barb.

Vince piped in, "And we got the fuel topped off and got this here oxygen machine for you and I got your friends at the Scotsburn United Church to fill your fridge with food. Heck, it's the least they can do for you." Vince said, and he meant it.

Vince had, casually or on occasion more forcefully, reminded everyone of the favors Kitty had done for them and pushed or embarrassed everyone into pitching in. The result was that the house was banked with more bales of hay than it had ever been before to keep it warm for the winter. The second floor had been closed off and Kitty's parlor had been turned into an intensive care ward and made warm and almost airtight. As far as Vince was concerned, Kitty would be comfortable if he had to knock heads all over the county to get it done.

"Horse trading," said Kitty to Barb. "Vince is a horse trader just like my mother was."

Barb stared blankly at Kitty for a moment then said, "Oh yeah, Vince is a wheeler-dealer all right," said Barb winking at Vince who blushed. "Sometimes it takes four or five deals to get something for free that would have cost ten bucks," said Barb.

"Yeah," said Vince, "but that's ten bucks you don't always have." Vince winked back at Barb and they all burst into laughter.

"It's good to stay in practice," said Kitty.

"Kit," asked Barb, "Do you want me to stay the night in case you need help? Do you think you can you make it to the kitchen and bathroom on your own?"

"I think so," said Kitty, who was a bit uncertain. "Yes, yes, I'm sure of it." Kitty was determined. "Besides, Vince's stew will hold me for a few days."

"Are you sure?" Barb demanded, holding Kitty's gaze.

"Yes, yes, I'm sure of it. Go home. I won't die of starvation, not with Vince's soup and besides, I think I've adequately demonstrated that I can get to the bathroom and back, haven't I?" Kitty was getting adamant.

Barb laughed, "Geeze, don't get yourself all worked up."

Turning to Vince, she said, "Get up you big lummox." She slapped him playfully with a rolled up magazine. Vince grunted and sat up quickly, too quickly, and he had to steady himself to keep from falling back.

"Want a snort," Kitty said with a smile holding up her oxygen tube.

Vince laughed and said to Barb, "Ah, come on, old girl. We'd better be going. I have to be at the yard at 6 am."

"I'll check on you in the morning. If you need anything call, OK? I'll send Vince right over," Barb said with a laugh.

After they left Kitty sat in silence for almost an hour sipping Vince's stew and eating the crusty bread. She tried not to "ruminate" on her condition, but she concluded that she couldn't ignore things much longer.

Determined, Kitty cleared her throat and picked up the telephone, dialed and said, "Hello, James."

"Hi Mom, what's up?" he said cautiously.

"James, I need you to come up here to help me put my estate in order," she said abruptly but rather weakly.

"Has your condition gotten worse?" Jimmy asked a little hesitantly.

"Well, James," said Kitty, "I'm on the slippery slope and it's getting steeper."

"Okay, Mom," said James. "Is the day after tomorrow soon enough?"

"That's plenty of time," said Kitty as she started to relax. "That's plenty of time," she repeated to herself after she hung up. That's plenty of time.

5

Old Money - Spring 1998

Two days later the phone rang. It was Jimmy. He was at the airport trying to rent a car. He'd be home in a couple of hours. He had said. Kitty laughed, "James is on his way from the airport, if he can find suitable transportation."

"Great," said Barb, "I'll fix up a room upstairs and open up the heating vents."

"That's a good idea," said Kitty. "Don't want my boy to freeze to death. After all, he's coming up from Boston in the deep, deep south."

They both had a good laugh at that. Barb suggested that she should start dinner for the both of them. "Thanks," said Kitty. "But when James gets here he can cook for me so you can have your life back."

"So, you're kicking me out, are you then?" said Barb with a smile.

"Yup," said Kitty. "You don't want to spoil James, but stick around at least until he gets here."

When Jimmy arrived five hours later, he was exhausted and angry. The car rental agency couldn't find his reservation, and they were out of cars anyway, as were all the other rental agencies, so he waited until a car was returned. It was a luxury sedan, a Cadillac and Jimmy wasn't sure if he was angrier because they couldn't find his reservation or because they insisted on charging him for a luxury car when all he wanted was a cheap sedan. Besides, Jimmy was embarrassed to be seen driving a Cadillac in Nova Scotia; Boston, perhaps, but not Nova Scotia.

Barb made Jimmy a cup of tea and fed him some currant scones. "Food calms the savage beast," she said to Kitty while winking at Jimmy. Both food and Barb's flirting calmed him down, and he went upstairs to unpack. First, there was his cell phone charger. Jimmy looked at the face of his cell phone and realized that "No Signal" showed on the screen. It was useless this far out in the country. Plug it in any way, he thought, it might work in Pictou. Next, he unpacked his laptop computer and took it downstairs. No high-speed Internet here, but there was always a phone connection. Kitty reminded him that she was on a party line. Jimmy cursed and threw up his hands.

"We do have books here," Kitty said hopefully. Jimmy gave her a sour grin. Kitty had forgotten how impatient he could be. He was a city boy, she told herself.

"Well, Mom," Jimmy said, "I guess we'll have to cook and tell stories."

That perked Kitty up, and she instinctively tried to get out of her chair, but a mild shot of angina reminded her why Jimmy was here. "Curses," she muttered under her breath as she fell back into her chair.

"I'll cook," said Jimmy. "Just tell me what to do."

"With that, I'll go home," said Barb as she put on her coat and left.

Jimmy wasn't used to cooking, and Kitty wasn't used to not cooking so they stared at each other for a moment before Kitty said, "I guess I'll have to teach you how to cook finally."

Jimmy smiled and said, "Okay but go slow and have mercy since I don't know what I'm doing."

"All right," said Kitty. "We'll start cooking everything in the house. With luck and some ingenuity, we'll empty this house of everything edible thing by the time you leave, or I go to Shiretown, whichever comes first."

Jimmy laughed from the pantry where he had gone to assess the situation. "There isn't much here except some canned beans and pasta," he grumbled.

"That should last us months," Kitty said with a smile knowing what was in the cupboard. "Bring me a cutting board, my paring knife, and some onions to start with. The onions are in a box beneath the kitchen table."

Jimmy complied with his mother's request and brought two large onions, some sprouting shallots, and three carrots he had found, for good measure. "Here you go," he said, "but it's not enough for a meal."

"How much do you plan on eating?" said Kitty.

"More than this," he said.

"Well," began Kitty slowly, "Put on a pot of water for some of the pasta you found and dig down into the freezer. At the bottom should be some old venison steaks and some frozen stewed tomatoes. There are turnips and potatoes in the basement as well as some red wine of uncertain provenance." She said rolling her 'r's' on provenance.

"There should also be some jug wine from the store that you might like to drink. I can't have any, but it needs to be drunk."

Jimmy returned from the basement grinning from ear to ear, carrying two bottles of wine and an unopened bottle of Martell VSOP cognac. He had never known a time when his mother would not have a glass of wine with a meal. 'One cup in the broth and one in the gullet' she used to say when he was little. "What are we making, Mom?" he asked.

"Br-r-r-aised Venison à la Bag End," Kitty stated with authority, rolling her 'r's.' "Bring me a pot."

Jimmy complied, and soon Kitty was cutting vegetables while Jimmy rummaged around the freezer to find the perfect cut of meat. "Mom, you need a walk-in freezer. How many dead animals do you have in here?"

"Well, as best I can remember there are parts of at least three deer, well hidden of course since it's out of season and they would now be considered poached. There is also a leg of mutton, and various loin and flank steaks from the last cow Earl slaughtered for me last year and a smoked ham and some chickens," said Kitty.

Jimmy stacked most of the meat on the kitchen table before finding various wrapped packages marked with a large "V" and containing dates and other cryptic markings he couldn't decipher. Kitty remembered exactly what each piece was, when it was shot, and by whom. She chose a cubed venison flank steak and told Jimmy to put everything else back in the freezer.

"How are we going to cook this?" asked Jimmy holding up a substantial lump of frozen meat.

"Braise it, very slowly," was the answer.

After browning the meat and deglazing the pot with cognac, Kitty told Jimmy to put the lumps of meat back into the pot with the stewed tomatoes and the vegetables she had been cutting. When Jimmy had finished Kitty pulled herself up and shuffled into the kitchen with her walker for a final inspection. Satisfied, she had Jimmy open one of the bottles of wine he had brought up from the basement.

"Sniff it," Kitty ordered. "If it's not vinegar we use this. Its apple, grape and raspberry wine, vintage 1985 or thereabouts."

"Ew!" Jimmy exclaimed. "Could it possibly still be any good? Was it ever any good?"

"I don't remember if this was any good or not. Pour me a glass, and I'll let you know."

"I thought you weren't supposed to drink anymore."

"I'm not supposed to eat meat either. Dr. MacKenzie says it might kill me someday. Pour me a glass," she ordered.

Jimmy laughed and handed his mother a glass of the dark red wine. It left the smell of raspberries in the air without a hint of vinegar. Kitty took the glass, held it up to the light, swirled the liquid in circles and took a long, loud sniff.

"Humph," she grunted, "good enough to cook with but I'm not going to drink it."

Satisfied with his mother's judgment, Jimmy opened the other bottle and poured himself a glass of store brand Burgundy wine. "I've tasted better," he said.

"I certainly hope so," said Kitty, "That was my stock cooking wine. It's been there for years."

Kitty gestured to Jimmy to pour the apple, grape and raspberry wine into the pot with the venison and vegetables. "How much?" Jimmy asked.

"Cover it about halfway, and don't forget the obligatory bay leaf or two," she said with an air of satisfaction. "We'll let it stew for a couple of hours or so."

They sat, mostly in silence, while their dinner cooked. When it was done Jimmy served them both in large bowls.

Kitty ate very little while she watched her son devour his meal.

"Are you okay Mom?" Jimmy finally asked when he noticed her food getting cold in front of her.

"I'm not very hungry," she said. "I'm feeling a bit off tonight."

After he was finished eating, Jimmy cleaned up the kitchen and put the uneaten portion of the most delicious meal he could remember, in the refrigerator. Then he went back to sit with a glass of wine and chat with his mother.

Jimmy made himself comfortable then looked up from his glass to meet his mother's eyes. Eyes that were open and staring at him with what Jimmy took to be panic. "Are you okay?" Jimmy repeated, very slowly this time.

Kitty looked at him and nodded. Although she could feel another attack of angina beginning and even with deep breaths, she didn't feel like she was filling her lungs with enough air. It was scary. It felt a little like drowning, she thought, and her anxiety showed. "I'll be okay," she gasped. "I get these little attacks every once in a while. It will pass."

It didn't pass, and Jimmy sat across the table from his mother who was staring back at him in terror. There was nothing he could do. "Shall I call the doctor?" he asked.

"No," said Kitty breathlessly.

They sat there in uncomfortable silence for more than an hour. Jimmy's eyelids felt heaver and heavier. He caught himself nodding off several times only to wake up with a start to see his mother's frightened eyes still staring at him. Eventually, he fell asleep in the chair only to awake in a cold sweat nightmare of corpses slowly swimming around him.

The angina attack had subsided, and Kitty had managed to move the four feet to the bed across the room from her chair. She was asleep, her rhythmic breathing accented by the gurgling of the oxygen machine. The oxygen tube that was still draped over her ears and plugged into her nose stretched from the oxygen machine to her bed across the room at an elevation sure to trip anyone passing.

When Jimmy noticed the oxygen tube, he made a mental note to avoid tripping over it as he crawled upstairs to bed.

"Time to get up," Jimmy heard from the bottom of the stairs. It was a familiar sound, and it reminded him of his childhood in which his mother always got up before he did and always roused him from a sound sleep from the bottom of the stairs with the loud and insistent refrain, "Time to get up, time to get up." "Oh, Mom," he started to say before he realized he had been dreaming. He could hear his mother shuffling with her walker in the kitchen, and it was the smell of coffee, not the sound of his mother's voice, that was waking him up.

"I thought you'd be down ages ago," said Kitty as Jimmy entered the kitchen. Kitty was sitting awkwardly but very erect at the kitchen table on one of her old Queen Anne chairs. "I was going to make you an omelet but got stuck here. It seems that I need to be reminded that I really can't do much anymore," Kitty said apologetically.

"That's okay Mom," said Jimmy. "What's on the agenda for today?"

"Well," said Kitty, "I want you to go into town and clean out my safety deposit box. I won't be needing it anymore."

"Okay, what am I going to find?" asked Jimmy.

"Oh, the usual stuff," Kitty began. "You know, all the junk I had when you were growing up. Barb convinced me that I shouldn't leave my valuables in the house, so I got a safety deposit box. Oh, and fetch my stocks."

"Your stocks," said Jimmy with surprise. "What stocks?"

"My uncle Chester, your great uncle I suppose, left me four thousand dollars and instructions to invest in Pfizer Pharmaceutical," said Kitty, "so I did."

"So what is it worth today?" asked Jimmy.

"I have no idea."

"What do you think its worth?"

"Well, they were worth four thousand dollars in 1968, so I suppose its worth, maybe, ten thousand today, but I really don't know. They keep sending me more and more paper that looks like stock certificates that say 'don't lose these' or something to that effect. So I suppose they might have split once or twice."

"Well, what did you pay for each share?"

"About forty dollars."

"And what are they trading for now?" Jimmy asked.

"About forty dollars, I think, but I haven't had to sell them."

After breakfast, Jimmy drove into Pictou in his rented Cadillac. The assistant manager at the Scotiabank was very deferential when Jimmy asked to see his mother's safety deposit box. When Jimmy put his mother's key into the lock of her safety deposit box the manager, wearing white cotton gloves, did the same. When the door was opened the manager pulled the overstuffed box from the vault and placed on a table. "Press this button if you need assistance," he said with more formality than Jimmy thought was necessary.

The box was 18 inches long by four inches wide and three inches deep. It had been well used given the dings, dents, and scratches on the old paint. The metal was soft like tin but slightly rose-colored. The top was held on with a spring clamp which Jimmy slowly pulled open until the top of the safety deposit box sprang open and flew across the room breaking at the hinge. "Damn," said Jimmy out loud. "That's going to cost me something."

On the top was a sheaf of what looked like computer generated stock certificates; indeed the top dozen certificates had a coversheet that read in large red letters, "Valuable Documents – Do Not Discard." Each certificate said Pfizer Pharmaceutical and the number of shares each piece of paper represented: one said 200 shares, another said 1000 while another said 400. Jimmy wasn't sure if one set superseded the other, but in his wildest dreams, he counted 7200 shares. That's pretty cool, he thought, while he struggled with the math, seventy-two hundred shares times forty — wow, something like $300,000. It's probably wrong, Jimmy thought, but hey, someone has to win the lottery. He was smiling.

Below the pile of Pfizer stock was another manila envelope containing another dozen stock certificates for companies Jimmy had never heard of. Below that was the jewelry which Jimmy had always assumed were his mother's most valuable possessions. Looking at the contents spread out on the table inside the bank vault they didn't look very impressive: a half-inch pile of stock certificates and a dozen items of jewelry. Wow, not much left to show for a couple of generations of wealth, he thought as he swept the jewelry on top of the stocks before jamming everything into a large manila envelope.

On his way out the door he asked the bank manager what needed to be done to close the account. "Your mother called, it's already been handled. All I need is the key," said the senior vice president with a bow. Jimmy bowed too, as he handed him the key. "Do you need an escort to your car?" the manager inquired.

Jimmy thought that question odd but remembered that he was carrying the contents of his mother's safety deposit box. Somehow, the small manila envelope just didn't seem that valuable so, with a shrug, he declined the offer.

Back in Poplar Hill, he spread the contents of the manila envelope out before his mother on the dining room table. "Tell me what I've got here," he said, "and what you want me to do with this stuff."

"How many shares of Pfizer do I really have?"

"I think you have 7200 shares of Pfizer and all these other shares too. What are these anyway?"

"That was my inheritance. Before I left for Germany, my father split up what was left of his stock portfolio between my sisters and me. I've never touched those shares, so I don't know what they're worth."

"I guess I'll have to look," said Jimmy. "What's the deal with all this jewelry? Is this stuff worth anything? I always assumed it was."

"It's all real," said Kitty somewhat defensively, "but most of it is Victorian in style and completely out of fashion."

"What do you mean?"

"Take this diamond and sapphire ring, its four carats worth of diamonds and two carats worth of sapphires. That sounds like a lot until you talk to a jeweler who will tell you that the old-fashioned cuts on the diamonds ruined them and the sapphires aren't of the best quality. I've had it appraised twice so I know it's only worth between four and ten thousand bucks ... US of course."

"You're kidding?" said Jimmy.

"Nope, its worth about the same today as it was in 1890 when my grandfather gave it to my mother. It was a real keepsake then. Today it's one step above costume jewelry.

Hold on long enough, and it might come back into fashion."

Kitty had a melancholy smile, "My mother cherished that ring. Don't sell it, pass it on," she said.

"I won't, Mom," said Jimmy. "What about your jade necklace?" he continued, holding it up.

"Oh, that," said Kitty with a smile. "The jade is real, so are the pearls, not cultured pearls, mind you, but real, natural ones. You can see the imperfections if you look closely. I think they may be worth a lot. My mother gave them to me so I could look respectable when I went to Germany in 1937."

"I see they made their way back into your safety deposit box. I guess they aren't paste after all," said Jimmy laughing.

"No, they're not," said Kitty emphatically with a wink. "No one believes they are real which is why I've always felt safe wearing them. I think they might be valuable but I've never had them appraised, I never really wanted to know.

"It's fun to wear them on swanky occasions. You can get a sense of who people are by their reaction. People who think they have arrived and you haven't will assume its all costume jewelry and will usually say so. On the other hand, the more insecure nouveau riche, you know, socially climbing ne'er-do-wells, will assume they are real and also say so. The 'old rich' and Nova Scotian farmers couldn't care less."

Jimmy was grinning, "I know, I remember your story of going to tea on Cyprus."

"That was the most fun I've ever had with my string-o-pearls and jade.

"Imagine what I must have looked like. I had one small suitcase full of my traveling clothes, and I'd been on the road for a month. I'm sure I must have stunk to high heavens. Then I met a snooty but otherwise charming English woman on the boat from Greece who invited me to tea. I think she was lonely and wanted to impress someone. People love to show off; it makes them feel good. I usually indulge people like that. You'd be surprised how far you can get with a smile and a few small compliments. Just acknowledge people for who they say they are and you will make most people very happy. I got a very lovely meal out of it.

"Anyway, I had my one outfit suitable for tea, so I wore it along with my string-o-pearls and jade. The old biddy was suitably impressed, and we had a grand old time. She was a widow who had married into some old but impoverished British aristocracy and inherited her estate on Cypress. She was keeping up appearances as best she could. I gave her all the kudos I could muster, and I think it made her feel swell.

"But her curiosity finally got the better of her, and she asked me if the necklace was real or not. I told her, 'heavens no, these are paste, a copy, the real ones are in the vault in New York.' You can imagine her reaction; she didn't know what to make of me. I enjoy that story every time I tell it."

Jimmy smiled and said, "I know."

"I guess I've told that story before," said Kitty.

"Yes, Mom," said Jimmy, "a lot."

The next morning, Kitty's stocks and jewelry were still on the dining room table when Barb walked in.

"Knock, knock," said Barb, "are you decent?"

"As decent as I'm going to get today," said Kitty.

"I didn't mean you, Kit. I wouldn't expect you to be decent," said Barb laughing, "I was talking about Jimmy."

"What are you talking about me for?" said Jimmy coming down the stairs.

"I was just hoping that you weren't naked," said Barb. "I don't need a fright today."

"Funny," said Jimmy sourly.

"Seriously," said Barb, "I'm heading to Pictou, so I thought I'd stop by to see if you need anything. I figured Jimmy could use his beauty sleep after his million mile journey. What's all this junk on the table?"

"It's me riches or what's left of it."

"Well your jewelry looks pretty darn good to me," said Barb examining the diamond and sapphire ring.

"It's supposed to," said Kitty, "but it's not worth a fraction of what you think it is."

"But it's not fake either," said Jimmy who had long since learned to trust Barb where his mother was concerned.

"Oh," said Barb a little bewildered, "I wouldn't know. What's all this fancy looking paper?"

"My stock certificates," said Kitty. "They may be worth a lot or a little, too. James will look into it." Kitty nodded to Jimmy who bowed to his mother.

"Hmm ... , I've never seen a stock certificate," said Barb as she turned to leave. "I'll bring you a loaf of French bread on my way back. Should be back by lunch."

"Barb and Vince are taking very good care of me," said Kitty to Jimmy.

"I know, Mom," said Jimmy.

Barb smiled as she closed the door.

Jimmy made breakfast for the two of them which they ate while staring at the pile of papers and jewelry on the table.

"I think I'll keep my string-o-pearls, but I want you to ship everything else out to your sister. She's my executrix when the time comes," said Kitty.

"Okay, Mom," said Jimmy. His Internet provider in Boston had given him a Nova Scotia telephone number that he could dial into. After breakfast, Jimmy set up his laptop computer on the dining room table and plugged the phone line into its modem. A few beeps and buzzes later, Jimmy watched the screen as it slowly filled up. "Jeez this is slow," he exclaimed.

"We're in the boonies," his mother replied proudly. Jimmy growled.

Quite a few minutes later, or so it seemed to Jimmy, a screen full of stock market symbols confirmed the value of Kitty's portfolio. Kitty was worth a lot of money. Not millions but a lot nevertheless. "You're almost rich," said Jimmy.

"Now you tell me," said his mother with a laugh.

"Seriously Mom, what do you want me to do with this?" asked Jimmy.

"Send it all to your sister Maggie, I don't need it and couldn't spend it if I tried," said Kitty.

Jimmy looked consternated then said, "How about a grand tour of the world. We'll hire porters to carry you around in one of those imperial basket things, you know, like the Queen of Sheba or something. You wouldn't have to get out of bed."

"Just send it to Maggie," Kitty laughed. "If I took off and did a grand tour it would probably kill me in a week, and besides wouldn't you like to spend some of me 'almost' riches?"

Jimmy looked hurt but agreed to pack everything up and mail it to his sister in Alberta.

Jimmy was bundled up and heading out the door to the post office in Pictou when Barb walked back in. "Where ya goin'?" she asked Jimmy.

"To the post office to mail Mom's stuff to Maggie," said Jimmy.

"I could have done that for ya," said Barb to Jimmy. He shrugged, turned and walked into the cold. "Kit, can I make you lunch?" asked Barb.

"No," said Kitty, "I'm not hungry yet."

"Okay," said Barb, "but I bought a sub. I'll cut a piece for you as a snack."

Kitty quickly ate the first and second pieces of the sandwich that Barb offered but declined a third making Barb smile. "I thought you weren't hungry?" she said.

"I guess I was," said Kitty. "I need your help in going through my stuff," Kitty continued with a stern voice.

"So what are we doing today to dismantle your life?" asked Barb.

"I believe the word is deconstruct, anyway I had a valise,

under the table that's full of stuff I collected when I was in Germany, before the war," said Kitty. "It's all my Nazi propaganda and some things I took from Germany that were strictly verboten."

"Ooh," said Barb, "sounds top secret."

"It is in a way, I suppose," said Kitty. "It's not considered proper to have a lot of this stuff. I mean some people would consider this stuff to be poison."

"What kind of stuff do you have?" said Barb, her eyes widening in anticipation.

Kitty put her finger up to her lips and said, "Shhhh! I have lots of photographs, and I have a Jewish armband with a yellow Star of David. I also have a poster that I ripped off the wall that said, in German of course, 'Jews forbidden' and ...," Kitty looked around suspiciously then, lowering her voice said, "I have a photograph of Hitler signed by the man himself and Herman Göring."

"Oh," said Barb pausing, "wouldn't that be valuable to someone?"

"It might be some day," said Kitty, "but I think you can go to jail, at least in Germany, for having that stuff or selling it." Kitty looked around suspiciously, "I don't know what the laws in Canada are but it's certainly politically incorrect to have this stuff around."

"Where, or rather how, did you get it? The photo I mean," asked Barb shaking her head.

"In Munich," said Kitty. "He gave it to me."

"Just like that?" asked Barb still shaking her head.

"Pretty much," said Kitty. "I used to go to the Café Heck with my friends after rehearsal. I studied opera while I was in Germany. I was supposed to sing the role of Papagena in Mozart's Magic Flute at the Munich Opera in the spring of 1940 but I obviously never got the chance." Kitty looked off wistfully, breathing a deep sigh.

"And?" Barb interrupted, waving her hands.

"I'm getting to it," Kitty protested. "... Anyway, as I was saying, I was studying opera, and Hitler loved opera, and he used to come to the Café Heck too. I saw him there all the time, so when he heard there was an American girl studying opera, actually there were a bunch of us American girls studying opera, he asked me over for a chat. I only talked to him that once and only for a few minutes. He didn't speak any English, but I spoke passable German and French, of course, so we were able to communicate. He was very charming and asked me all about my studies and how I liked Germany and all that.

"He had a very magnetic gaze. He would look you straight in the eyes with that piercing look; it felt like he could look into your soul. It was more than a little frightening, creepy. Most women I knew there were mesmerized by him. I can completely understand the effects he had on people. In the end, we all agreed that he and the whole Nazi group were sleazy.

"Anyway, on the night before Kristallnacht, he smiled and waved to me as I was leaving and he was coming in with his cronies. He sent one of his henchmen chasing after me with that picture. I met Herman Göring a couple of weeks later, also in the Café Heck, and got him to sign the same picture."

"Wow," said Barb in astonishment, "you're history."

"No, I certainly hope not," said Kitty correctly, "but I did see some history being made while spending my father's money."

"I thought you were poor during the Depression, what's this 'Spending your father's money' all about,'" said Barb.

"We were cash poor; we had the 'big house' but very little income. My father had left some money in Germany, so I went there to spend it."

"How did that happen? Couldn't you just write a check or sell the stuff?" Barb asked.

Kitty took a deep breath and began, "Right after the First

World War, when Europe was a colossal mess, my father invested some money in Germany, and his investments did very well. But the German Government blocked access to the Mark, which prevented anyone from transferring cash out of Germany. That meant that my father lost all that income and capital. Anyway, when I got out of high school I went to Germany to study opera and spend that money before the war started and, believe me, everyone knew another war was coming."

"Wow, how much money did you have?"

"I started out with about a million Reich marks. I'm not sure what that would have been in dollars, several hundred thousand I think. It was a lot of money then, and today I would guess that it would have been at least a few million bucks, 'US' but I really can't say ... it was a lot of money."

"Cool," said Barb. "Did you spend it all or was there some left when you skedaddled?"

Kitty's face broke into a grin. "I was pretty efficient, and I don't think I left more than a couple of hundred marks. I did everything First Class."

"Wow, what was it like?" asked Barb.

Kitty smiled and said, "Did you ever see the movie Cabaret?"

Barb nodded.

"Well, my life in Munich was really like that. It was a pretty decadent place, and I was Sally Bowles only I had a lot of money." Kitty was very proud of herself for coming up with that.

Barb sat quietly thinking about Kitty living the wild life in Nazi Germany. "Yup, I can see you there," she said. "So where is this state secret?"

"All that stuff is in a valise, that was tucked under the table here," Kitty said.

"Oh that old thing," said Barb, "I tossed that," but the grin on her face announced her lie.

"Well go get it from the trash then," said Kitty with a polite smile.

"I put it in the cold room, behind the wall with the expensive china. I'll go fetch it," said Barb.

When Kitty first moved to Poplar Hill, she had Vince turn the front room into a combination library, front parlor, and antique shop by putting up bookshelves and built-in cupboards. The small sign over the front door still read, "Bag End, Notions & Antiques." She had Vince create a hidden, secret compartment behind the built-in cupboards so that she could hide her more valuable possessions like her Limoges china and Tiffany trinkets.

When Barb returned with the dilapidated suitcase, Kitty had turned pale and had begun to hyperventilate. "Oh, Jeez, are you okay?" she asked, very concerned.

"I'm having an angina attack," said Kitty breathlessly. "I think I'll be all right in a bit. I took some aspirin and another nitro pill."

Barb and Kitty sat staring at each other for nearly an hour. When the angina attack finally passed Kitty was exhausted and told Barb that she really just needed a nap. Barb put a blanket over her and asked, "Which opera do you want me to put on?"

"Der Meistersinger. It's already in the machine," said Kitty, her eyes already closed.

As the Prelude began its crescendo, a dreamy smile came over Kitty's face while Barb put on her coat and tiptoed out of the room.

6

The Valise - Spring 1998

Jimmy could hear the unpleasant sound of an operatic soprano screaming from the house as soon as he opened the car door. He hated opera as much as his mother loved it. When he was a child, she would sing along with whatever opera was playing on the radio. It was all she listened to, and when she wasn't listening to opera on the radio, she would play one of her three thousand 78s, all opera. When she washed dishes, she would daydream of her dramatic debut at the Munich Opera, or sing the same refrain, over and over again, from the chorus of Beethoven's 9th Symphony.

Now, however, Kitty was deaf, and even with her hearing aids, she had trouble hearing or understanding people when they weren't right in front of her. When it came to music, though, Kitty hated wearing her hearing aids; they distorted the sound of music, she said, so she would unplug her hearing aids and crank up the volume as high as it would go. Since her heart attack, she no longer had the breath to sing at operatic volume but would occasionally still hum along or just sing the refrain softly.

Jimmy entered the house with his hands over his ears and turned the volume down to a level he didn't find painful. The sudden absence of sound woke Kitty with a start.

"Oh, you're back from town I see," said Kitty. "I was just listening to some Wagner."

"I know," said Jimmy. "I could hear it halfway to Pictou."

"What?" Kitty asked not realizing that she had taken her hearing aids out.

Jimmy laughed and pointed to his ears with both hands.

"Oh, that's the problem," said Kitty as she plugged her hearing aids back in. "Did you get everything off to Maggie?"

"Yes, Mom," said Jimmy. "I see you had Barb drag out your old suitcase. What do you want me to do with that?" he continued.

"I'm not sure," said Kitty. "I told Barb what's in it and she thinks this stuff is valuable and it might be after my generation is gone, but right now I think it may unnecessarily open old wounds," Kitty continued then paused for a moment and said, "You keep it."

"Okay," said Jimmy, "but that stuff means something to you, not to me. Do you want to go over it, so I know what's what?"

"Oh, that would be fun," said Kitty rubbing her hands together, "but first let's make dinner. We shall make crepes tonight."

Of course, Jimmy ruined the béchamel sauce, but the results were delicious nonetheless.

As Jimmy cleaned the dinner dishes, Kitty sat staring at the small suitcase.

It had been years since she had looked at its contents, but James was right, she thought, if she didn't talk about it now the history contained in the valise would be lost forever.

"You're staring at it," said Jimmy as he came into the room from the kitchen. "Shall we open it and take a look?"

"I was just thinking," said Kitty wistfully as she opened the valise, "that I should have written a book."

Jimmy smiled and said, "Are these pictures in any order?"

"At one time they were in chronological order, but I wouldn't count on that anymore."

"Who's this?" asked Jimmy holding up a small black and white photograph of a young man in a business suit.

"Oh, that is Herman the Vermin," said Kitty with a quiet 'humph.' "He was a Nazi SS officer assigned to keep tabs on us." Kitty looked sad for a moment, "We managed to get rid of him for good."

"How did you know that?"

"Simple, we had lots of parties, and Herman always managed to show up uninvited. We had our suspicions, so Betty Hofeldt and I talked Herman into throwing a party at his apartment. While one of the girls kept Herman occupied, Betty and I snuck into his bedroom and discovered his SS uniform hidden in the back of his closet. We kept a close eye on him after that and sent him on wild goose chases when we didn't want him around. We got rid of him for good eventually."

"When was that? How did you get rid of him?" asked Jimmy.

Kitty thought for a moment then with some sadness creeping into her voice, said, "Well for one, we didn't want him around when we biked passed the Dachau prison just outside Munich, and I took photos for the Chicago Tribune. We sent him to Berlin to watch opera with Betty Hofeldt. They had a wild weekend in Berlin, on Herman's nickel. It was our first strike against the Third Reich.

"I need a scorecard to keep track of all these people," said Jimmy. "Who's who?"

"Okay," said Kitty, "you know about Herman the Vermin. I mentioned Betty Hofeldt, she was studying opera and spending her family's money just like I was. I think my father knew her father, so somehow I managed to have an introduction when I arrived in Munich. I can't really remember anymore but that's how we met. Betty and I were roommates back in New York during the war when we both worked for the Pennsylvania Railroad. Then there was Kozie, his real name is Manouchehr Kozimere. He was a first cousin of the Shah of Iran and had some kind of diplomatic passport but he was basically in Munich to spend money too. Kozie was also a part-time spy for the British, or so we all thought. If he really was a spy he was an amateur spy and did it for the fun of it. Then, of course, there was Chauncey Joseph Medburry III. Joe was also a spy, of sorts, I think, and also in Munich to spend his family's money. Peggy Sweeney was there too but she was a violinist. Then there was dear Sam Anderson. We went everywhere together. Whenever there was a crisis we'd get out of town together. Sam was in Germany studying German and Slavic languages. He spoke everything, German, Polish, Slovenian, you name it. There were lots of others that came and went but that group was the core and they stayed till the bitter end."

"What was the bitter end?" asked Jimmy.

"Well, let's see," said Kitty. "Betty left a week before the Germans marched into Czechoslovakia on the ides of March 1939; I tried to leave the next day but got stuck in Trieste with Sam when all the borders were closed. That's when we hopped on the refugee boat heading to Palestine; it was the only way out. We went back to Munich when things quieted down, and the war obviously hadn't started, which we all expected it would. I don't know where Peggy, Kozie and Joe Medburry went during that Czech crisis but I do know that Kozie was called home but didn't actually leave Germany until sometime in late 1940 or '41. Peggy went to London and stayed through the Blitz, and Joe was in Paris when the Germans marched in. He got back to the US on a Spanish freighter. Sam put his reporter's hat on and went to Paris with Joe, then to London for the Blitz."

"Wow," said Jimmy, "that's pretty cool. And you left just before the Germans invaded Poland, right?"

"Yup," said Kitty. "I spent just about all the money I had left to get that ticket home, First Class all the way. I made it back with a 1000 mark note in my pocket. It's in the valise someplace. The black market for money had dried up by then so leaving on a German ship was pretty much my only option.

"We were two days from New York when the ship's Captain announced at dinner that he had been ordered to turn around and head back to Germany because England was expected to declare war any minute. We had a parley with all the First Class passengers, and he decided that he was going to ignore that order and continue on to New York. We had lifeboat drills every couple of hours after that. I think the captain expected to be sunk by the British or Canadians at any moment. We were all scared to death until we saw the Statue of Liberty then everyone, including the German crew, cheered." A small tear ran down Kitty's cheek.

"What's the matter, Mom?" asked Jimmy.

"That man," Kitty said quietly. "That man ruined everything. He really ruined everything."

"Hitler, you mean?" asked Jimmy.

"Yes," said Kitty turning away. "Yes, Hitler."

Jimmy didn't know what to say, so he sat in silence while Kitty picked up and examined photographs one at a time. He could see tears in his mother's eyes even as she hid them. "It's time for bed," she announced suddenly....

The next morning, Kitty had already been up for several hours and had made coffee and scones. She was sitting in a chair by the kitchen table buttering her creations when Barb pounded on the back door. Before Kitty could say "come on in" Barb was already in the kitchen sniffing the air.

"Yummy," exclaimed Barb. "What are you up for today?" she asked.

"It's a good day already," said Kitty pointing to her walker. "I made it from me bed to the kitchen, but I don't think I'm up for Pictou."

Before Kitty's heart attack, Saturdays meant that Barb and Kitty would set off for town. Kitty would shop for groceries then spend a couple of hours at someone's house hooking rugs. Barb didn't have the patience for rug hooking so she would drop Kitty off with the "hookers" while she shopped at the mall in New Glasgow. Kitty loved telling callers that she was unavailable on Saturdays because she was hooking that day. It always caught them off guard.

"I think I've hooked me last rug," said Kitty quietly.

"Okay, Kit," said Barb, "I don't have much to do today. We can just hang out if you want."

Just then Jimmy crashed into the kitchen in search of coffee.

"Welcome to the world of the living," said Kitty. Jimmy grunted.

"Late night carousing?" asked Barb with a smile as she handed Jimmy a cup of coffee and a scone.

"I think I'm going to go into town to see if I can find out what happened to the companies you have stock in beside Pfizer. I want to know what happened to some of those companies, they may have merged or something," said Jimmy.

"Murdered? Who got murdered?" asked Kitty.

"Turn up your hearing aids, Mom," said Jimmy pointing to his ears as Barb giggled.

"I'm going to go to the library, to research some of your strange stock certificates," Jimmy yelled.

"I can hear you, I can hear you," said Kitty turning down her hearing aids which were squealing.

"Hey Jimmy," yelled Barb, "we can hear you."

Jimmy rolled his eyes and went back upstairs to get dressed.

"Kit," said Barb, "what would you like to do today? I have all day. Do you need anything done?"

Kitty thought quietly for a moment then said, "Have I ever told you about the valise in the other room and how I got to Germany?"

"Yes," said Barb laughing, "a few times, but it always gets better every time you tell the story so let's hear it again."

"Oh, dear, when Stan was alive, he used to tell the same stories over and over again, and they got awfully repetitive after a while. Are you sure I won't bore you?"

"Kit, you've never told a boring story, and I doubt you've told the same story twice."

"I haven't made any of it up," Kitty protested.

"I didn't mean that. You tell different parts of the same story, but I don't think I've ever heard all the parts of any one story, so I've never gotten bored. Besides, I never did very well in history, so I learn a lot."

"Oh, well, that's different then," said Kitty.

The two sat in silence sipping coffee until Jimmy left for town, then Barb helped Kitty back to her chair and put the oxygen tube around her neck. Kitty took several deep breaths and said, "I'm feeling a lot better today. I was unplugged from this machine for almost three hours, but it feels better breathing oxygen."

"Your color is better too," said Barb.

"Splendid altogether," said Kitty sinking deeper into her chair. "I want to tell you about ... the valise." Kitty pointed with a weak flourish at the small weather-beaten suitcase sitting on the chair next to her.

"I'm all ears," said Barb taking a bite of her scone.

"That little suitcase has a very long history," Kitty began slowly.

"I'll bet it does," Barb interrupted.

Kitty smiled and continued, "This belonged to my mother when she was in convent school as a child. They teach you to live very sparingly in the convent. When I went to the convent school in Grenoble, my mother gave me this valise. I always felt it was a sacred gift of sorts."

Kitty paused to think about what she had just said then continued, "My mother was very, um, je ne sais quoi, not really wild, but more adventurous, and I guess she knew that I would be too, so I always took the gift of the valise as a symbol of the wanderlust we shared, a passing of the torch, as it were, or in this case the valise."

Barb nodded.

"Of course that makes no sense unless you knew my mother. She was the youngest of three girls; I am the youngest of three girls. I'm not sure that matters, but, anyway, my mother was the first woman, in recorded history, that is, to climb Mont Blanc. She did that when she was 20. That was in 1905. Before that she traveled alone, overland from Paris to Shanghai then sailed back to London via India. She met my father in Paris at the American Embassy where they threw a party in her honor. My father said it was instant mutual infatuation. He was in Paris trying to write his doctoral thesis on French jurisprudence."

"What's that?" asked Barb.

"Jurisprudence?" asked Kitty. "He was studying the French system of justice."

"Oh," said Barb, "so keep going about the suitcase."

Kitty paused for a moment and deeply inhaled oxygen from the tube in her nose before continuing. "When my parents deposited me at the convent, I was six or seven, and all my worldly belongings were in that valise. The convent supplied uniforms, so I didn't need anything besides underwear, a couple of sweaters, and a coat. When I traveled home seven years later, I had this valise and one other small suitcase that showed up when I was sent home. I learned to travel very lightly.

"When I went to Germany to study opera I went with a steamer trunk full of clothing - I had to be sociable after all - and this little suitcase. But whenever I had to beat it out of Germany during some crisis or other, all I took was this valise. There were times I wished I had brought more though. When Sam and I went from Trieste to Istanbul third class, steerage, there was no way to wash clothing. We had to wear the same clothing for four days. Phew!"

Kitty held her nose before continuing, "Everywhere else was just fine. Even up in the mountains, in the traveler's inns, you could wash your underwear and hang it to dry."

"I don't think I'd like to travel like that," said Barb.

"Most people traveled like that back then," said Kitty. "Only the ostentatiously rich had dozens of trunks when they traveled. Of course, well-appointed travel was a lot easier back then when everyone traveled by boat and railroad. My father liked traveling in style, but my mother preferred to travel 'fast and light' as she called it, and so do I.

"It's funny, but, if you traveled first class on a train in Europe in the 1930s only the Americans and occasionally the British traveled with lots of baggage and a retinue. The image of the loud, brash, uncultured American was, and is, quite real abroad. Pictou is not a swanky destination, so you don't get many of those types here. Halifax maybe, but I doubt it."

"Did you always travel first class?" asked Barb.

"Only when I could pay in German marks," said Kitty, "otherwise I had to trade what I could on the black market, and that wasn't always much. The closer we got to war the more expensive other currencies became. By the time I decided I had better skedaddle home, in the summer of 1939, I couldn't buy an American dollar at any price, but I could always buy a train ride or a ship ride out of Germany, and I always bought round-trip tickets and always first class because they do treat you better in first class," Kitty was grinning.

"I'll bet they do," said Barb.

"Yup," said Kitty, "that's the point of first class, but once I was out of Germany I had to buy local currency on the black market, and that was a problem. We might arrive someplace by first-class train then have to stay in a hostel because we couldn't find anyone who would exchange our marks. That's why Sam and I went steerage from Trieste to Istanbul, it was the only way out of Trieste, and we had to leave because no one would take German marks. Steerage was the only way we could afford to travel. It took all the cash we had in our pockets. It's also why we had to hike across the border into Switzerland, up a valley and then up a mountain during one crisis or other ... I can't remember which one right now. Sam, Peggy, Betty, Joe, Kozie, and a bunch of others I can't remember, spent a wonderful week at a Swiss excursion inn. The innkeeper was grateful to have anyone with cash, even if it was German marks, and we were grateful to be out of Germany. Everyone won.

"I learned to ski there. Our crowd included about a dozen women and half that number in men. The Swiss army was out, maneuvering on skis, and after a few hours of blowing things up and shooting at things in the valley below us, they'd come and join us at the inn for food and drink. The Swiss army was well equipped with food and beer when they visited. I'm not sure they made us any safer, but the Germans did leave Switzerland alone, and I don't think they could have walked in as they did in Austria or Czechoslovakia without a bloody nose."

"I didn't know you knew how to ski," said Barb.

"I don't anymore. That was the first and last time I was ever on skis, but at the time I thought I got pretty good at it. Joe was a phenomenal skier."

Kitty sighed, "There were a lot of things I might have done if the war hadn't come along. On the other hand, there are a lot of things I wouldn't have done if the coming war wasn't obvious to all."

They sat quietly for a few minutes before Barb asked, "Where else has this suitcase been?"

"Just a minute," said Kitty breathlessly, "I need to catch up."

Kitty looked pale, so Barb got up to look. She wasn't sure what she was looking for, but she felt she had to do something. "Ah ha," Barb exclaimed while holding up Kitty's oxygen tube, "a kink in the tube. This should do ya better."

Kitty slowly and deliberately inhaled the renewed flow of oxygen, and her pallor returned to normal, or at least what passed for normal with Kitty whose 'normal' color had slowly assumed a slightly ashen shade since her heart attack.

"Well," said Kitty slowly, "when I got home from Germany I lived in New Canaan and worked at the French Institute, the Alliance Française, in New York as a translator and tour guide. When the Japanese finally forced us into the war, I had to move to New York, to Manhattan, because the trains were reserved for the boys going off to war so I couldn't commute anymore. I lived uptown in an apartment my mother kept at 325 East Seventy-Ninth Street so that I could walk to work on East Sixtieth. I worked there from October 1939 to March 1941 then I joined the Pennsylvania Railroad as a 'passenger representative.' I ran the trains while the boys were off at war." Kitty sat back and smiled, very pleased with herself.

"You were talking about this here suitcase," said Barb in mock annoyance.

"I was," said Kitty looking surprised, "Oh!"

"And, ..." said Barb waving her hands.

"Well, I suppose I used this little valise throughout the war years. I managed three trains, 'The Twentieth Century Limited,' from New York to Chicago, 'The Broadway Limited,' from Washington to New York and 'The Capitol Limited,' between Chicago and Washington. I made a counterclockwise loop starting in New York. There were twelve girls running those trains and we hot-bunked in three apartments. My apartment in New York was our New York base. Betty Hofeldt was my official roommate in New York, and she always ran the train ahead of me, so she always knew what was happening in Chicago or Washington before I did. Six of us went clockwise, and six went counterclockwise. Oh, and the valise was all I took for the week-long trip: New York to Chicago, then Chicago to Washington DC, then back to New York and a couple of days off. I met Stan on The Washingtonian to New York leg."

"It's pretty beat up," said Barb. "When did you stop using it? Did you stop using it?"

"Stan bought a new one for me when we were dating. He thought this one looked a bit too shabby, so I relegated it to keeping my memorabilia in. It served its purpose well; it is, after all, close to 100 years old now."

"Wow," said Barb shaking her head. "I can't imagine anything I own lasting 100 years."

Kitty shrugged, "Would you mind helping an old girl into the shower?"

Part of the transformation of the first floor of Kitty's house included a shower stall with a fold-down seat that Vince had put into the pantry while Kitty was at the hospital. Kitty preferred a leisurely bath and had never lived in a house with a modern shower. Now, of course, she couldn't climb the stairs, and there wasn't enough room for a bathtub in the pantry, so Vince installed a prefabricated shower stall 'straight from the Simpson-Sears Catalog.'

Kitty could get used to anything, and a shower was a delightfully new experience. It was not that she'd never taken a shower before, it was more that when she had a choice, she always preferred a bath. Now a shower was the only option, so she was determined to enjoy it, and she did, often sitting under the shower head until all the hot water in the tank had been exhausted, and her already wrinkly skin had assumed the texture of a prune. Secretly, Kitty could still sing loudly enough in the shower to enjoy herself.

When Jimmy came home from Pictou, Barb was sitting at the kitchen table sipping tea and reading the Canadian edition of People Magazine. Kitty was clearly and loudly enjoying her shower.

"I hope she doesn't slip in there," said Jimmy.

"Naw," said Barb, "she's sitting down, I checked. She'll call when she wants out."

Jimmy leaned back in his chair and poured himself some tea. "Thanks for taking care of her," said Jimmy.

"Aw, jeez," said Barb, "What are friends for?" Barb paused for a minute then said, "I've been wondering something about your mom for years that I just can't figure out."

"What's that?" said Jimmy.

"I'm not sure how to say this," said Barb, "but, well, I've known Kit for about 30 years, and I've never quite figured out why some people treat her like royalty. I mean your mom is a nice lady, down to earth, has her own opinions and all that, but why do so many people 'bow and scrape' as your mom would say?"

Jimmy laughed. His mother was singing at the top of her weak lungs, "Oh Susanna, now don't cha cry for me ...."

"Well," said Jimmy, "it's sometimes a delicate topic, and one that I'm not sure Mom could explain herself, but I asked her old friend from New Canaan, Mrs. 'O' the same question once, and she explained it this way:

"Every society is stratified, even Communist societies. In America, and I guess also in Canada, there are 'blue collar' and 'white collar' or 'middle class' and 'upper-middle class' but there is a lot more to it than that. The reality is that, in America at least, and I suspect everywhere else too, the rich set the pace for the rest of society to follow."

"Yeah," said Barb, "I know about working class and middle class and all that."

"Right," said Jimmy, "but it's more complicated. At the top you have the old rich who have the money to buy everything but no longer have the desire, mostly because they have discovered that they already have enough of everything, so they stop spending money, they become cheap. Next, you have the newly rich. They have the money to buy everything and do, but don't really have the social maturity or taste to know what to buy so, they look to the 'old rich' to set the standards and teach them how to behave. Movie stars and rock stars fall into this category. Then you've got the average upwardly mobile middle-class man or woman who gets their clue from the TV or magazines. Of course, journalists fall into a category in between, so they often take their lead from the newly rich and totally gauche, those who make the most noise."

"Like who?" protested Barb.

"Like Donald Trump," said Jimmy with a little disdain in his voice.

"Oh, I see," said Barb giggling to herself.

In the shower, Kitty began singing, 'Oh Christmas tree' in German. Jimmy and Barb both laughed. It was mid-autumn.

"So why do the ladies of Pictou and New Glasgow kowtow to your mom?" asked Barb.

"I was getting to that," said Jimmy. "Mrs 'O' and my mom are the last of the 'old rich' even though they don't have much money anymore. Somehow people sense that she's old money. It's a special kind of self-assurance that comes with having good taste and a bit of a devil-may-care attitude. Mom can tell the difference between a real Gucci bag and a Chinese knockoff but is perfectly content to use something she found at a thrift shop.

"Mrs. 'O' and Mom were young New York socialites back when it really made a difference. They ran the show. Take fashion. There are two centers of the fashion universe, New York, and Paris. Only the 'old rich' and the 'new rich' can afford thousand dollar outfits, but it's the 'old rich' that get to decide what's fashionable. That's the social elite of New York City, and Mrs. 'O' and my Mom were part of it. They got to decide which designers were 'hot,' what authors or artists were 'in,' and what charity to support or not and the rest of the world followed along like puppies.

"She's a natural leader, but she doesn't have the kind of ego that makes enemies."

"I think I know what you mean by Kit's attitude," said Barb thoughtfully. "She looks everyone in the eye and treats everyone as an equal. So if I think I'm hot stuff and Kitty treats me as an equal, then Kitty must be hot stuff too. And since

Kitty really is hot stuff then people who get to know her feel totally cool when they hang around her."

"Yeah, something like that," said Jimmy laughing. "She knows who's who in the world and what is hot, what's fashionable, and what's not. She knows - or at least knew - the names of all the writers on the best sellers lists and has met a lot of them, same with art.

"She also knows what fork to use for what and how to properly address a Roman Catholic Archbishop or the Governor General of Canada, or the Queen of England, but not the Prime Minister of England, apparently — but that's another story. And she does all these things effortlessly and mostly without drawing attention to herself. If she doesn't know the right way to do something she'll make it up on the spot and never offends. I'm always amazed.

"She was no more impressed by meeting Hitler or Neville Chamberlain than she was repulsed by penniless Jewish refugees traveling to Palestine. Don't get me wrong, she's always said that the trip in a refugee boat was a disgusting experience, but did she ever tell you that she kept track of some of those refugees and helped them come to the US after the war? When I was a little kid some of our neighbors had been on that boat with her. No one is above her, and no one is beneath her. She really believes in *liberté, égalité, fraternité*.

"So the ladies of Pictou want to be like her, and that makes her the queen."

"Okay," said Barb not quite sure she understood. "So why are the two of us such good friends then?"

"Ah," said Jimmy, "that's easy, you're simply friends. She's not 'on' when she's around you. You don't care what fork is the right one to use or if Picasso or Degas is the more important artist, or which wine is the correct one at the moment so long as it tastes good. Mom really just likes to live day to day, minute by minute. The two of you have a more

basic relationship, a friendship that goes beyond proper appearances. She can talk to you about baking a simple cake
or the politics of Pictou or whatever it is that the two of you
talk about. That stuff is really more important to her than
stuff like 'can you wear white after Labor Day?'"

"So what happened to you?" asked Barb. "And I don't mean
that as an insult," she quickly added. "I mean, you're not like
Kit that way."

Jimmy said quietly, "It's hard enough for me to just make
a living. Have you heard the old saying 'it takes three generations to go from rags to riches?' Well, it works the other
way around too. My grandfather was rich, and I'm not. Now
I am thoroughly, completely and hopelessly struggling just
to stay in the middle class."

Barb nodded and thought quietly for a moment. "Sometimes I feel like I'm inside the castle of a princess," said Barb
with a wistful look that made Jimmy shake his head and
smile.

"You are, Barb," said Jimmy. "You are."

In the shower the hot water had been exhausted and was
now well water cold, but Kitty was determined to finish one
more refrain, "Oh, ye'll tak' the high road, and I'll tak' the
low road, And I'll be in Scotland afore ye; But me and my
true love will never meet again, on the bonnie, bonnie banks
o' Loch Lomond."

7

Another Mouth to Feed
Summer 1998 (May 1937)

Jimmy was going into town again, this time with his laptop computer. He was determined to discover the value of the stock certificates he had found in Kitty's safety deposit box. He found it hard to believe that they had no value at all. Kitty had just shrugged her shoulders when Jimmy had told her that none of her stocks were still traded. "Ah well, *c'est la vie*," she had said. She had said the same thing years before when Jimmy had tried in vain to discover if his father's estate had any hidden gems stashed away someplace. Jimmy couldn't believe that so much money could just disappear.

Barb came in with groceries as Jimmy pulled out of the driveway in his rented Cadillac. "Where's Jimmy going in such a hurry?"

"Oh, he's off tilting at windmills just like his father."

"I thought Stan was a big deal businessman," said Barb not fully engaged in the conversation as she put cans in the cubbard.

"He was an inveterate entrepreneur," said Kitty.

Barb looked at Kitty, paying attention, "A what?"

Kitty started off slowly, "Stan was more of an entrepreneur than your average business executive. I don't think he would have been happy running the Bank of America, but he jumped at the chance to try to save Continental Coal Corporation. Stan ended up presiding over the biggest bankruptcy in American history, up till then anyway."

Barb laughed.

"Of course, the collapse of Continental Coal was nothing compared to what followed, like the Pennsylvania Railroad bankruptcy.

"Stan always believed that executives should have some 'skin in the game' as they say, to justify the salaries they receive so he went 'all in' when he took over Continental Coal. It didn't work out, and I think it ultimately killed him. Stan was optimistic till the end but really, how do you start over at 70?"

"I didn't know you were really *that* broke," said Barb with a shrug.

"Oh, yes, we were."

"What happened, I mean besides the Continental Coal thing?" asked Barb as she brushed Kitty's thinning hair.

"Well, Stan was quite well off when I met him. He owned several houses and a half dozen horses up in Ardsley Terrace, New York. He also had a sea plane moored on the Hudson. When his only daughter, from his first marriage, got married he gave her most of his belongings as a dowry. I certainly couldn't object. Besides, Stan had a very good job working for the government."

"I didn't know Stan had a first wife; did they get divorced?"

Kitty laughed, "No, I wasn't the ingénue out to wreck homes. Stan's wife died of cancer just after I met him. We didn't date for a couple of years after that."

"Oh, so what happened then?"

"Stan retired from his government job and resurrected his old investment banking business after we married. His investments gave us a nice income but, he was itching to do something big. Stan loved huge engineering projects so when Continental Coal came along with its three hundred mines and a hundred thousand employees he jumped in without looking very closely, without due diligence, I think they call it. He put five million dollars of his own, our own, money into the business before he realized they were over

200 million dollars in debt. None of his banking or investments buddies were willing to help, so the whole venture
foundered, and we lost every last cent Stan had."

"Wow, that's a lot of money," said Barb. "So is that how
you ended up in Nova Scotia?"

"It wasn't that simple; besides that was in 1957, I think,
well before I ever thought of moving here," Kitty protested. "We did have to move out of New York City and back
to New Canaan. Stan still commuted to New York during
the week, but he never did rebuild his business. We moved
into a cheap basement apartment. Then, when it got flooded
during a hurricane, we moved into the coachman's cottage
on my father's estate where we lived until Stan died and I
moved here. We were poor but happy." Kitty was smiling,
"Stan was a wonderful man."

"How did you meet again?" asked Barb. She couldn't remember if Kitty had told her the story but thought she might
have. There were times when the two of them would just
chat about nothing for hours, and Barb would walk away not
remembering a thing they'd said, but now Barb was paying
attention.

"It was during the war. One of my jobs running the train
was to manage the radiotelephone between stops. Everyone
has a cell phone today, but back then there was one radiotelephone on each train. We made reservations in fifteen-min-
ute increments to use the phone, and I used to double book
because at five dollars a minute no one ever talked for long.

"Stan and another fellow booked a reservation at the same
time, and the other fellow showed up first, so I placed his call.
Stan showed up and threw a fit. It turned out that his wife
had terminal cancer and she would get a shot that knocked
her out at five thirty p.m. Stan tried to call her every day at
exactly five p.m. You can imagine the stink he made. The
other fellow gave up his reservation and Stan had his call. I
didn't see him again for five years, but we remembered each
other when we did meet again."

Barb nodded her head; she *had* heard the story before.

Kitty giggled to herself and began to sing softly, "Passengers will please refrain from flushing toilets while the train is standing in the station, I love you."

"What was that?" said Barb in astonishment.

"Oh, that was a little ditty I made up," said a distracted Kitty.

The valise was still sitting on the chair in front of Kitty, and she started poking at the items on the surface. "Humph," she said, "I wonder where my air-raid warden's arm band is?"

"What's it look like?" asked Barb taking a renewed interest in the small suitcase in front of them.

"It's khaki with an air-raid warning symbol sewn on, a red triangle inside a black circle. I applied for the job when I was still in high school, but some general wrote back saying what a marvelous idea it was but that he had no money for it."

Barb looked at Kitty, blinked and said, "What on earth are you talking about?"

"This," said Kitty holding up the Civil Defense armband. "I asked for this in 1936, well before the war started and before I went to Germany. Everyone knew that a war was coming. But it took until the middle of 1942 before the Civil Defense was really organized."

"Why did you ask for this in 1936?" asked Barb a little confused.

Kitty explained, choosing her words carefully, "My father was, what you might call, a rabid anti-Communist. He tended to see a Communist conspiracy in almost any movement outside of the Connecticut Republican Party. He thought Roosevelt was a traitor to his class, which I suppose he was in a way ... but that's beside the point.

"Anyway, my father had read Hitler's book *Mein Kampf* where Hitler said exactly what he had in mind. He said that Germany needed room to grow, *Lebensraum* they call it, and that the primary causes of Germany's problems were the Jews, to put it succinctly."

"Go on," said Barb in disbelief. "Really? We have lots of room in Canada, and it hasn't helped us all that much."

Kitty laughed, "No one said he was right."

"Go on, go on!"

Kitty took a deep breath from her oxygen tube; she was on a roll. "It was clear that the Fascists were not very nice people. They had already taken over Germany, Italy and were taking over Spain and everyone knew what they were all about.

"Germany and Japan had already agreed to divide the world between them. So although my father was an anti-Communist, he firmly believed that the Fascists were the greater danger. It turned out he was right."

Kitty took another deep breath, "Anyway, by the time I graduated from high school in 1937, Hitler had already remilitarized the Rhineland, which is a strip of land between Germany and France, and no one but the French said a word. I think it was clear that they would take over more and more until a war was inevitable. Hitler was going to expand Germany at his neighbor's expense, and caution be damned.

"Hitler really thought that the French would give in and that England and the United States would eventually align themselves with Germany. He said so in his book. It was all right there for everyone to see.

"He was only right about the French, of course, but that was only because the French had terrible leadership at the time. In another France, he would have been very, very wrong. Think of Napoleon."

"Oh," said Barb, "how come I never learned this stuff in school?"

"Well, I don't think anyone is interested anymore. It's all ancient history now I suppose, isn't it?"

Kitty shook her head then held up the Civil Defense armband and said, "So after one of my father's Saturday morning lectures on current events I wrote a letter to the General in charge of the Connecticut National Guard suggesting every neighborhood should form defense committees. He replied that it was a great idea but that he had no money for it. I finally got my Civil Defense armband in 1942."

"I'll never remember half of that, but it's a good story," said Barb who thought for a moment then asked, "So if you knew a war was coming, why did you go to Germany? Why would your father let you go?"

"For one," said Kitty with a laugh, "we were broke. My father had already developed as much of the estate as he could. We were down to three and a quarter acres in a four-acre zone. That was down from almost 400 acres. We could see our neighbors in the winter, which was something my mother did not like.

"So after I graduated from high school, I was another mouth to feed and since I couldn't afford to 'come out'...." Kitty thought for a moment then laughing, said, "It meant something different back then."

"Oh?" said Barb with a wink.

"Anyway, the expedient thing for me to do was to go to Europe, Germany in particular, and spend my father's money." Kitty was animated and close to hyperventilating oxygen.

Barb could see Kitty smiling and breathing heavily, so she said, "Slow down before you pass out on me. I know you went to Germany to spend your father's money, but why did he have money there in the first place?"

Kitty took a deep breath and began the story, "Right after the First World War Germany experienced hyper-inflation. A day's pay was a million marks if you had a job and starvation poverty if you didn't. My father had sent an old friend an American ten-dollar bill after that friend had said he was having financial difficulties. Later that year that friend wrote back to tell my father that the ten-dollar bill had paid for a two-month vacation on the Baltic Sea. My father smelled an investment opportunity. He invested a few thousand dollars in Krupp, the big German industrial giant.

"Krupp largely rebuilt the German economy and profited handsomely when Hitler began to re-arm. We had enjoyed the rise in the value of, and dividends from, this and other investments in Germany. That is until Germany blocked the mark by restricting the flow of money out of the country.

"Anyway, both my sisters were married, and my parents didn't want to go, so I was the only choice," said Kitty.

"But you still haven't told me why your father let you go?" demanded Barb.

"Oh," said Kitty, "that's easy. I wanted to study opera and Munich had a well-respected school. Plus there was lots of money in Germany and, as my father said at the time, 'Armies are like big, ponderous pachyderms — they move very slowly, only a snail couldn't get out of the way.' He was wrong, of course; the German army could move very quickly, but there was still plenty of warning, like the earthquakes that happen before a volcano erupts.

"Secretly, I liked to write, and some friend of my father set it up so that I was accredited to the Chicago Tribune as a stringer. It was an opportunity to be a part-time journalist which gave me the excuse to travel. I thought of myself as a petty spy. A lot of us thought of ourselves as petty spies." Kitty was grinning.

Barb shook her head, "I don't think I would have gone and I don't think I would have let my children go either."

Kitty shrugged, "I left New York City aboard the SS Europa in the middle of May. I didn't stick around for graduation because I was eager to get to Germany.

"I remember the date, May 16th, 1937, because there was a big to-do about the survivors of the Hindenburg going home, all the media were there. I left for Europe tourist class and returned first class."

Barb interrupted, "Hey, I thought you only traveled first class?"

"Only when I could pay in German marks," said Kitty with a laugh. "It turned out that I could have paid in Marks since I was traveling on a German registered ship, but I didn't know that until I was already in my tourist cabin. The bursar informed me of that fact when I had to pay for meals that I didn't have the cash for. I gave him my account number for the bank in Munich, he wired ahead and informed me that there would be no further problems. Welcome to the cabaret," said Kitty with a flourish.

Jimmy came crashing through the back door just then breaking the spell Kitty had cast with her story.

"They are worthless," said Jimmy looking dejected, "totally worthless. Every single one of those companies went broke during the Depression."

"It doesn't surprise me," said Kitty, "but are you sure? I've put those stocks up for collateral, more than once, and no one objected."

Jimmy laughed. "Yeah, they are pretty worthless, but this one is so well done it's worth $40 ... as art." Jimmy waved a blue bordered stock certificate worth 500 shares in Midland Oil Corporation. "Who took these as collateral anyway and when?"

"Well now let's see," said Kitty thoughtfully, "I had you bring that package of stocks to Mrs. 'O' when I bought this place. I wrote a check to Mrs. 'Pat' for $6,000, and I asked Mrs. 'O' to cover it and used these stocks as collateral. I put them up as collateral again when I co-signed for our neighborhood tractor with the Scotsburn Co-op."

"Oh, yeah," said Jimmy, "I remember riding over to her house on my bicycle with these when you were up here. She gave me a check to deposit. I think I was about 15, but I never made the connection then because I didn't know you had bought this place until two weeks later when you came home and said,' We're moving.'

"You know, of course, these were as worthless then as they are today, don't you?"

"I had no idea. I paid everyone back, so I never found out."

"Or they never found you out," said Barb laughing.

Between deep breaths from her oxygen tube, Kitty said, "People will believe what they want to believe. People think I'm rich, evidence to the contrary notwithstanding."

"They also think you grow pot," said Barb still giggling.

"What?" said Jimmy.

"Nothing," said Kitty, "it's a long story."

Jimmy shrugged it off; he was used to bizarre stories from his mother, and this one sounded like just another strange story where his mother had bluffed her way out of one situation or another. "What happened?" he said more than asked. "Did the RCMP catch you smoking pot, or did someone plant pot in your woods?"

"Oh Jimmy, your mom and I used to smoke up a storm right here in this kitchen, but we never got caught, except by Earl," said Barb winking at Kitty.

Kitty started laughing so hard she began coughing.

"Mom, you didn't, I mean you weren't, were you?"

"Why? Would it bother you?" Kitty asked between laughs and coughs.

"Did you tell him about the motorcycle gang that came to buy pot from you?" asked Barb in near hysterics.

"I was sold out when they came," said Kitty trying to get control of herself.

"You're kidding me, right?" Jimmy had acquired a terrified look.

"Well, sort of," replied his mother regaining her composure.

"Mom!" said Jimmy, but before he could continue his protest Barb interrupted.

"Calm down Jimmy. I found a bag of what I thought might be pot in my daughter's room so I brought it here to ask your mom what I should do."

"And we smoked some of it to see if it really was reefer," said Kitty.

"Reefer? Was it? ... and how would you know?"

"If it was reefer," said Kitty with renewed vigor and a laugh, "it wasn't very good."

"But how would you know?"

"I know what reefer smells like, but I can't say it ever did me any good ... or harm for that matter," said Kitty, but before Jimmy could respond she waved him to sit down and continued, "When I worked for the Pennsylvania Railroad I spent one or two nights a week in Chicago, and I used to spend all of my free time in the black jazz clubs. The porters took me to them all the time. That's where the cool music was. Reefer was more common than tobacco, and I've smoked both. Neither one is very good for you I think."

Jimmy was relieved then asked, "But you said Earl caught you smoking?"

"Well you know, Jim," said Barb with a sly smile. "Earl rolls his own tobacco, so we asked him to come over and roll a marijuana cigarette for us. The three of us sat here puffing away, but nobody got stoned. At least I didn't, and I don't think Earl did either but you would never know would you?" Barb made a sad face before breaking into a grin.

"Humph," said Kitty. "I wonder if old Earl told someone who told someone that we smoked pot and that's how the motorcycle gang found out?"

"Oh, now that could be," said Barb nodding in agreement.

"I don't think I want to know anymore," said Jimmy shaking his head. "Anyway, what were the two of you cackling about so wildly when I came in? I didn't mean to interrupt you."

"I was on my way to Germany to study opera," said Kitty.

"I don't think you got off the boat yet," said Barb, then looking at Jimmy she said with a smile, "but we got sidetracked, I think we got stoned."

Jimmy gave Barb a sour smile and said to his mother, "I've never heard the whole story either so don't let me interrupt."

8

Rumors of War - (Summer 1937)

"I didn't go to Munich right away. It was summer after all, a time to explore, a time for lounging in outdoor cafés and for personal *lebensraum*. With no lofty academics, I spent the summer of 1937 exploring first Berlin then the magic kingdom of Bavaria, then Czechoslovakia. Prague was wonderful, and finally Hungary. Budapest was my favorite city. Then I went back to Munich in August to register for the opera school." Kitty was smiling.

"Registering for school took two weeks. It was a long, very Germanic, process, made more frightening by the looming presence of Nazi officers scrutinizing every application — Jews need not apply. For the first time in my life, my standing in society was questioned, something to which I took great exception. How dare they?"

Barb nodded her head.

Kitty was almost laughing now, "Fortunately there was someone from the American Consulate who could vouch for my provenance. An addendum was made to my passport noting that I was of pure Aryan stock. This last was accompanied by half a dozen official stamps — both rubber and paper — that were signed and counter-signed by officials in Nazi uniforms. The deed done, the officials stood up, looked at each other, clicked their heels, gave the Nazi salute, and proclaimed loudly, and in unison, 'Heil Hitler.'

"I thought this last business was very comical and I started to laugh when the panicked attaché took me aside and explained that these were not your friendly, bumbling *Burgermeisters* portrayed in literature but very serious, and very dangerous Nazis."

"All summer long we heard rumors of wars in far off places. Franco was winning the war in Spain, and the German air force was helping openly, as were the Italians. Russia and Italy were in a tiff in the Mediterranean. The Japanese had invaded China, and it looked like the Russians might go to war with the Japanese ... again. But that was all very far away from the beautiful Bavarian capital, the Bavarian Opera Company, Bayerische Staatsoper, and its school where I expected to spend the next few years mastering the craft of operatic soprano. It is all in the breathing, you know." Kitty sighed.

Barb waver her hands and said, "... and?"

"Oh, by October 1937 it was beginning to look like a war was coming again. The British government had reaffirmed their intention to protect Poland, but there had been a referendum in Poland that suggested that a good portion of what had been Prussia wanted to reunite with Germany. The Polish government didn't like that one bit and began to mobilize its army."

"Well," said Kitty slowly, "you can imagine what a fly in the ointment that was. Hitler was beaming with satisfaction the first time I saw him at the Café Heck.

Barb shook her head. "I wish I could follow you, Kit. You're going to make me read more history than I ever read in high school. But keep going."

"Later Chamberlain came to Munich when I was there, too," said Kitty, "in late 1938, I think, when he did his 'Peace in our time' speech. I was there.

Kitty giggled. "Heads of state and potentates didn't travel with hundreds of bodyguards like they do today," said Kitty.

"Well, of course, they had their retinue, and some of them may have been secretly armed, but if you didn't appear to pose a threat and could get past the uniformed police, you could go shake anyone's hand if you extended yours politely. That's how I shook Chamberlain's hand. I walked right up to him, shook his hand and said, 'Magnificent, Sir Neville, magnificent.' To which he replied, 'Humph, I didn't know there were any Americans left here.'"

Kitty was in her glory and beaming from the best telling of one of her best stories.

"Wow," said Barb.

"The funny thing is," said Jimmy to Barb, "I never believed her until I saw the TV show 'The Twentieth Century,' and they showed a young woman run up to Chamberlain and shake his hand. Mom was standing there and said, 'See!'"

Kitty was grinning from ear to ear. After a few minutes, she said, "It was years before someone told me why Chamberlain knew I was an American. It was because the Prime Minister is a member of the House of Commons so he can't be a Sir anything."

"Oh, I didn't know that," said Barb.

"That's a very modern tradition," said Jimmy. "There were some Prime Ministers named Lord this or that in the past. I think it was a Lord North during the American Revolution or maybe he was just a general — I forget."

"There weren't many Americans left in Germany, but the bulk of us were there to spend our family's money one way or another. Sam was there to study German and Slavic languages, and Joe was just there being Joe and, we all thought, being a spy."

"What made you think that?" asked a curious Jimmy.

"Because," said Kitty slowly, "all Joe did was spend money. Betty and I and the others had opera; Sam had his studies. But Joe and Kozie were full-time tourists. The first time Betty and I talked about Joe Medburry being a spy was when

Joe told us about a meeting at the American Consulate in Munich that we all should attend. All the consular officials knew Joe very well. The meeting was called by the Consulate to tell all the remaining Americans that they really should be going home or at least leaving Germany. I remember about thirty people at the meeting, but I don't think anyone went home just then. After all, we had 'Peace in our time,'" Kitty was grinning. "But what did we know?"

"Mom, I think the 'Peace in our time' thing was later in 1938. You're talking about the fall of 1937, right?"

"Oh," said Kitty frowning. "Well it's been fifty or sixty years, I can't remember everything."

Jimmy laughed at the confused look on his mother's face.

"Anyway, the Consulate had weekly tea parties that we were told we should attend. I learned the art of understatement by listening to the consular officials' chit-chat as they mingled. The first few times we all went to the tea parties were very strange. I don't think I ever talked to the same person twice, but it became obvious that the state of the roses in the Consulate garden was intended to be read as a metaphor for the state of international affairs. Dead roses were a state to be avoided at all cost. As war came closer, we could tell the state of affairs by the flowers in the window of the Consulate entrance. These were changed daily. When the Consulate was finally abandoned after *Kristallnacht* every flower pot in the building was left outside on the lawn to wither so anyone wandering by could see lots of dead flowers. I guess it was a universal sign of sorts. I lived north of the Consulate and walked by it every day.

"Our whole world, Betty's and mine at least, revolved around a six-block area. At the far north was our apartment at No. 69 Koeniginstrasse. We walked past the American Consulate at No. 5 Koeniginstrasse, a few blocks further south was our opera school and in the middle the Café Heck where Hitler hung out when he was in Munich. We made it a point of *not* going to the Café Heck after the affairs at the Consulate on the assumption that we would undoubtedly talk about what was said or unsaid there and that was not for Nazi ears. If the weather was good enough we would wander through the 'English Gardens' and talk about what happened at the Consulate — Betty, Sam and I with Joe or Kozzi tagging along as the occasion permitted.

"Herman the Vermin showed up in early September I think, at one of the Consulate parties, not the teas the Americans attended but at a formal party that included English, French, Czech, Poles as well as Germans. Herman said he was a journalist but demurred whenever anyone asked who he wrote for.

"I remember the *Chargé d'affaires* introducing Herman as Herman von Min. Apparently the *Chargé d'affaires,* at the time, I can't remember his name, they kept changing, had a high opinion of Herman. He was apparently rich, a bit of a playboy and loved parties. I found him a bit vulgar and boorish, and we all assumed he was spying on us, and it turned out he was, but he was also a lot of fun before things turned ugly," said Kitty with a faint smile. "We had a cocktail or dinner party at the drop of a dime and Herman was quick to supply the booze, always the best French or German wine or schnapps. He tried very hard to be the life of the party, but he always had that Germanic stiffness that comes with military life. He was as rigid as a broomstick. He just could never really relax, even when we got him dead drunk." Kitty was enjoying this.

Jimmy was frowning, "If you knew he was a spy why did you hang out with him?"

"I was thinking that too," said Barb.

Kitty had a quick answer, "Simple. Herman was fun to hang out with. Anyway, we weren't at war with Germany and Hitler had gotten everything he had asked for, so why should we worry?" Kitty laughed. "And we didn't have any real secrets for Herman to steal, at least not then." Kitty winked at Jimmy.

Kitty thought for a minute then added, "You have to look at the times. On the surface, what Hitler was asking for didn't look that radical, except, of course, for his totally insane attitude towards Jews, gypsies and people like that, but that was different. Look at it this way: after WWI Europe was full of completely made-up countries. Almost half of Poland was German-speaking, the city of Danzig was completely German speaking so was Alsace and Loraine in France, the Sudetenland in Czechoslovakia as well as most of Austria and half of Switzerland. Hitler said over and over again that all he wanted to do was unite the German-speaking peoples. He said that all he wanted to do was finish the work of Bismarck. It may have looked frightening to the English and French who had had recent nasty experiences with Germany, but to us Americans, it looked very reasonable. Germany felt a lot more like America than France or England did so we were very comfortable."

"So you knew what was coming?" asked Jimmy.

"Yes, well sort of. My father pointed out that when Texas became mostly English speaking, we had a war with Mexico that brought Texas into the United States. It's hard to imagine now, but to most Americans in 1937, England was viewed with more suspicion than Germany. America's love fest with the English is a post-war thing. At the time the Communists were thought of as being far more evil than the Fascists. So as Americans in Nazi Germany we had no fear at all. And besides, Herman the Vermin was something of a joke."

"When did things turn ugly?" asked Barb.

"They were ugly when I got there," said an unsmiling Kitty.

"No, really ugly. When did you begin to feel threatened?" asked Jimmy.

"I never felt threatened myself, but I suppose I realized how ugly things could get for the Jews when our piano tuner's daughter, I think she was about 12, begged us to help her family escape from Germany. Until then I really had no idea how badly the Jews were being treated."

"I thought *Kristallnacht* was the beginning of the attack on the Jews," said Jimmy.

"Oh heavens no," said Kitty with surprise. "Hitler had been bad-mouthing the Jews for years. In his book, he blamed all of Germany's problems on the Jews. I think, just before I got to Germany, the Jews were stripped of their local citizenship, and that triggered an exodus of Jews.

"Germany was strange that way; you could have local as well as national citizenship. Losing your local citizenship meant you weren't welcome 'here' which, of course, meant you weren't welcome anywhere. The only option available to you was to get a passport and leave but without money where could you go? And remember, you couldn't take any money out of Germany if you still had any left. I remember reading once that some big high Nazi *muckety-muck* proposed sending all the Jews to Madagascar, but that was before they came up with their 'final solution.' Still, anyone with half a brain could see where the Nazis were going, and almost everyone who wasn't an 'Aryan' was trying to get out if they could."

"You know, very few countries helped the Jews," said Kitty with a look of disgust, "and most were downright hostile to them. Even the United States rejected a boat full of Jewish refugees, but that was later on. When I first got to Germany most of the professional Jews — you know doctors, lawyers and people like that — had already left. The only Jews left were shopkeepers and tradesmen.

"There were two choice destinations for German Jews — New York City and Palestine. Little Sophie Goldberg, our piano tuner's daughter, wanted to go to New York but her parents had the Jewish bug for Palestine. In the end, they never got out, and I don't know if I could have helped them any more than I did, but after the war, I found Sophie in a refugee camp in France, and I helped her get to New York. She lost both her parents.

"James, you might remember her as your babysitter — do you remember the woman with the numbers tattooed on her arm?"

"Oh, yeah, that Sophie," Jimmy said with surprise. "She tried to teach me Yiddish."

Kitty laughed, "She *did* teach you Yiddish. You used to run around the apartment building chatting up a storm with everyone ... in Yiddish."

"Oy," said Jimmy with a laugh, "I remember that. The doorman was the only other person in the building who spoke any English, besides you and Dad."

Kitty nodded. "Yiddish was their common language, some were German Jews, some Polish and some Russian and there was a French couple. I spoke passable German which was close enough to Yiddish so that I could understand everyone. I tried to teach everyone English. We had classes in our kitchen. Don't you remember?"

"I thought you used to argue about books," said Jimmy.

"We did, that's how I taught them English. We would take turns reading a book then try to talk about it in English, but we often resorted to German or Yiddish or even French. Everyone got a bit animated on occasion."

"So what did Sophie say to you that made you realize how bad things could get?" asked Barb.

Kitty began slowly, "Sophie always came with Joseph when he came to tune our piano. Sophie told me their story over cookies and tea while Joseph did the tuning in the other room.

"Joseph Goldberg, Sophie's father, had been a music professor with the Berlin Philharmonic. He taught conducting.

They had been living on a professor's salary which wasn't much, but they had university housing, so they had a nice middle-class existence. But because they were Jewish, he lost his job. They were thrown out of their apartment and told that all their possessions belonged to the university, so they left without much beyond the clothing on their backs. They came to Munich and were living with Joseph's brother Saul who had an antiquarian bookshop. Joseph was working on the side tuning pianos as a way to make enough cash to get to Palestine. That's how I met him.

"By the way, my friend Sam Anderson bought a lot of Saul's books and Saul, and his wife did make it to Palestine eventually. Sam paid for their passage out of Germany and Saul bought jewelry with the marks he had and used that to bribe his way into Palestine right after the war. One of the books Sam bought from Saul was a 15th-century manuscript that made Sam's career later on, but that's neither here nor there."

Kitty felt tired but happy. It had been years since she had relived her early days in Munich. "Heck, even knowing what I know now I did everything I could think of to help the Goldbergs ... but in the back of your head, you always wonder."

Barb had brushed and braided Kitty's hair and had helped her put it up in the tight bun that had been Kitty's trademark. Kitty's hair had gotten very thin since her heart attack and her arthritis had gotten in the way, so Barb had volunteered to braid her hair for her. "Well, Jimmy," said Barb, "are you going to make us a lunch or are we going to starve?"

"I have a craving for liverwurst canapés," said Kitty out of the blue.

"Huh?" said Barb.

"Liverwurst canapés," repeated Kitty.

"Yuck," said Jimmy. "What on earth do you want that for?"

"I just remember that liverwurst canapés were just the

thing at diplomatic receptions, and I would like to have some liverwurst canapés, and I happen to know there is some liverwurst in the fridge that's never been opened."

"How old is it?"

"Young enough."

"I'll try it too then," said Barb without hesitation.

"Okay," said Jimmy, "but I'm having peanut butter and jelly."

"I'm not supposed to eat liverwurst," said Kitty with a big grin, "it might kill me someday with all that cholesterol and fat. Here, bring me the bread and some mayonnaise."

They mostly ate in silence except for the rhythmic thump, thump, thump of Kitty's oxygen machine.

"You know," said Kitty between bites, "there were several times when I was a little scared in Germany but only one time where I really felt terrified. Looking back it's silly, given what happened, but at the time, well...." Kitty shook her head.

"It was Joe's idea to go to the Nuremberg rally. It was a week-long Nazi extravaganza full of prancing about and marching and speechifying. It was right after Betty and I started classes and we had a long weekend off because of the Nazi goings on. Both Joe and Kozie said they were going to go to Nuremberg to see what was up, so Sam, Betty and I decided to tag along. So did Herman the Vermin.

"I'll tell you the Nazis knew how to put on a show and when we got there the show was in full swing. There was a parade that lasted all day and was full of soldiers, sailors, army trucks, tanks and more airplanes than I have ever seen at one time, before or since, thousands of everything. Sam and Kozie took lots of pictures. That night we went to the biggest rally of the week. They said there were a million people there, and I'm not exaggerating either. There were a thousand spotlights ringing the stadium and when Hitler walked in, all one thousand spotlights turned and focused on him while everyone in the entire place yelled 'Heil Hitler' at the top of their lungs three times followed by dead silence. It was frightening, terrifying. That's when I realized how unprepared the rest of the world was and how big this war was going to be when it finally got started. I was very scared. I looked at Sam, and I must have looked terrified because he put his finger to his lips and said 'shush' and nodded at Herman. We took the train home in silence. I think that's when we all realized just how much control Hitler had over Germany. It was a very sobering moment."

"So why didn't you go home then?" asked Barb. "I would have."

"Well, for one I hadn't spent all the money of course, and we figured we probably had a few months before all hell would be set loose. Besides, if Nuremberg was a sobering moment we didn't stay sober very long." Kitty was giggling again and started to sing, "Welcome to the cabaret old chum."

"What do you mean," asked Jimmy, "... seriously?"

"I'm not sure how to explain it, but the pace of life quickened. We had more parties, we spent more money more quickly, and so did the Germans, especially those in the arts. Life got decadent, 'Live today for tomorrow we die' became everyone's unspoken credo. We listened closely to the news on the radio, especially the *BBC*, read the *International Herald Tribune* cover to cover and listened carefully for rumors and watched the flowers in the Consulate window every morning and evening. We kept our escape money and tickets at the ready. I had my four $50 gold pieces and each of us knew what we would pack on a few minutes' notice. I even practiced packing my little valise a few times."

"I don't think I could live like that," said Barb, "the worrying would drive me crazy."

"It drove a lot of people crazy," said Kitty, "but you learn to live with the angst, you change your behavior, you listen for signs of trouble, you cope. But everyone has their limit and whenever I reached mine, I left Germany for a while, until things quieted down, usually with Sam. Not everyone could do that."

"You mean like the Jews?" said Jimmy.

"Yes," said Kitty slowly, "but it was a lot more complicated than that. Not all Jews wanted to leave and not all Germans wanted to stay. If your home was in Germany where would you want to go? Where could you go? Some people thought that it would all blow over after Hitler got everything he wanted. Chamberlain certainly thought so. I was very lucky I had lots of options and money to spend."

There was a crashing and banging on the door to the kitchen. "Earl is paying us a visit," said Kitty with a laugh as the kitchen door swung open.

"Hooch, lady, you're looking good today."

"Thank you, Earl. To what do we owe this pleasure?"

"Huh?"

"She means, what's up Earl?" said Barb.

"Oh," said Earl followed by his usual awkward silence, "I've been meaning to ask you if you will be needing your lane plowed this winter? I mean seeing as you're laid up and all ... and not driving." Earl shuffled back and forth, looking at his feet.

Both Kitty and Barb sensed that there was more to the question and both women decided independently to let Earl stew for a moment. Finally, Kitty said, "Well, I expect to be hauled back and forth to the doctor a few times this winter so yes, I expect I will need to have the lane plowed."

"Oh, lady," said Earl shaking his head, "I don't know."

Kitty let the awkward silence fill the room before answering, "Well Earl I will be needing it plowed. Is your plow broken?"

Earl looked at his boots and shuffled uncomfortably. "Hooch, lady, it's the hydraulics. They're gone on me truck."

"Well, how do you plan on plowing your own lane then?" asked Barb.

"Hooch, I don't know."

"I think Vince should take a look at it and figure out what needs to be done," said Kitty.

Barb rolled her eyes. "We can't have the neighborhood plow broken can we?"

"What's it going to cost?" asked Jimmy with no real interest in the answer.

"Oh, I don't know," said Earl still looking at the floor. "It might be $800."

"Canadian," said Kitty and Barb in unison, laughing.

"I never heard of any hydraulic system costing that much to fix," said Jimmy. "I mean, a pump might cost $100, 'US' and bleeding the lines might cost another $100. If all the lines are rotten, then I can see it maybe."

Earl stood awkwardly in silence.

"Well let's have Vince take a look at it shall we?" said Kitty.

"Well, I'll be in me barn," said Earl turning towards the door with more than his usual dour look, "milking me cows."

After Earl left Jimmy asked, "Did he really expect you to pick up the tab for his truck?"

"Yes, actually. He has always paid me back, but this time I suspect he was thinking about a 'terminal' loan. ... But I plan on surprising him." Kitty giggled to herself.

"No wonder he doesn't make eye contact," said Jimmy. "He's a grave robber."

"Yes," laughed Kitty, "only it was hard for him to negotiate with the corpse, but I suppose we'll have to help him out somehow."

"What a hoot," said Barb shaking her head. "Just wait till I tell Vince that Earl's trying to be a grave robber."

"Jeez, Mom, do you have to save the world and everyone in it?"

"Yes, James," said Kitty sternly. "Noblesse oblige, James, noblesse oblige."

9

First Flight
Summer 1998 (August - December 1937)

Kitty was not feeling particularly well this morning. She hadn't gotten up to make coffee. She wasn't hungry, and she didn't have to pee. The shades on the windows were still down and, although she could see day seeping in from under the edges, she was not in a daylight mood. She didn't even feel like taking a shower. Damn, she thought, I'm one of those little old ladies that can't get out of bed and stink to high heaven. She sniffed the air around her. There was a vaguely medicinal smell in the room which she attributed to her own rotting flesh. There was also a hint of ozone and oil from the oxygen machine throbbing at her side. The place, no she, didn't smell healthy, she thought.

When Jimmy came down the stairs, he found his mother still in bed with the oxygen tube stretched across his path to the kitchen. He growled under his breath.

Kitty saw the look of annoyance on her son's face and, trying to sit up, said, "I'm sorry, I guess I've slept in today." Kitty quickly found out that she did not have the strength this morning to sit up without help. "Curses," she mumbled to herself. "Help me up would you, James, help me over to my chair. I need a cup of coffee to revive me body and soul." Jimmy did what he was told, and he helped his mother into her chair then started the coffee and put a pastry in the microwave.

Jimmy was angry, he never liked his job or his boss, but it was an important rung up the corporate ladder for him. He needed this job but the night before he had been in Pictou where he had called his boss in Boston who told him in a rather impolite tone that he had used up his vacation time and any goodwill leave he might have accumulated; his job was on the line. He had to return to Boston today, or he could forget about his career. He changed his open return reservation to the 4:00 p.m. flight from Halifax. By his calculation this was an international flight, so he had to be in the Halifax airport by 2:00 p.m. and it was a two-hour drive so he had to leave by noon, no later. Better get it done now, he thought, finding the nerve to tell her that he had to leave.

"Well, that's one heck of a how-do-you-do," she said without much emotion.

Jimmy was thankful for that. He had prepared himself for an argument.

Kitty noticed the look of disappointment on her son's face, so she quickly added, "I launched you into this world to soar not to be dragged down like an albatross by the slow fade of an aging diva. Go make your mark on the world, and with my blessing." Kitty admired her own dramatic flair for a moment then nodded her head with both authority and a smile. It broke the spell, and they both laughed.

"Well, I can't stay here forever," said Jimmy looking more optimistic. "Will you be okay without me?" he asked.

"Of course, Barb will help me." Kitty looked at her son with a smile and successfully fought back a tear.

"Oh, all right, I was feeling very guilty halfway through your soliloquy, but now I'm ready to go back and conquer the world. What shall I do with all the money I'm going to make? Shall I build you an enormous mausoleum?" Jimmy winked at his mother knowing he could always hit a sore spot with her.

"If you do it will be a waste, like the Great Pyramid, an

empty sarcophagus," said Kitty. "I've arranged to be disposed of properly."

That took Jimmy by surprise. "What on earth are you talking about?"

"I've donated the r-r-remains to science," said Kitty rolling her 'r's' and with a small flourish of her hand. She was surprised at how weak she felt. "With luck, there'll be nothing left but some bone shards and ash to be scattered on Potters' field." Oh, now that was good, she thought.

Jimmy scowled. He didn't like to be reminded that his mother might die and, in fact, might die soon.

"I am here," Kitty said pointing at her chest, "I am not the remains. Once I'm gone, I have no further use for this." Kitty pulled up the aging skin that sagged from her arm in disgust. She had once been a very robust woman standing five feet eight inches, very tall for her times, and weighing over one hundred and seventy pounds, little of it fat. Stan was only an inch taller but more portly. Now her body, or as she would say, what remained of it, had been reduced to a frail five feet six inches and a mere one hundred and fifteen pounds. She had shrunk, her skin had not, and it annoyed her.

"And don't forget to take the valise that's under the table," Kitty said with the sound of resignation in her voice, "I just want to take a couple of pictures out of it. The rest you can do with as you please."

A tear rolled down Kitty's cheek as she picked up, first, a picture of her dear Sam Anderson when they were on the refugee ship together. Then, after a deep sigh, she picked up the picture of Herman the Vermin. She nodded, and under her breath, she whispered, "I really wish I could say I'm sorry."

Jimmy packed his rented car and went back to say goodbye to his mother. He thought she looked a little gray but attributed it to the dim lighting in the room and the fact of his imminent departure. 'Time cures all ills' his mother would say, and Jimmy was able to convince himself that all his mother needed was time to heal. After all, she had made remarkable progress in the six months since her heart attack; given another six months, she might be able to take care of herself, perhaps even drive again. That would be nice he thought, perhaps she can come for a visit to Boston next year.

Jimmy was out the door by 10:30. He felt relief; he had plenty of time, enough to get breakfast on the road before entering the numbing world of Halifax's airport. He was in Truro before he remembered the pastry in the microwave. *Oh well,* he thought.

Kitty, for her part, felt a mixture of relief and anxiety. James had gotten restless in the past few days and had ceased being fun. Barb had been busy, and James had stopped listening to her stories. She had begun to feel alone even before James abrupt departure. Now she felt a strange mixture of relief and dread. So long as she could tell stories, she didn't need to look into the abyss. It was depressing, and she was depressed. Damned either way, she thought. She was almost 80 years old and in poor health ... *she was going to die.* Yes, she said to herself, that is an undeniable fact. She had avoided thinking about death for years. She knew it would come, but it had always been a long way off. Not anymore!

Kitty's mother, Katherine, had been lucky. She died of a quick heart attack, no pain, no fuss, doing what she most loved which was playing bridge in her kitchen. She had been 79, the same age Kitty was now. That would be a nice way to go, thought Kitty, perhaps next time I know I'm having a heart attack I'll just let it go. No, that's cheating, she thought. She mentally slapped herself on the wrist, but that didn't dispel her gloom.

On the other hand, her father, Archie, had a slow lingering death starting with a mild heart attack followed by a dozen mild strokes that slowly robbed him of his essence. I suppose that's like Alzheimer's, she thought, but in more discrete chunks. It had been a relief when the nursing home called to report that Archie had passed away in his sleep one night. By then there was nothing left of him, thought Kitty. I suppose the worst would be Alzheimer's disease, knowing that each day the lights dimmed just a little bit more until the darkness settled over you. That's not for me, thought Kitty with defiance.

Kitty sat there satisfied for a moment, but what if? She was thinking: What if, like her father, she still had all her faculties but a stroke robbed her of speech? What if she could still think, could still be present while the world decayed around her? What if she could watch while they pulled the plug? Kitty broke into a cold sweat; a rush of adrenalin overcame her. Panic! That would be like being present at your own execution. What a gruesome thought!

She wondered if any of her friends had died that way. Kitty shuddered at her thoughts and resolved to try to think of more pleasant things, but that proved difficult.

A tinge of angina brought her back to the present. The clock on the wall said about 1:35 pm. Kitty couldn't remember if the clock was slow or fast, but it was right within about ten minutes. The imprecision of timepieces always bugged her. It was past lunch, and she had not had breakfast. She couldn't remember if she had given herself insulin or not. Kitty suddenly felt very confused. I'd better eat something, she thought, but as she made an effort to stand up she felt faint and passed out, falling back into her chair.

#

When Barb walked in, the clock read about 2:15 pm. Kitty was still passed out, but Barb thought she might be sleeping until she came close enough to see how pale Kitty was, almost gray. When Kitty didn't respond immediately to being gently shaken, Barb called for the ambulance which would take about 45 minutes to arrive. In the mean time, keep the patient upright if possible. Barb pulled Kitty to a more upright position, but she slumped at an awkward angle. Kitty's breathing was shallow, and it occurred to Barb that she might have low blood sugar. Kitty had shown Barb how to check her sugar by pricking a finger and placing a drop of blood on the test strip. Kitty's blood sugar meter read 2.3, well below the 5.0 Barb knew was considered normal and well below what Barb knew would make Kitty grumpy.

The solution was to get sugar into Kitty as quickly as possible, but pouring juice down Kitty's throat was not the best idea. She could drown. There was the Glucagon kit in the bathroom that Kitty had told Barb to use on just such occasion. A shot of Glucagon would cause the liver to release sugar into the bloodstream and bring someone out of a diabetic coma. The label on the kit announced an expiration date some four years earlier. I don't think this will poison her, thought Barb: even though it's outdated there should be some chemicals that still work.

Barb's hand shook visibly as she drew the distilled water from one vial into the needle then injected it into the second vial containing a thin white wafer which dissolved instantly. After drawing the fluid back into the needle, Barb held her breath while she plunged the needle into Kitty's leg and injected its contents. Kitty didn't flinch as she often did when Barb injected her with insulin. Barb withdrew the needle and said a small prayer of encouragement, "Come on, Kit, wake up."

Almost instantly Kitty grumbled something that sounded like, "Damn it all I can do it myself." This was followed by a mild thrashing about as a disoriented Kitty slowly regained consciousness. Kitty pulled the oxygen tube from her nose made an effort to sit up which failed as she fell back into her seat. "Oy vey, I feel like I've been run over by a truck. What happened?"

"I just got here," said Barb. "You were passed out so I

checked your sugar and you were two so I shot you up with this here Glucagon."

"God, this feels like the worst hangover I've ever had — and I've had some doozies."

Barb made Kitty drink some grape juice and made her a sandwich, but her color didn't improve. "Where's Jimmy?" she asked.

"Oh, he left."

"What?" said Barb sounding angry.

"Oh, it's okay. He had to go back to work. I don't mind. He was beginning to stink up the place."

Barb laughed but said, "You still don't look very good. The ambulance will be here in half an hour, and I think you should go with them."

"All right, I *am* feeling under the weather."

Kitty didn't feel or look any better when the ambulance arrived. The EMTs checked her blood sugar, her pulse and her blood pressure announcing over their radio, "Patient is a stable diabetic with a history of heart disease: neighbor reports a recent low blood sugar incident requiring Glucagon injection; current blood glucose 8.4, patient reports a bad headache, pressure two twenty over one fifty, pulse one twenty, transporting to Aberdeen, ETA." The EMT looked at his watch and shook his head, "seventeen thirty."

"I guess I overdid the Glucagon," said Barb.

Kitty nodded.

\#

The next time Barb saw Kitty was almost a week later. Kitty had been in intensive care where visitors had been strictly forbidden. Now, Kitty had an IV bottle, several in fact, hanging from a hook over her bed. The heart monitor beeped with every diastolic pulse, and the oxygen feed hissed softly. Barb passed Dr. MacKenzie in the hall but made no effort to engage him.

"I won't ask how you feel 'cause you might tell me," said

Barb. "I saw Dr. MacKenzie in the hall. He didn't say anything."

"I'm on me last legs," said Kitty softly. "Congestive heart failure he said."

"Oh," replied Barb disappointed.

They sat in silence for several minutes. Finally, Kitty broke the spell by saying, "I want to tell you my life's story. It is interesting, at least I think it is, and you might enjoy it. It's a story that, so far, doesn't have an ending and I was just musing that if I tell it, it won't have an ending and that's a desirable outcome don't you think?"

Barb gave Kitty a strange look and began to say, "What on earth," when Kitty interrupted her. "If you think about it, it makes perfect sense."

"Okay," said Barb, shaking her head. "If you say so. I'll go along with it. The last story you told, you had just gotten to Germany, and you and Herman the Vermin went to some big Nazi rally, and it scared the bejesus out of you."

"Oh, that; that was the big Nuremberg rally. The Nazis really knew how to put on a show. It was very impressive.... Herman, that ...."

"Go on, so what happened next?"

"Well, nothing really, Peggy studied violin, Betty and I studied opera, Sam studied German and Slavic languages, and Kozie and Joe snooped around. I was sure they both were spies."

"I remember that," said Barb with a laugh.

"Well," said Kitty taking a deep breath, "The big excitement that fall was a bicycle expedition Joe and Kozie organized to ride out by the Dachau concentration camp, which was right outside Munich, and take pictures."

"You mean you were there when they had concentration camps?" asked Barb in disbelief.

"Sure. They had them ever since the Nazis came to power, I think, since 1933 or 34. Dachau was the oldest. When we rode by, it was mostly for political prisoners, you know, Communists, labor leaders, and people like that. But it's also where they put all the Jews they rounded up on *Kristall-nacht*."

"Okay, so what happened?"

"Well," said Kitty getting warmed up, "They were in the middle of building an enormous extension to the camp, doubling or tripling its size. I guess they had already decided on the next to final solution. We picked a Sunday morning to go.

"Joe and Kozie organized the expedition. About 30 bicyclists met in the 'English Garden' down the street from the American Consulate. All the expats I knew including Joe, Peggy, and Sam were there as well as a couple of dozen people I didn't know, but who looked somewhat familiar, probably from the American and British Consulates. Joe gave me a camera and told me the plan."

"Oh, this is going to be good," said Barb rubbing her hands together.

Kitty smiled and continued, "We rode out from the "English Garden" single file with Joe leading the way; I was right behind him with Sam behind me. Kozie brought up the rear. The plan was to ride out to the Dachau camp then ride by on the access road while I photographed it with the camera Joe had given me.

"Just past the front gate was an intersection where five roads converged. The plan was that when we reached the intersection, I was to toss the camera over my shoulder. If there was trouble, and there was, the pack was supposed to split into four groups, each pedaling down a different road."

"You really did that?" asked Barb incredulously.

Kitty nodded her head before continuing, "Yeah, well sort of. It took an hour of easy pedaling to reach the far end of the camp. As we road past the camp, I took a picture every hundred feet or so. I ran out of film just as we neared the main entrance. When we biked past the guards, we must have looked like any group of young Germans out on a bicycle ride because no one stopped us, questioned us, or even acknowledged our presence. I think one workman looked up and waved, but that was it."

Kitty took a deep breath of oxygen, "When we arrived at the five-way intersection a car pulled in front of us with a driver and a military officer in an SS uniform and tried to block our path. The SS officer gave the Nazi salute and commanded us to stop in German. A few of the group who spoke German stopped and engaged the SS officer, who didn't speak English. He was obviously rattled that the rest of us didn't stop. I just kept peddling and let the camera drop on to the road. I never learned who picked up the camera, but Joe later told me that one of my photos made it into the *Chicago Tribune*, without attribution, of course, since I was still in Germany at the time.

"Later we got together to try to figure out how the SS knew we were going to photograph Dachau and our only conclusion was that Herman the vermin found out somehow. Lose lips sink ships."

"Wow," said Barb, "that was pretty brave of you."

"Only in retrospect; in fact, it was a rather foolish thing to do, but I was young, American, and invincible." Kitty was grinning again and continued, "I did a lot of foolish things that fall."

Barb was shaking her head. "Oh, do tell, I can only imagine."

"Did I ever tell you about the time I was declared *persona non grata*?"

"What's that mean?" asked Barb.

"Basically it means that they kick you out of the country," said Kitty, "which is the nicest thing the Nazis could do to you."

"Oh, did they kick you out?"

"They would have but the consulate made a stink, not on my behalf in particular, but in general, so I didn't get the boot."

"What happened?"

Kitty had to think for a moment before starting, "Hitler was rattling his saber, and we all thought he was about to go to war with Czechoslovakia over the German-speaking minority in the Sudetenland. The Czech president was ready to go to war too, so there was a lot of huffing and puffing all over. The trouble was that everyone was completely intertwined just like in World War One.

"The French and the Poles backed the Czechs while the Italians and the Romanians backed the Germans and the English backed the French ... sort of. No one was ready for a war, not even the Germans. It would have been a mess but especially for the Czechs." Kitty paused to think about what had happened and shook her head, "It was very confusing and after reading some of the histories written since ... it's still rather confusing." Kitty's attention drifted off as she shook her head.

Barb laughed, "And ... you were getting thrown out of Germany, right?"

"You know," Kitty suddenly continued, "the problem is that the Czech crisis lasted almost two years. It began with not-so-veiled threats in 1937 and came to a head in 1939. We had the crisis of the week with rumors of wars almost every week. If it wasn't Czechoslovakia, it was Austria, if it wasn't Austria it was Poland and the Danzig corridor."

"And ...?" Barb asked, waving her hands.

"And what?"

"And how did you almost get thrown out of Germany?" asked an exasperated Barb.

"Oh, I lost my train of thought." Kitty looked bemused for

a moment before continuing, "Roosevelt gave a speech that said 'the aggressors' had to be quarantined. Everyone knew that 'the aggressors' meant Germany and Japan, so it was the first time America got in Hitler's face. He didn't like it one bit, and the embassy and all the consulates made a big deal of it, so did we.

"After the Italians officially joined the Fascist axis community someone printed up handkerchiefs with the German, Japanese, Spanish and Italian flags. So when the Consulate had a formal party, I arrived with that handkerchief sewn to the seat of my dress." Kitty was grinning from ear to ear, "The Germans took umbrage, and I was quickly shown the door. Apparently, the *Chargé d'affaires* at the consulate got nose to nose with Herman Goering who was there, and in the ensuing brouhaha, they forgot all about me. I was banished from attending consulate parties for a couple of weeks after that."

"That's it?" said Barb with a laugh.

Kitty frowned, "Oh no, that was hardly the end of it. Just after I was told that I was *persona non grata* at the consulate and possibly in Germany, the word went out that the consulate flowers were dying and that all Americans should leave. The consulate began preparations to evacuate everyone, but that turned out to be a bluff. Still, Joe announced an "expedition" to Switzerland so Sam and I booked a first-class round-trip train ride to Zurich. Of course, I paid for the train tickets in blocked marks."

"Wait," said Barb, "So you didn't get thrown out after all, you left anyway. Right?"

"Well no," said Kitty, "but we left anyway. We all hopped on the train to Zurich, but the train only got as far as the Swiss border, and the Swiss wouldn't let us go any further, at least by train, so we got off, and Joe led us up a mountain trail to a beautiful Swiss chalet. We stayed there for about a week. By then the crisis had blown over, and they had forgotten about my flag decorated bottom so we all hoofed it back down the mountain and back to Germany."

"I would have left then and there," said Barb, "but I guess you couldn't take a hint."

"Things calmed down, and the Consulate remained open. Still, we had a crisis every few weeks, but the real crises didn't come until a few months later after Hitler took over Austria then got everything he wanted from the Czechs. That time, Sam and I ended up on a refugee boat, which was awful."

"What, wait, when did all this happen?" asked Barb.

"The hike up the Swiss Alps or the boat ride to Hades?" asked Kitty.

"Oh God Kit, I don't know. You were *persona non grata*," said Barb a bit confused.

"That was when we went skiing in Switzerland just before Christmas in 1937."

"Ok," said Barb, not sure if she got it all, "So what happened next?"

"Just after we got back, the Nazis began to really intimidate the Jews. The Nazi police started to picket Jewish shops at random. Four or five *polizi* in uniform would walk back and forth in front of a Jewish-owed store with signs saying things like 'Don't buy from Jews,' or usually something more impolite. If you looked like you were going to walk in, they'd yell "Jew" at you. They did that to me once, and I told them off in English, but fortunately, they didn't understand me. Sam hauled me back as I was haranguing the cops." Kitty let out an audible "harrumph" which made Barb laugh.

After a satisfied pause, Kitty continued, "The intimidation was haphazard, but it scared Saul Goldberg half to death. He closed his bookshop and he and Sam Anderson wrote letters to Sam's academic friends trying to sell whatever Saul had in his shop, which apparently included some pretty rare books. Sam was mailing books to the U.S. almost every week. Finally, Saul had enough money to leave Germany for Palestine, but his brother Joseph and his family stayed in Munich until Joseph was carted off to Dachau.

"Anyway, just before Saul left, Sam and I were invited to a Hanukkah dinner with the entire Goldberg clan. Joseph's wife, I can't remember her name, told me what to bring and where to get it since they were terrified of visiting Jewish shops."

Kitty had a smug smile when she continued, "Sam and I went on a scavenger hunt looking for just the right kosher items. Most of the Jewish stores were closed by this time, so we had to buy whatever resembled items on the list. Sam managed to find a rabbi who blessed everything we found even though some of it wasn't really kosher. I guess he made everything kosher by blessing it." Kitty shrugged, "He gave us a note to give to the Goldbergs, written in Hebrew that said, after Joseph translated it, 'We eat unleavened bread at Passover because then we did not have the time to leaven it. Today we eat any bread we can find because there is no one left to bake it. Remember this day.' The Goldbergs burst into tears. When we had Passover with Joseph and his family a couple of months later, we couldn't find that rabbi. He had either left or had been arrested.

"I never forgot that dinner during Hanukkah, it was really moving. All the Jews knew they were in for a *pogrom*, but no one believed they were in for what actually happened."

"What's a *pogrom*?" asked Barb.

"A very sad time for Jews," said Kitty. "They knew their lives would be turned upside down again, just as they had been throughout history."

A nurse entered the room and announced that it was time for Kitty to be taken downstairs.

"Whatever for?" asked Barb looking at Kitty who shrugged her shoulders.

"You are going to have an angiogram dear," explained the nurse.

Oh," said Kitty surprised, "Dr. MacKenzie never said anything?"

"His orders are right here, Missy."

Kitty leaned over the clipboard and made a face when she recognized the fuzzy outline of her doctor's signature. "I guess its okay," she said with a whimper. The drug the nurse had already injected into Kitty's IV was beginning to have its effect. "Goodbye, Barbara," said Kitty with a drunken flourish.

An hour, maybe two, later Kitty found herself in a room that looked to her like a jungle. Things were crawling from place to place overhead. A plant that rose from a pot near the floor climbed to the ceiling then ran along the ledge leaving a trail of leaves and flowers in its wake appeared to say, "Hello, Catherine, are you feeling better?"

My, how interesting, thought Kitty, *I didn't know that rose-scented geraniums could talk.* "Hello yourself," said Kitty, "and how are you feeling today? It can't be that great with all this artificial light. Do you get enough fertilizer?"

"Ha! The hospital food isn't the best tasting, but it *is* nourishing," said the plant as another stalk spread over Kitty's head. *How interesting*, thought Kitty, *I wonder how many people know that they have a talking plant in the basement here.* Kitty faded out again.

She woke up once more in the room she had started out in that morning. Her leg ached where the catheter had been inserted to inject X-ray opaque dye into her heart, and when the nurse came in Kitty complained loudly.

"I'll give you a little something to take the edge off," said the nurse.

"Splendid altogether," pronounced Kitty as the drug quickly took effect.

Kitty was snoring when Barb entered and woke her up.

"Did you know that they have a talking plant in the basement of this hospital?"

"Do tell," said Barb giving Kitty a strange look.

"Oh, yes, it's just like the one I have at home. You know, the rose-scented geranium that is planted in the little pot above the sink and meanders along the ceiling sconce along to the window above the kitchen table?"

"Oh yeah," said Barb, "that straggly looking thing. I'm surprised that you've kept it alive."

"Exactly," said Kitty emphatically, "but the one I have at home doesn't talk, at least not to me. Has it ever talked to you?"

"No," said Barb shaking her head, "I can't say that it has. By the way, what drugs are you on?"

"Whatever is in the bag up there," said Kitty pointing to the IV drip above her head.

Barb was giggling and shaking her head when a nurse came in.

"How are you feeling dear?" asked the nurse to Kitty.

"Splendid altogether," said Kitty with a weak flourish.

"No pain?" asked the nurse.

"Oh, it hurts like hell," said Kitty, "but I don't care at the moment. Did you know you have a very articulate plant in your basement?"

"No, Miss Stevenson, I didn't know that," said the nurse with mock surprise. "I think I should turn this morphine drip down," she said winking at Barb who was still laughing.

"Yes, quite remarkable," said Kitty and turning to Barb continued, "Do you think we should call the newspapers? Would they be interested?"

"Oh, I don't think so," said Barb, "talking plants are an everyday occurrence don't ya think?"

"Oh," said Kitty yawning. "I've never had a conversation with one before, but I'm hungry. I've been told that the food here is quite nourishing."

Barb and the nurse looked at each other and laughed. "I'll order you a healthy breakfast," said the nurse.

"Splendid altogether," said Kitty as she drifted off to sleep.

10

Spiraling Down - Autumn 1998 (early 1938)

Gavin MacKenzie, M.D. was angry with himself. He was losing a patient. He was questioning his own judgment: Should he have been more aggressive, proactive and more insistent? Would she have listened? The answer was unknowable. He knew that but still, he thought, he shouldn't be losing *this* patient. She was a friend; he'd known her for over 30 years. He was taking it harder than she had.

When he told Kitty that she had had another heart attack and that this one had done as much, perhaps, even more damage than the last one she was sanguine about it. He had expected her to cry or otherwise display grief as other patients had when he told them they were dying, and that there was little he could do about it, but Kitty had only shrugged and extracted a promise that when the time came he would provide enough of the right drugs to keep her out of pain.

Did she realize that her kidneys and liver were "compromised?" Did she understand that her heart was barely pumping enough blood to keep her alive? Yes, she had said, she understood and had come to terms with it. He had not, so when he left the room and saw Barb, he had deliberately avoided her eyes for fear that he might lose his professional demeanor and burst into tears.

Kitty had suggested but not requested that he post a "do

not resuscitate" order on her charts, but Doctor Gavin MacKenzie could not bring himself to do that. Instead, he vowed to make her remaining visit, that's how Kitty had put it, as comfortable as possible. As he sat in his office alone he knew that Kitty could not be discharged, she needed 'round-the-clock care. He also knew that Kitty was waiting for a room to open up at the Shiretown Nursing Home, and a call confirmed her status but the helpful director suggested that she be admitted as a hospice patient. Dr. MacKenzie hadn't thought of that, but it was appropriate. Kitty would have to live in a double room but could receive round the clock care. Dr. MacKenzie could hear Kitty saying, "Splendid altogether," so it was set.

Two days later Kitty was feeling a lot better. She could sit up in bed with help, and she was relatively free from pain. She was looking forward to the nursing home. "It will be a new experience for me," she had told one of her nurses who was reluctant to say goodbye. Neither Barb nor Dr. MacKenzie had arrived when the orderlies came to get her, but prolonged goodbyes had allowed her to stall just long enough for Barb with Dr. MacKenzie in tow, to arrive breathless with a "travel kit" consisting mainly of pajamas, bathrobes and several shirts, pants and a long skirt sufficient to be presentable on occasion. Barb had hurriedly stuffed Kitty's "kit" into one very large suitcase.

"Good Lord," said Kitty looking at the suitcase. "I'm going to Valhalla, not Paris."

Barb giggled, "Well it's not your valise, but it's the smallest suitcase *I* have."

"Well then, it will have to do," Kitty said with resolve then turning to the orderlies said, "Onward gentlemen."

With that command, Kitty led a procession, as she later put it, worthy of an oriental potentate, out of the hospital. The parade, consisting of Kitty in the lead on her litter followed by Barb and Dr. MacKenzie with his staff and his medical students, the attending cardiac surgeon and his staff, and at least a dozen nurses, passed through the hospital, gathering admirers as they went. The main entrance was lined with the entire kitchen staff, almost the entire union of Haitian orderlies, janitors and assorted bystanders wondering who the celebrity was.

Kitty's arrival at the Shiretown Nursing Home was far less glamorous. Only the Shiretown administrator was there to greet Kitty and to fill out the paperwork. Kitty was alone; Barb had been held up for almost half an hour by construction on the causeway while Kitty's ambulance was allowed to pass through. By the time Barb arrived the ambulance had left, so she had to inquire about Kitty at the front desk.

There was no information on the computer about Kitty so all the clerk at the front desk could do was offer Barb a cup of coffee while she waited for the director to appear. This proved to be a long, three-cup, wait.

Aberdeen Hospital had not forwarded Kitty's medical history to Shiretown, so the Director sat on Kitty's gurney and manually took her medical history. It was complex; yes, her primary medical problem was cardiac, but her immediate problem was her type 2 diabetes. Yes, she knew what her insulin doses were; yes, the director could confirm everything with Dr. MacKenzie if she wanted to. Yes, she had had cancer. No, it was considered cured, it had been 40 years with no recurrence. Next of kin to notify? Well James and Maggie, of course, but please also notify Barb as well. Satisfied, the director left saying that she would send someone to get Kitty settled in.

Kitty was on a gurney, tightly packed in a blanket for traveling in cold weather. She was propped up at an awkward angle, not up enough to see anything interesting but not so far back as to only see the ceiling. Pillows blocked her side view.

She had been left in a large room with windows on three sides, a "solarium," thought Kitty. Straining to see without her glasses on she looked for signs of life. Nothing! *Well,* thought Kitty, *if I have anything to say about it I'll soon have those windows full of colorful flowers, perhaps even talking geraniums.* That thought stopped her for a moment; did she really encounter talking geraniums back at Aberdeen Hospital? *That's silly*, she thought again, *Barb must have been just humoring me.*

From where Kitty lay she could look out of the window on one side and see the wall of the old Pictou hospital. On her other side, she could just make out an empty office and a doctor's office lounge chair, the kind that looks comfortable but isn't. She wasn't alone, the quiet murmur of indistinguishable human voices drifted in from places beyond her vision. She heard but could not see the passage of at least two self-propelled wheelchairs and, although Kitty could raise her head a few inches for a few seconds at a time, she was unable to make any contact with other humans in the room.

"Are you here to kick the bucket or just for a short visit?" a familiar voice asked.

"Robert MacDougal, is that you?" asked Kitty of her old neighbor in Poplar Hill.

"Oh, I don't know, might be, might be, I'd have to look at my name tag, but it's upside down."

"Well, Robert, I'm here as a hospice patient, so I guess I'm here to kick the bucket." Kitty thought it would bother her to say that, but it didn't.

"Oh, pay that no mind," said Robert. "I'm here for that too but I've been here for four months, and they can't get rid of me even with the rat poison they call food. It's not like yours, you know. While you're here could you teach them how to cook?"

"I see you've already got a boyfriend," said a very pretty and very young nurse, "and you've got visitors, too."

Kitty blushed. "Prop me up, would you," asked Kitty, "so I can have a decent conversation, and find my glasses."

Once she had been cranked up to a full sitting position

and put on her glasses, which had been hiding in a bag of her belongings, Kitty could see a room full of patients in wheelchairs or shuffle by with walkers and several more on gurneys but not a single green plant. *That's depressing,* she thought, *I'll bet most of the people here were farmers and the rest had gardens.*

"So, there you be," said Barb entering the room with the director. "I've had so much coffee waiting to see you that I'm vibrating, see." She held her hands out and shook them back and forth in mock convulsions.

"Dr. MacKenzie has sent me all your prescriptions including an IV drip he wants you on, so we'll have the phlebotomist drop by shortly," said the director.

"No need," said Kitty holding up her right arm, "My IV's still intact, just shoot me up with a little heparin to clear things out."

The director laughed, "So you're a nurse, too. Well then, let's get you settled." She pulled on the foot of Kitty's gurney and wheeled her around, rather abruptly thought Kitty, and headed off towards one of the wings. "Your roommate is named Elizabeth. She has senile dementia, Alzheimer's, and has had a stroke which has left her unable to speak but she loves her soap operas and watches them virtually all the time. I understand you are quite deaf," said the director pointing to her ear.

"Only when I take my hearing aids out," replied Kitty. "Is this Elizabeth a hospice patient too?"

"Why, yes," said the director, "she has advanced Alzheimer's."

"Oh," said Kitty, "I didn't know it could kill you."

"It's a progressive neurological disease very much like Lou Gehrig's disease except that Alzheimer's begins with the higher cognitive centers while Lou Gehrig's disease starts with the motor nerves. It's more complicated than that but ...." the director trailed off not wanting to get into greater detail.

As they approached the room, there was a commotion. A bottle of something flew out and crashed and broke on the linoleum floor. A middle-aged man backed out of the door cursing while a nurse and two burly orderlies rushed in.

"Oh, my," said Kitty with surprise, "you have a lively bunch here I see."

"This might not be the best place to be," said Barb.

"Why not?" asked Kitty.

"Well, for one, you can't defend yourself here," said Barb punching the air.

"I hadn't planned on fisticuffs."

"But did you see that?"

Kitty was laughing. "Yes, I'll bet it's some annoyed child trying to take something away from the old biddy, and she objected. It will make my stay interesting." Kitty paused, then added, "If I don't overstay my welcome."

"This isn't going very smoothly," said Barb nervously.

Kitty regained her composure and authority. "Well, Barb, it's the bumps and unexpected turns that make life interesting."

It took several minutes to reestablish order in the room. It was a private matter, Kitty was assured by the director, that should have no bearing on Kitty's stay at the home. Kitty was not convinced but, given her lack of choices, she smiled as best she could when she was wheeled into the room. One, two, three and she was lifted off the gurney and swung into her bed, and the gurney wheeled out of the room. Barb put Kitty's things away and, after apologizing profusely for having to leave, did so. Kitty was alone with a woman who, minutes before, had exhibited violent behavior toward some relative. The "better part of valor" rule dictated that, for Kitty, the best idea was to simply try to go to sleep.

Kitty was on the point of dozing off when she noticed that the volume of the television, which had been on but low enough to be meaningless noise, was now audible enough to distinguish voices. *It must be loud,* Kitty thought, *maybe she's both deaf and mute.* Without rolling over Kitty turned down her hearing aids. The volume went up again almost instantly, and Kitty could now distinguish voices clearly again. *Wow,* she thought as she rolled over to see an angry face glaring back at her. As soon as they made eye contact her roommate deliberately and dramatically turned up the volume again. The angry face glaring at Kitty challenged her to do something about it.

Kitty looked at ... "Elizabeth isn't it?" she asked in a loud but non-threatening voice. "I understand that you can't speak but can you hear? Just nod your head."

Elizabeth's angry face dissolved into a smile and she nodded vigorously.

Kitty removed her hearing aids and continued almost yelling, "I'm as deaf as a stone, so if I take these out I don't care how loudly you play the TV, but others with more intact hearing might object."

Elizabeth's smile turned into a scowl again, and she raised the remote again, threatening.

"You know," said Kitty, "if you keep playing it too loudly they might take the remote away from you."

Elizabeth thought about it for a second then defiantly turned the volume up as far as it would go.

"Fine," said Kitty who grabbed the nurses call button and with as threatening a scowl as she could muster held the button in one hand while raising an eyebrow. "Your choice," she yelled. They stared at each other for several seconds before Elizabeth turned off the TV and rolled over with a "humph." Moments later a nurse and two burly orderlies rushed into the room. "I believe we're all set for the moment," said Kitty as she turned out the light.

Elizabeth was in the shower when Barb arrived late the next afternoon. "I hear you tamed the savage beast," she said to Kitty.

"Shhh," said Kitty, "she's not as daffy as people think. She hears perfectly well. We merely arrived at a sort of détente. The war may not be over. It's best we talk down the hall."

Barb helped Kitty into a wheelchair and pushed her down to an empty solarium.

"How are things going?" asked Barb, just to get the conversation going.

"The food is dreadful. They seem to think by feeding me the blandest food possible they'll prolong my life, and they may, for a month or two or until I commit murder or mayhem for lack of taste bud stimulation. They even take the salt packets out of the plastic wrapped forks before I get them. Could you go into a restaurant and sneak me some salt?"

"Would I be aiding and abetting a suicide?" asked Barb who was unsure if Kitty was kidding or not.

"Heavens, no," said Kitty who was actually unsure herself. "If you can't enjoy the music, or can't enjoy the touch of a massage, or can't smell the flowers, or taste the food you eat, you might as well be dead. What is the value of life if there's nothing left to enjoy?" It had just come out, she hadn't thought about it, but there it was, her new philosophy of life. Kitty brought herself up as best she could thrust out her jaw, put on her most determined face and declared, "Well there you are!"

Barb saluted and said, "Yes ma'am!"

They both laughed at that but Kitty was still determined, she had made up her mind. "So you will get me some salt packets then?" she more demanded than asked. Barb nodded. "Well, that's settled then," said a satisfied Kitty.

They sat in silence for a few minutes then Barb remembered that she had a present for Kitty. "Kit I brought your opera collection, at least the CDs, and I also stopped and bought a portable CD player."

"What for?" asked Kitty. "I'm not going anyplace."

Barb laughed, "It's got these earphones you can put on,

turn the volume all the way up and no one will hear. Of course, it doesn't have the equivalent silencer if you want to sing." Barb grinned knowing that Kitty would have a hard time not singing along with her favorite operas.

Kitty gave her a quizzical look then 'got it' and burst into a grin too. "You know, people almost paid to hear me sing."

"Yeah," said Barb, "almost?"

"No, really, one more year in Munich and I would have been a professional opera singer. I was studying the part of Papagena in Mozart's 'Magic Flute' and would have understudied the part in the Munich Opera, but they canceled the performance in March 1938 when all the male leads and their understudies were drafted into the army. I might have opened in that role in 1940 if the war hadn't gotten in the way." Kitty sighed, "Damned Hitler."

"You can say that again," said Barb. "What was it like to study opera in 1938?"

"I suppose it's not much different than studying opera today," said Kitty who was trying to think what differences there might be. After a few moments, she said, "I suppose there were fewer electronics. The only time I ever saw a microphone was in a cabaret where most of the singers couldn't produce enough volume to fill the hall, and one other time when I sang in the chorus when the Munich Philharmonic made a record of Beethoven's Ninth.

"We used to laugh at the cabaret singers. They smoked, drank themselves into oblivion and whored around. That's both sexes I might add. You know the movie *Cabaret*?"

Barb nodded. She had heard parts of this story a hundred times and normally would tune it out, but today she was interested.

Kitty nodded too, "*Cabaret* was a pretty realistic portrayal of the decadence of the time. The closer we got to war the more bizarre things got." Kitty's eyes sparkled, "One time there was an act that included a love scene. I had seen it

before, and it was pretty tame but once both 'performers',"
Kitty used her fingers to indicate quotation marks, "got very
drunk and proceeded to attempt real fornication on the
stage. The manager thought it was hilarious, so did we. But
eventually, the MC went over and poured a pitcher of cold
water on them when they started puking on stage." Kitty
was laughing to herself, "Apparently sex on stage was okay
but throw up wasn't."

Barb laughed, "What other decadent things happened?"

Kitty blushed, "Well, I think it might ruin my image to go
into great detail but let it suffice to say that the consumption
of both booze and 'French Safes' went up exponentially as
war approached. 'Live today for tomorrow we die' was very
real, even for those of us who had a way out."

"Kitty Stevenson I'm shocked, shocked I tell you."

"Why? Every generation has had an excuse for wild abandon at some point. Your generation just did 'it' because you
could, with 'the pill' and all that. My generation didn't stop
just because the war was over. We just stopped using con-
doms and had babies, lots of babies instead. You know, 'Baby
Boomers.'"

"Oh, I hadn't thought of that. It makes lots of sense I guess."
Barb paused to regain her composure after a few moments
of giggling to herself. "If things got scary enough for your
'wild abandon,' I'd still like to know why you didn't leave
Germany at that point."

"Well," said Kitty starting up slowly as she thought through
what she was going to say. "For one I hadn't spent all the
money, and for another, I was young and invincible, and I
didn't think a war would happen any time soon. It turned
out I was just about right in my estimates, but I could just
as easily have been dead wrong. A lot of other people were
dead wrong, unfortunately. Joseph Goldberg was one of
them." Kitty paused.

"I guess we're we back in Germany today? What happened

to Joseph?" laughed Barb.

"Well, I offered to pay for Joseph and his family to go by train to Trieste where they could hop on a ship that would take them to Athens and from there to Jaffa, but that would only get them halfway. The trouble was that the British were only allowing a small number — I think it was 15,000 a year — to land in Jaffa so the majority of refugees that could afford it got off at Istanbul and traveled overland to Palestine. The British only counted those who landed in Jaffa, not those arriving overland. Joseph wanted to save up enough money to get to Palestine overland and to start a new life once he got there. He was totally unrealistic, and it cost him and his wife their lives. His daughter Sophie made it through the war, but just barely."

"I think you told me that part," said Barb. "I still don't get it. I would have been out of there fast."

Kitty smiled and shook her head, "The closer we got to war the more pigheaded Joseph became and the more cautious I became," Kitty paused shaking her head. "It's not like he didn't have any warning.

"Joseph's brother Saul left for Palestine just before Christmas. Technically, Saul sold his bookstore to Sam Anderson, Joe Medburry and me, but Joseph Goldberg and his family still lived there. So when the Gestapo, not so quietly, started rounding up Jews at the end of January 1938 they passed them by. We had a real Passover a couple of months later."

"I thought," interrupted Barb, "that the Germans didn't round up the Jews until that crystal night you keep talking about."

"That's what everyone thinks," said Kitty. "That's when they made a point of breaking the windows of every Jewish shop that was still open and hauling off the eldest member of the family. That's when Joseph Goldberg was arrested; but starting in January of 38 the Gestapo started to arrest anyone that made a noise including Jews, gypsies, students, anyone that said pip against the Nazis. Most of the rabbis that were left were arrested, and the rest went underground, and all the synagogues closed their doors. I also think that's when any Jewish professionals that were left in Germany were arrested and their business confiscated. Saul would have been arrested and his shop confiscated if Sam, Joe and I hadn't bought it first. So many friendly Germans 'bought' Jewish shops that the Nazis passed a law making it illegal for 'Aryans' to front for Jews. It worried us, but the Nazis didn't do anything about it for a while.

"I remember Joseph whispering to me when he was tuning my piano that the pogrom had begun. He knew what was happening, everyone knew what was happening. We were all scared for them."

"So what did you do?" asked Barb.

"We had a yard sale," said Kitty, "or the German equivalent which was to place an ad in the newspaper. After all, the contents of the building were his brother's even if we did officially buy it from him. That 'yard sale' was Joseph's undoing I thought. In Germany, you needed official permits for everything and Joseph went and got the permit without telling us. He had to show an identification card that showed his address. He went from invisible to visible, but by then the Germans were preparing to invade Austria. I think Hitler was worried that there might be a real war during the Austrian Anschluss, so he mobilized the entire German army. Even that SOB, Herman the vermin disappeared for a while. Anyway, they put Joseph on hold, but they knew where he lived."

"If everyone knew that why didn't he just leave?" Barb was shaking her head.

Kitty nodded, "To get out of Germany at that point, if you were in Joseph's shoes, you needed gold. That was the magic currency everyone needed, and there was almost no gold to be had. Everyone had the same idea: hoard gold, jewelry, francs, pounds, U.S. dollars, anything that could buy your passage outside Germany. I think we raised almost a thousand marks at our yard sale and he was able to buy just enough gold jewelry to probably get from Trieste to Istanbul but not much more. Unfortunately, we had our yard sale the week before Hitler took over Austria. The Anschluss effectively closed the door for Joseph. I suppose he could have tried to get out through France or Switzerland or even Czechoslovakia, but the odds and cost prevented it."

"I thought you had a lot of cash and there must have been other things you could barter with," protested Barb.

"Our cash was all in German marks, and the black market was quickly drying up, and besides, there wasn't much you could buy that had any real, portable value: the shelves were bare. The only things that were plentiful were food and alcohol, and we consumed as much of the latter as we could. Booze was available right up until the war began, but food started to get expensive in the summer of 1938 when Europe began drafting their farm hands and animals into their armies. I think it can be safely said that the European harvest of 1938 was a bust."

"I can't imagine living like that," said Barb.

"No one could," said Kitty, "that was part of the problem. Even those that lived through the First World War couldn't imagine what they were in for. But remember, to most Germans Hitler was still a shining light; his demands seemed reasonable, he was the reincarnation of Bismarck. And while everyone knew there was some a war coming no one expected what actually happened.

"The week we had our yard sale there were German soldiers marching this way and that. What I thought was strange was that it appeared that as many soldiers were getting off trains as were getting on. Joe and Kozie thought that Germany was going to march into the Sudetenland. The Czech prime minister was becoming rather bellicose, and the Brits announced that they wouldn't go to war over the Czechs. So when things felt like they were coming to a head, I got a little scared and bought myself a first-class round-trip ticket to Vienna to get out of the way. I left right after voice practice on Thursday. I took my valise." Kitty was smiling.

"What's so magical about Thursday night?" asked Barb, unsure of where Kitty's story was going.

"I can remember it well," said Kitty. "It was Thursday, March 11, 1938, the day before Hitler invaded Austria ... and I was on a train to Vienna. I could see miles and miles of army trucks and trains on sidings waiting to move. Well, needless to say, the Germans didn't let the train into Austria, and we were shunted onto a siding in a little village that was right on the border. I knew someone who lived there, so I used a pair of gold earrings to bribe my way off the train and spent a wonderful weekend in the Bavarian countryside. I was able to telephone Sam and tell him I was all right and ask him to pass a secret message on to Joe that the war machine was headed to Austria."

"How did you pass a secret message to Joe?" asked a wide-eyed Barb.

"Simple," said Kitty, "I simply told Sam to tell Joe that the flowers had died on the way to Vienna." Kitty was beaming. "Another strike for the good guys. Of course, I don't know if it did any good or not, but I enjoyed being a secret agent."

"So what happened?" asked an excited Barb.

"Well, nothing really," said a somewhat surprised Kitty. "By Saturday afternoon the Germans had peacefully taken over Austria, to a lot of cheering I'm told, so they let the train go on to Vienna. I spent the night there with friends and came back to Munich Sunday afternoon."

"That's curious," said Barb. "I always thought that 'history' with a capital 'H' moved at a slow but inexorable pace."

"*Inexorable*, that's a mouthful," said Kitty with a smile.

"I learned it from a TV show on World War Two," said

a proud Barb. "They used the phrase 'inexorable march to-wards war' a few times, but it sounds a lot more like fits and starts from the way you tell it. I looked it up, by the way."

"I think it was a lot more like fits and starts," said Kitty. "Everyone held their breath while the Nazis lurched for-ward then afterward had to catch their breath while the Nazis digested what they had just eaten. After every lurch toward war, everyone was relieved that the war hadn't ac-tually started. After Austria, there was a worldwide sigh of relief. That was misplaced of course, but I remember some fellow traveler saying, 'See, all Hitler wants is to unite the German people and he's almost done.' Well 'almost' was the problem because we all knew that meant the Czechs and the Poles were in for it sooner or later and Hitler was talking about *Lebensraum* in his speeches again, which meant that the rest of Eastern Europe could feel his hot breath, too. I think we all knew that war was inevitable but we all hoped it wouldn't start until next week or next month or next year."

Barb could tell that Kitty was winding herself up to tell more stories when a young orderly walked through the so-larium ringing a tiny, high pitched but loud bell.

Kitty's eyes darted all around the room. "Oh," she ex-claimed, "it's that damned dinner bell. I can barely hear it and it's more painful than auditory, like a dog whistle; you don't hear it, but you do register pain if you are too close to it."

Barb laughed, "Shall I push you to the cafeteria or back to your bed?"

"I suspect I've missed the call for dinner in bed so let's meander over to the dining hall," said Kitty.

Barb and Kitty quickly found themselves in a traffic jam of self-propelled wheelchairs all intent on getting to the cafe-teria before everyone else. "I wonder if only bad drivers end up here. I don't remember this kind of traffic at the Oddfel-lows, but of course, I was in the kitchen," said Kitty. Soon a platoon of nurses and orderlies arrived to sort things out, and Barb and Kitty found themselves sitting at a table with two older gentlemen.

The waiter/orderly gave Barb and Kitty a curious look.

"What?" protested Barb

"Are the two of you new," the waiter asked glaring at Barb with more than a little condescension.

"She's the patient, and she's new," said Barb. "I'm the friend that punches people like you out if they give her any grief."

The two older gentlemen grunted their approval as Kitty loudly intervened, "I'm sorry we haven't had the pleasure of meeting. I'm Catherine Stevenson, and I arrived last night, and this is my friend Barbara. She gets grumpy if she hasn't been fed. I trust the food here is excellent?" Kitty brought herself up as best she could and paused to let the waiter adjust to her assumed authority. "Is there a menu?" she asked.

"Yes ma'am," said the waiter as he handed her a soiled Xeroxed sheet containing the week's menu.

"I see there are not many choices," said Kitty slowly. " I'll take the boiled ham and peas with apple compote for dessert. Barb would you like that or the squash pie?"

"I'll take the pie," said Barb. "I don't know how they could ruin that."

"You'd be surprised," said one of the older gentlemen.

They all giggled at that as the waiter resumed his sour attitude. "Very well," he said. "Mrs. Stevenson have you arranged for an account; I don't see you on my list."

"I didn't know I had to," said Kitty.

The waiter grinned slightly and said, "I'm afraid ...." but Kitty interrupted him, "Young man bring me some food or I shall die on the spot, and it will be blood on your hands and call the *maître d'* and I shall set up an account immediately." Kitty was feeling haughty and enjoying it.

"Me too," said Barb.

"Samson," said one of the old men angrily, "if you can't make arrangements immediately then put these lovely ladies' dinners on my account."

Samson smiled slightly, bowed slightly, and left to take orders at other tables.

"He's my nephew," said one of the older gentlemen. "He doesn't like working here; he thinks it's beneath him, so he pretends that he's a waiter in a four-star restaurant."

"Ha," said Kitty, "so that's it. Well, let's hope the food lives up to the reputation portrayed by our young actor."

During the meal, Barb was about to comment on the food when Kitty interrupted her saying, "Shhh, I am in Paris, do not break the spell."

11

Estate Sale - Late winter 1999

After dinner, a meal memorable primarily for its lack of texture, Kitty announced on her way back to her room that she needed to have an estate sale.

"Is that going to be like a yard sale?" asked Barb.

"No," said Kitty, "I've called an estate agent. If you can spring me this Saturday afternoon so that I can supervise, he'll come to clean out my house, remove anything of value and throw away everything that isn't."

"Sounds drastic," said Barb.

"Well under the circumstances...." said Kitty.

"Don't talk like that," said Barb.

"It's reality," said Kitty quietly. "I'm not leaving this place."

Barb and Kitty returned to Kitty's room in silence.

Saturday morning arrived cold and raw. A nurse had helped Kitty get into her green flowered dress, the one she had bought to match her 'string-o-pearls' and wheeled her to the front door wrapped in a blanket. When Barb arrived with Vince in tow Kitty was ready. Together, Barb and Vince lifted Kitty and her oxygen tank into the back seat of her car, put the folding wheelchair in the trunk and headed to Poplar Hill.

The fields were still brown and gray in the late winter twilight, and the trees showed no signs of swelling at their still dormant twig tips. Kitty often looked for these first signs of spring. Back in Connecticut the sap in the sugar maple trees often began to rise in mid-February and budding would be evident a week or so later. Occasionally, during an early spring, crocuses would poke their purple and yellow heads through the last inch or so of snow. Winter lasted longer in Nova Scotia, and the sap rarely rose before mid-March, and crocuses never bloomed before mid-April. It was mid-March already, and spring could be years away from the evidence Kitty could see from the moving car. I'd love one more walk through the woods, she thought, to look for signs of bears awoken from their slumber or of newborn deer. Winter is not the dead season people think it is, she mused; there is life out there that you can't see from a car window. Kitty let out an audible sigh.

"Are you okay, Kit?" asked a concerned Vince.

"I was getting nostalgic," said Kitty. "There are woods out there I've never explored and likely never will."

"Woods is woods," said Vince. "One bog is as good as the next."

Kitty allowed as how that was very likely true but that there were always surprises to see in nature and she didn't get to see much from her hospital bed.

The truck from the auctioneer had backed into the driveway, so Vince parked next to the old barn. "I guess we'll carry you to the house," said Vince in a low key voice.

"I'll ask the boys to lend a hand," said Barb.

Barb waved the auctioneer over and introduced him to Kitty. It was immediately decided to bring Kitty in through the front door and that Kitty could give a tour of the house on her way to the kitchen.

Vince ran inside and opened the front door while two burly movers carried Kitty in her wheelchair from the car to the front porch. Once they were inside, the auctioneer inquired as to the provenance of the contents. At first, he was a bit dubious about valuing any of the items. "Fake Tiffany lamps are a dime a dozen," he said with a slight derision in his voice.

Kitty smiled and said simply, "I assure you everything in here is the genuine article. The Tiffany wall sconces were converted from gas lamps and came from the house in Newport. If you know your Tiffany, you'll appreciate the fact that they came from very early in the movement. Indeed these sconces were privately made by one of the "Tiffany Girls" for my grandmother who was always on the lookout for talent for Mr. Tiffany. They are very rare. The lamp next to the telephone in the other room is a classic 'Venetian' lamp. It weighs a ton.

"The couch you are sitting on is very uncomfortable which is why it's intact. It's horsehair and is from the French 'Louis Phillipe' period. It came from my mother's bachelorette collection when she was at Vassar College. My grandmother went to Vassar too.

"Vince, would you show the gentlemen the secret compartment?"

"Sure thing, Kit," said Vince as he mimicked the movements of a magician and said "abracadabra" before opening the "secret" compartment in Kitty's bookcase. "I'll be in the kitchen if you need me," he said.

The auctioneer's eyes widened as a treasure trove of China was exposed before him.

"Where did you get this and why is it in a secret compartment?" asked an astonished auctioneer.

"Some people think I'm rich," said Kitty, "so they invite themselves inside when I'm in town. They miss the obvious like the Tiffany lamps, artwork and silverware but wouldn't miss the gold-rimmed Royal Doulton china you see before you."

"Remarkable," said the auctioneer. "Where did you find this?"

Kitty let out an audible 'humph,' "Growing up we had seven sets of silverware and nine sets of China. My daughter has the two good sets of silverware, and I've kept what's left of my grandmother's bachelorette set. When we go into the kitchen, I'll show you. It's a beautiful set that has the theme of grapes and other fruit. I always liked it, so I've used it as my everyday set. The Royal Doulton you see here was my parents' luncheon set. They have never been washed by a dishwasher, always by hand. Same with the Limoges."

The auctioneer raised his eyebrow.

Kitty noticed and said, "Oh, yes! At one point we had houses in New York City, New Canaan, Connecticut, Newport, Rhode Island and Bar Harbor, Maine and there were two or three sets of china and silverware in each house. Plus my mother and grandmother each had a bachelorette set. The house in Newport burned down, so most of the china there was ruined. The house in New York had the oldest stuff. There were sets of China from Spode and others from Minton and Wedgwood. My sisters split that up. The Bar Harbor house was carefully boxed up and stored in a warehouse in New York. My father sold all that during the Depression. What was left, you see here. The Doulton and Limoges were left over from the New Canaan house and my mother's bachelorette set. Hers was the Limoges."

"... and the furniture?" asked the auctioneer.

"The bulk of the family's furniture was sold at an estate auction after my father died and we sold the New Canaan house. What you see here is what I had taken for the cottage we lived in before moving up here. The horsehair sofa was my mother's, the ball and claw chair was from my father's den. The bureau and armoire came from my bedroom as a child. I am not sure of their provenance. I do know that the table in the other room once belonged to John Ewing who was seven or eight greats ago. The table must be from about 1750 as John Ewing was a contemporary and friend of Ben Franklin. The kitchen table is from the same era but in worse shape."

"... and what about these trinkets?" asked the auctioneer, pointing to items on the shelf above the china.

"Oh, that. That's my inventory," Kitty said with a smile. "When I first moved here I had visions of opening a store to fleece the tourists out of their pocket change. I bought lots of local artisans' work.

"I can't remember the name of the fellow, but I liked his work, so I bought a lot for the store, but I didn't sell much. Eventually, I gave a lot away as presents, and I finally realized that buying inventory for the store was just an excuse to buy the things I liked."

"I'll have to do some research," said the auctioneer, "but I think your inventory is surprisingly valuable. Your Inuit soapstone carvings alone are valuable as are these handmade mittens. I'll have to do some research, but I believe the artists are known."

Kitty shrugged. "I can't remember who they are anymore, but if they are known, then I must have good taste."

"Exquisite," said the auctioneer as he motioned to his helpers to start moving the furniture.

"I emptied the drawers," said Barb. "The boxes are in the barn if you'd like to go through things."

"No, no," said Kitty with a sigh. "James and Maggie have taken everything they want so everything else should go to charity. Barb, did you go through the closet in the unheated bedroom upstairs?"

"Yes, it's all boxed," said Barb.

"Well, I saved that for you. I think that stuff will fit you."

"Aw, Kit, that's nice of you, but I have more clothes than I know where to hang them."

"I know," said Kitty, "but there is some nice classic designer clothing in there. Just try it on before handing it over to the United Church in Scotsburn."

Barb looked at the floor and said, "Thanks, Kit."

There was an uncomfortable pause that went unnoticed by the bustling movers and auctioneer who was busy tagging items and writing notations in his notebook. Vince, who had disappeared earlier, came bursting through the door to announce that he had made lunch.

"Splendid altogether," said Kitty as Barb pushed her into the kitchen.

Vince had warmed up some venison stew he brought with him frozen in a Tupperware container, and some cornbread Barb had made earlier that morning. It was delicious, and the three sat quietly eating while the movers and auctioneer swirled around them. Having cleaned out the rest of the house, the movers descended in the kitchen.

"Ah ha," exclaimed the auctioneer as he plucked the sterling silver from Barb, then Vince then finally Kitty's hand. "We must keep the set together as much as possible," he said.

Kitty shrugged and pointed to a set of cutlery hanging from a stand sitting on the top shelf over the kitchen sink. Barb got up and brought the stand to the kitchen table, handing out soup spoons as she went.

"Oh, my God!" exclaimed the auctioneer.

"Not yet," Kitty replied with authority.

"Do you know who you're eating with?" asked an incredulous auctioneer.

"You mean besides Barb and Vince?" said a slightly annoyed Kitty.

Barb and Vince looked at each other and shrugged.

"You," the auctioneer began breathlessly, "are eating with a Lukas Peet original."

"Yes, I know," said Kitty still annoyed but slowly breaking into a smile. "I bought them for my inventory. And?"

"Lukas Peet is one of Canada's premier sculptors!" said the auctioneer interrupting as he grabbed the soup spoon from Kitty's hand, "Museums will pay thousands for this set ... in good condition."

"Oh," said a surprised Kitty, still staring at her bowl of stew.

When the auctioneer left the room carrying the Lukas Peet cutlery set with him, Barb turned to Kitty and said, "I'm sorry Kit, when I cleaned up I threw away a box of plastic utensils."

Kitty looked at Barb and shrugged then put the microwave and oven proof Corel bowl to her lips and slurped down the rest of the stew. Looking at Vince, she exclaimed, as the movers took the antique kitchen table away from in front of her, "That was delicious. I've never had a better, more delicious meal."

Vince broke into a grin; it was Kitty's recipe.

12

Hope Springs - late winter 1999
(Autumn 1937 - Summer 1938)

An old dog-eared black and red copy of the New York Social Register was jammed under the screen door at the front of the house to keep it open. As they left, Kitty asked Vince to stop for a moment while she looked at the ruined book. She laughed, turned to Barb and said, "Looks like someone finally found a use for that thing after all, but any one of a thousand objects could have served the same purpose. There is irony in that isn't there?"

Barb nodded and smiled, not aware of what Kitty was talking about. As they drove off, there was something the auctioneer had said that stuck with her. He said something like "this was the most valuable estate he had ever seen in Nova Scotia." Barb wasn't sure what to make of it. Kitty obviously had some money, but she was also the most frugal person she knew. She hadn't bought the items in her estate, she had inherited them, and it was "just the leftover junk." Barb's eyes widened as her imagination caught a glimpse of the vastness of the wealth Kitty's estate once represented. "Wow," she exclaimed aloud.

"What?" asked Kitty, almost yelling from the back seat.

Barb turned her head to face Kitty and said, "The man said you were the richest person he ever met in Nova Scotia."

"That's not quite right," said Kitty a little perplexed. "I think he said something like it was the second or third most

175

valuable stash packed into such a tiny house that he had seen. He said it might be worth $100,000 ... Canadian." Kitty giggled at that, "I can't imagine there aren't a lot of houses with more stuff than I have in Nova Scotia. He will just have to wait a few years to have a go at them I guess."

Barb wasn't sure about that; it was the tone of the man's voice, he had sounded ... awestruck. Kitty was rich! Everyone knew it, and it wasn't just her demeanor that said she was rich, it was also ... What? Barb had to stop and think. She always had money when tax auctions came up. That's how she had bought her square mile of land. Actually, it was more than a square mile, 820 acres, more or less. That had to be worth a fortune now that the timber had grown back. And she had all those stocks too, lots of stocks, thought Barb. She must have more money than she knows what to do with ... that must be why she's so generous. Well, no, that wasn't quite right either, thought Barb. Kitty rarely gave away anything, but she had given Barb her car, and she was always willing to help ... within reason, but there was always some kind of contract involved even if it wasn't written. Kitty called it a *quid pro quo*, whatever that meant, thought Barb. Vince always negotiated the deals. Kitty never got rich from the deals, but she never lost money either.

Barb laughed to herself, everyone thought they got the better of any deal with Kitty, except Earl, of course, but Barb always wondered if Kitty was a lot shrewder than she let on. Vince and Barb had once argued about it years ago after they discovered that they had built their house on her property.

Kitty hadn't thrown them out as they had feared; she didn't sue them or even charge them rent. Instead, she had loaned, no given, them enough money to finish building the house with the agreement that when they were ready to move on she would sell them five acres (at market rates) and they could pay her back ... without interest. Vince had come home convinced he had found his patron saint. Barb had been dubious, but Vince had convinced her that this was the best possible solution for everyone, even Kitty.

Kitty had helped everyone around Poplar Hill, sometimes with money, sometimes with influence and sometimes with her simple willingness to listen and engage in conversation without being judgmental. Barb always liked that. Kitty treated everyone as an equal, even small children. Kitty had become the patron saint of the entire neighborhood, and now, the empty house reminded Barb that she was leaving Poplar Hill for good. That thought brought a tear to Barb's eye, and she turned to look out the window at a darkened landscape punctuated only by the glow of windows as they passed by the infrequent farmhouses.

"I used to like the desolation here," said Kitty from the back seat.

"It's getting pretty built up," said Vince. "A lot of new people."

"I don't think I'll miss the winter," said Kitty, "but I do like a good blizzard and the sparkling white afterwards and the smell of wood burning. I wish they had a wood burning stove at the home or even a fireplace."

"Last time I was in New Glasgow they had cedar incense. Smelled just like an old wood burner," said Vince.

"I couldn't burn that, not with the oxygen, it might explode."

"Yup," said Vince as they drove on in silence.

Few words were exchanged when they dropped Kitty off at the Shiretown Nursing Home. It was late and all Kitty wanted was to get in bed.

On the way home to River John, Barb asked Vince, "How long do you think Kit will live?"

"I don't know. She's been a real friend and good to us."

"And we've been good to her too."

"Yup, I know what you're thinking, but she's got family, and we've all been fair traded."

"I know Vince, I know," said Barb, "but sometimes you hope you win the lottery...."

Barb and Vince both got up at 5:00 a.m. It was very early for Barb, but she couldn't sleep after Vince got up and for some reason, her muscles ached. Barb had made Vince lunch the night before but rearranged it again before sending him off to work. On his way out the door, Vince asked casually, "Are you seeing Kit today?"

"Yup," said Barb. "I want to see as much of her as I can. I want to hear all her stories."

"I don't think there's enough time in the world for that," said Vince with a wink as he closed the door.

As Barb sat at her kitchen table drinking coffee and thinking about Kitty, something Vince had said popped into her head: "Don't look at the ledger," he had said, "you might not like the balance." That's silly, she thought, Kit and I don't have a *quid pro quo*. Of course, we do, said the other voice in her head. She could have the entire argument sitting by herself at the kitchen table. Vince would always take Kit's side, and that little voice of doubt inside her head would argue.

"Kitty made a lot of money selling us those five acres," said the voice.

"Yes, but she had to sit on it for thirty years while we lived there to earn it," said the voice of Vince.

"We banked her house with hay every winter," said the voice in her head.

"Yes, but she gave us hay from her field, and wood too," said the voice of Vince.

"We had to drive her everywhere after her heart attack," said the voice in her head.

"Yes," said the voice of Vince, "but she gave you her car, and when you had cancer she took in the kids and cooked and cleaned for you when you were too weak to manage. What did she get in return?"

Vince was right. Kitty was more than a neighbor, she was

Barb's best friend, and Barb had gotten a lot. "Enough of that!" thought Barb with determination, Kitty is my friend and I enjoy hanging around with her and that's enough. Barb put her coffee cup down with a bang.

The day was still young, and the nursing home discouraged visitors before 10:00 a.m., so Barb decided to stop at the River John Library to find a book on pre-war Germany. The book selections were meager, but Barb managed to find a book with a two-page timeline which she Xeroxed rather than check out because it was mostly about the war, and she wasn't interested in that.

By the time Barb got to the Shiretown Nursing Home, it was almost noon. Kitty would be wondering where she was so she hurried past the front desk to Kitty's room. Kitty was already dressed but still sitting on her bed reading.

"Hello, Kit," said Barb.

"Hello, yourself," said Kitty. "I've ordered dinner in bed, but I can call and get you something too if you like."

"No," said Barb, "I made a sandwich, it's in the car. I'll eat on the way home." Barb lied; she didn't have a sandwich in her car but didn't want to put Kitty out, and besides, the food at the home wasn't very good.

"Well, now that you're here I suppose we could go to the solarium and watch the plants grow."

"I guess we could if there were any plants to watch," said Barb as she helped Kitty out of bed and into a wheelchair.

"I had a dozen geraniums delivered this morning."

"That's nice but what can we do about your oxygen?"

"They have some new oxygen machines that you can take with you," said Kitty. "They are an engineering marvel. We can get one at the nurse's desk."

By the time Barb had helped Kitty into the wheelchair and hung her IV bottle, Kitty was out of breath. By the time Barb had pushed Kitty to the nurse's station she was gasping for breath and staring, wide-eyed, into the distance. Barb quickly hung the oxygen machine on the back of Kitty's wheel-chair with the help of the nurse and placed the tubes over Kitty's head. Kitty shook her head as she inhaled as deeply as she could as the fresh oxygen blew into her nostrils.

"Are you sure you're okay?" asked Barb.

"No, I'm not okay," Kitty said between breaths, "but it will have to do. I'll be back to normal in a few minutes." Kitty waved "calm down" slowly at Barb who sat across from Kit-ty with a worried look. "I'll be okay in a minute," she added.

Barb wasn't so sure as they made their way to the solari-um. She had never seen Kitty so ... tired. "You know, I can come back another time if you like," said Barb.

"Heavens no," said Kitty looking a little less ashen. "Once I catch up I'll be okay. So what's new?"

Barb was thinking ahead and almost interrupted, "Your stories got me thinking so I went to the library and found this." She had spoken too soon; the Xeroxed sheet was lost in her purse. As Barb fumbled in her purse, Kitty gave her a "you must be nuts" look. "Its history," protested Barb, final-ly retrieving the sheet. "See, it's a timeline that lists all the events you've been telling me about." Barb pointed and said, "See here, it's 1938, and you were there."

"Ah, so I was," said Kitty whose color had come back.

"I've even checked off the stories you've told me about; see, there's the Anschluss," said Barb. "I tried to find a map of Germany, but they didn't have any that were that old. They said they only kept current maps."

"Libraries hold on to things, you know books, maps and things like that, for twenty or thirty years at most then throw them away. Then fifty years later they cry about all the things that have been lost and the cycle begins anew. No one ever learns."

"Okay," said Barb looking at her list and not actually pay-ing attention, "so what happened after the Germans went into Austria?"

"Well, I'm not really sure. What does your list say? As best I can remember the Czech crisis simmered along all spring and summer of '38. I remember Neville Chamberlain waffling every time he could. At one point he said that Britain would never go to war against Germany over Czechoslovakia and another time he announced that he wouldn't go to war over France or Poland. So there's no wonder Hitler eventually went to war. The Germans and the Austrians looked at him as the new Otto von Bismarck, a new Otto the Great. He was at the height of his popularity then."

"Oh, that sort of explains why you didn't leave."

"There wasn't any reason to leave at that point, and I wasn't Jewish." She paused, thinking, for a moment then added, "Hitler was uniting the German-speaking people, and the rest of Europe, while they might have complained, really didn't have the will to resist. As Americans, we were neutrals; we didn't have any reason to worry. As Stan used to say, we didn't have any skin in the game. I am quite sure that everyone knew what was coming but, I think, most Germans deluded themselves into thinking that Germany could get what they wanted from Europe with bluster and intimidation alone. And they almost did.

"It's hard to see now, but in 1938 almost everything Hitler was asking for looked reasonable to Americans. He was just asking to unite the German-speaking people wherever they were and that, of course, meant good chunks of Poland and Czechoslovakia had to go. It was not his aims but his methods that scared people. Everyone knew that Hitler was brutal, if not lethal, to those he perceived to be in his way.

"You know, I remember that April, right after the Anschluss, was very scary. The Austrians voted unanimously, or so they said, to join Germany. We, I mean Sam and me, had Passover with Joseph and his wife and daughter right after that. We had to do it in secret. We used saltine crackers for unleavened bread, they are sort of like matzos, and we improvised everything else. My Sam, Sam Anderson, couldn't find the rabbi he found at Christmas, so Joseph declared that we had a kosher meal anyway and did his prayers in Hebrew. It was a very sad and moving moment. The next time I went to a seder was in 1954 or 55 in New York after I managed to help Sophie Goldberg get into the United States. After that, I think the next seder was up here in Nova Scotia with the Steins — you remember them don't you?"

Barb nodded her head; of course, she remembered the Steins. Barb and Vince were at the seder too, thanks to Kit. All Barb could remember of the evening were dabs of horse-radish, sweet red wine, as bad as they serve in the Catholic Church on Easter, and flatbread crackers instead of bread. She remembered the incomprehensible mumblings in Hebrew were just like the incomprehensible mumblings in Latin. "Yup, yup, yup," said Barb waving her hands for Kitty to continue the story.

Kitty nodded too, "The biggest scare of all that year came when the Nazis announced that 'Aryans' —that meant us — could not act as fronts for Jewish business. You'll remember that Sam, Joe and I bought the book business from Saul Goldberg but we let Joseph and his family stay there. Apparently, a lot of good Germans had the same idea we had. The consulate told us to rent the place to the Goldbergs for a few thousand marks a year. We did, officially, but never actually collected any rent. Another strike at the Third Reich!" Kitty was pleased with herself although a tear ran down her cheek.

A nurse brought lunch on a tray to the solarium and adjusted Kitty's oxygen machine. "Splendid altogether," said Kitty digging in with gusto.

Barb watched impatiently as Kitty slowly and carefully ate the meal before her. Kitty's dentures had grown loose and eating anything, but mush had become a chore, but she had refused to give in and ordered regular meals, not the boiled monstrosities like the ones she used to prepare at the Odd-fellows.

Barb watched Kitty carefully cut tiny pieces from the strip of beef on her plate, thoroughly chewing each piece making sure that none of the food ended up under her dentures. When she was finished with the meat, Kitty carefully ate each pea and sliced carrot one or two at a time, leaving the soupy mashed potatoes for last. Finally, she pushed the plate away pronouncing the meal, "Splendid altogether." Barb let out a long-held sigh.

"Let's see, what else happened that spring," said Kitty thinking out loud. "I think the Nazis required all Jews to register their property, but of course the Goldbergs didn't have any, so that was easy. Joseph still tuned all our pianos so he had a steady but meager income and we all helped him and others like him out as best we could."

She paused, "Sometime that spring, I'm sure it was after we had Passover, Joseph received a letter from Saul that made him very upset. It seems that Saul had made it to Trieste without a problem and had taken a ship to Istanbul where the authorities stopped everyone attempting to get to Palestine. They were completely broke, but somehow they managed to obtain transit visas through Baghdad to India and were now stuck in India where the local Jewish counsel was trying to feed and house them as best they could. I think Joseph realized that the door was shut after that, so he turned inward and became a social hermit, preoccupied with his own thoughts. Sam Anderson said that he thought that Joseph was trying to make himself very, very small in the hopes that no one would notice him. I think most of the Jews left in Germany probably did the same thing.

"About that time we became preoccupied with our own scare as well. The Czech crisis developed its own rhythm with the bottom of each cycle getting deeper and scarier. I think it was in May when all of a sudden it bubbled up again and we all thought war was about to start any minute. It was the real start of the Sudetenland crisis."

"Hey," protested Barb, "I thought we already went through the Sudetenland crisis?"

"It festered for months," said Kitty. "I'm sure I've talked about it before, haven't I?"

"Helloo, Catherine," boomed a familiar voice.

Kitty turned to look. "Oy vey!" she exclaimed.

"Aw, Christ," said Barb who burst out laughing.

It was Mandy Betts looking like an overstuffed Michelin man with a huge down jacket over her uniform, flowered moo-moo. Behind her was a small runt of a man who, even with a winter jacket on, looked a quarter her size. His clothing suggested a Pentecostal preacher, a light blue shirt with a clerical collar, but otherwise, he looked rather shabby and someone more used to working in an auto garage than a pulpit.

Mandy leaned over, grabbed Kitty's head and forcefully kissed her on the cheek. "Well, hello yourself," said Kitty with obvious annoyance in her voice. Kitty looked at Barb and rolled her eyes. Barb shrugged.

"We heard you were convalescing in hospice here," said an out of breath Mandy. "This here is Jeff Goode. He's the assistant pastor over at Stellarton. We're here to pray for you and all that live here." Mandy was still waving her arms in the air as she spoke.

Kitty was taking deep breaths of oxygen again, and Barb knew that meant that Kitty's blood pressure was getting dangerously high. She had seen it before, and the doctors warned her that very high blood pressure might lead to another heart attack or worse, a stroke. "Hang tight," Barb said to Kitty with a wink who nodded as Barb walked swiftly to the nurse's station.

"Have you placed your trust in the Lord?" the puny minister asked, waving his Bible above his head. Kitty rolled her eyes then nodded affirmatively. Mandy closed her eyes, raised her hands above her head, Reverend Jeff followed suit, and began to sway back and forth and moan something Kitty couldn't understand even with her hearing aids turned up. She turned them down.

When Barb came back, a nurse in tow, it looked to her like some pagan ritual as Mandy and Reverend Jeff moaned and danced circles around Kitty. The only thing missing, thought Barb, was incense and naked dancing virgins.

"There'll be no more of that," said the large and very muscular nurse Barb had brought back with her. "Catherine is in a delicate condition, and we can't have you go and get her excited, so stop that this moment or I'll have to ask you to leave." The voice was big, not loud but carried with it enough authority to make Mandy and the Reverend Jeff stop in mid-incantation and drop their arms like deflating balloons.

"We're just here to save a soul," protested Mandy.

Reverend Jeff Goode stepped in front of Mandy, brought himself up, and asked the nurse as authoritatively as he could muster, "Have you been saved?"

The nurse, who towered over him, turned to stare him down and replied, "I'm a practicing Roman Catholic."

Barb and Kitty, who had been left out of the confrontation, looked at each other and giggled under their breath. "I'll place a bet on who's going to win that argument," Barb whispered to Kitty.

"I don't think I'll take you up on that bet," Kitty whispered back.

"We love Kit," said Mandy, pleading her case. "We would do nothing to hurt her, believe me."

"Can we pray quietly with her?" asked Reverend Jeff.

Kitty looked at the nurse wide-eyed and vigorously shook

her head no. The nurse shrugged her shoulders and said to Reverend Jeff, "Okay but just five minutes then I have to take Catherine back for treatment."

Barb looked at her watch. Twenty minutes later the nurse returned with two even larger orderlies to shoo Mandy and Reverend Jeff from the room. "The patients will be returning from lunch," she said, "and we have quiet time, so you'll have to go. There is a chapel down the hall for your use if you like."

"Goodbye, Kit," yelled Mandy as she turned to leave. "Stay well. We'll be back to see you soon."

"That's what I'm afraid of," mumbled Kitty under her breath as she smiled and waved back.

Reverend Jeff put his hand on Kitty's head and mumbled, "Lord Jesus, keep this kind woman in your thoughts as we will in our prayers, Amen." He left, following Mandy out the door.

After they left Kitty said, "I'd rather they didn't bring me to anyone's attention. I'm perfectly happy hiding among the multitudes."

Barb thought for a few moments then said, "That didn't help your friend Joseph did it?"

"Who?" asked Kitty raising her voice because she had forgotten to turn her hearing aids up again after Mandy left.

Barb pointed to her ears, and Kitty turned up her hearing aids and said with annoyance, "I can hear you."

Barb laughed, "Hiding among the multitudes didn't help your friend Joseph Goldberg in Germany did it?"

"Oh," said Kitty a bit sourly, "that's what you meant. No, No I suppose it didn't."

Barb winced at Kitty's reaction. "I didn't mean to ...," Barb began before being interrupted by Kitty.

"Don't worry Barb; it's just that those ... Pentecostals," Kitty said the word with distaste, "just drive me to distraction. They don't even know their own church history and couldn't tell me the difference between the United Church, the Presbyterian Church, the Methodist or Baptist churches or the difference between Catholic and Orthodox churches if their lives depended on it. But you can be sure they have all the answers." Kitty was fuming.

"I don't know anybody that could do that," said Barb. "Could you?"

"As a matter of fact I could if you'd care to listen," said Kitty. It came out as a challenge.

"I believe you," said Barb who threw her hands in the air in surrender.

"It's a very dry topic," said Kitty, "and there are lots more interesting things to talk about," she paused then continued, "like the weather ... or golf." Kitty was working herself up again.

"Oh, you're feeling your oats; I didn't mean to get you started about wasting time watching golf on TV."

"Well," said Kitty in a pontificating voice, "There are games meant to be watched, and there are games meant to be played. Golf and tennis are meant to be played not watched."

"I've never played or watched either; I watch hockey though."

"I can't follow hockey."

"That's okay Kit; I have trouble following your history lesson."

"Tell me to stop anytime; my story isn't unique, really."

"You're like listening to a good mystery novel being read, the kind you can't put down."

"I hope you don't put me down," said Kitty with a sheepish smile.

Barb laughed, "Got it. You're not ready for the glue factory yet. Besides you've got too many stories in you and you, yourself, said that you couldn't kick the bucket as long as you had a story left to tell. Vince says I don't have enough lifetimes to hear them all."

Kitty laughed, "Did I say that? Well, it must be so. What stories haven't I told you yet?"

They both laughed. "Well what happened to you during the rest of 1938, that's the year we were on I think," said Barb.

"Oh," said Kitty thinking, "remind me, what does it say on your list?"

Barb read the list slowly:

23 April—Czechoslovakia: German citizens of the Sudetenland, a Czech province, demand their independence.

24 April—Europe: German Jews are required to register their property with the government.

19 May—Czechoslovakia: Britain and France jointly reject Hitler's demands for Czechoslovakia.

20 May—Czechoslovakia: Czechoslovakia mobilizes its armed forces in response to German aggression along the border.

"I remember," said Kitty, "Can't you see the rhythm in the Czech crisis? The Nazis foment trouble then it quiets down then it flares up again. During this particular Czech crisis, Sam and I booked ourselves on a tour down the Adriatic Sea. When things began to warm up during the second week in May, and we all thought there would be a war by June, Sam rented a car in Germany, and we drove to Trieste in Yugoslavia which was only about two hundred miles or three hundred plus kilometers, about six hours in the car. From there, we drove down the coast to Zadar then Split and finally one of the most beautiful cities in the world, Dubrovnik." Kitty delighted in rolling her "r's" in Dubrovnik.

"We were in Dubrovnik when we heard that the Czechs had declared war on Germany. Of course, no such thing had happened, but rumors like that were rampant all over Europe at the time. Sam managed to telegraph the American Embassy in Athens to find out that the Czechs had mobilized their armies but that the British and the French had defused the situation. Still, we were cautious, so we continued down the Adriatic coast until we got to Greece. Gasoline was getting scarce because people were hoarding it. We stayed in some beautiful little towns and inns. Fortunately, Sam spoke the language nearly everywhere we went. I think he had some trouble in Albania, but he found someone who spoke Slovene, so we were okay. By the time we got to Athens the scare was over, so we drove back by way of Sofia Bulgaria, Bucharest Rumania, Budapest and finally Bratislava in Hungary. We had a most memorable three weeks, a glorious grand tour of Eastern Europe, the likes of which could not be had again until a few years ago. I'm not sure you could even do it today."

"How did you do that?" asked Barb, "I mean, you couldn't take money out of Germany and all that, could you?"

"Ah," said Kitty, "When we left, the borders were quite porous, and there was a vigorous black market. Sam knew people everywhere so he would arrange to buy items in Munich that we delivered in Dubrovnik for example. Of course we paid for as much as we could in marks before we left, like the car and some of the hotels, but still, we were pretty broke by the time we got back to Munich.

"By then the crisis had died down, and everything returned to normal. I had missed a week or so of classes, but we were down to just a few students, so our teachers were flexible." Kitty laughed, "They had to be since there were few Germans studying opera by then and we were the school's bread and butter."

Barb laughed, "I might have stayed in school too if I could come and go as I pleased. I don't think Vince would have stayed if they paid him."

"Don't get me wrong, I love opera, I love singing opera. I hoped to make a career in opera but the times made opera secondary, it was something I did between crises. What's next on your list? You know this makes it a lot easier to remember what happened, your list I mean."

"Let's see," said Barb trying to remember what exactly they had covered. She read down the list:

24 May—Europe: all Jew-authored and remotely anti-Nazi books removed from Austria libraries and bookstores.

30 May—Europe: Hitler publicly announces his aim to destroy Czechoslovakia.

Kitty jumped in, "See the rhythm? Hitler made noises, and we all figured that the next crisis would be at the beginning or middle of August. Go on."

Barb continued:

7 June—Europe: Germany signs non-aggression pacts with Estonia and Latvia.

14 June—Nazis order Jewish-owned businesses to register.

2 July—Europe: Nearly 40,000 Jews in Austria are taken into "protective custody."

5 July—Europe: A conference begins at Evian, France to discuss the problem of Jewish refugees from Germany.

6 July—Nazis prohibit Jews from trading or providing a variety of specified commercial services.

Kitty interrupted again, "Selling books was one of those trades that were banned. Saul got out at a good time. It was a very bad time to be Jewish, everyone in the world knew it, yet the entire civilized world stood by and did nothing." Kitty looked off into the distance with disgust. She nodded at Barb.

Barb continued:

11 July—Europe: The French prime minister is given the authority to rule by decree in the event of war.

12 July—Czechoslovakia: France recommits herself to the independence of Czechoslovakia.

21 July—Europe: The German government passes legislation to require identity cards for Jews.

25 July—Jewish doctors are prohibited by law from practicing medicine.

"What your list doesn't say," interrupted Kitty angrily, "is that Gentile, that is non-Jewish doctors were also prohibited from treating Jews. It was the beginning of Hitler's final solution, but that first version of the final solution didn't kill Jews fast enough for him. And the Austrians went along by building a concentration camp of their own. I think Italy followed soon after if memory serves me." Kitty was shaking her head, angry and out of breath.

Kitty was looking very pale when a nurse walked by to check on her. "Catherine, your blood pressure is 240 over 160. That is not good," said the nurse shaking her head. She injected something into Kitty's IV drip hanging from a metal post over her head. Kitty calmed down almost immediately.

"Jeez," said Barb, "I don't want to kill you, Kit. Maybe you should tell me what you did after the war instead."

Kitty slowly regained her composure and her color. The nurse came by every ten minutes to check her blood pressure which was dropping nicely. Kitty turned to Barb and said, "I used to be able to control my blood pressure, sort of. I would just close my eyes and chant to myself one of those Buddhist chants that they had in that TV movie I saw about Tibetan Buddhism. I don't know what the chant was all about, but it was the rhythmic chanting that calmed me down. It doesn't work anymore." Kitty made a sad face.

"I remember that," said Barb, "I used to wonder what in the heck you were doing. So tell me what you did after the war?"

"It was understood that when the boys came back from the war, we girls would lose our jobs, so I stopped working for the Pennsylvania Railroad in 1948 and went back to work at the French Institute and started writing for newspapers again. That's how I learned about the refugee problem. It wasn't in the newspapers, but the French were dealing with lots and lots of displaced persons as they called them then. So I volunteered.

"That's when I decided to look up the Goldbergs and discovered that Saul and his family had finally made it to Israel but that Joseph's wife didn't make it out of Auschwitz alive. Joseph's little daughter Sophie had survived and was in a French refugee camp. Of course, Joseph didn't make it past Kristallnacht. Stan pulled some strings, and we got Sophie to New York. The brave, little twelve-year-old girl I knew in Munich had turned into a shell-shocked twenty three-year-old.

"So Stan had connections?" asked Barb.

Kitty nodded, "Our building was owned by a Jewish gentleman who let Sophie stay in the apartment across the hall from us for free until we could find some relatives. She eventually found a cousin or someone she knew in Chicago. We managed to fill up half the building with refugees. The city paid for some, relatives paid for others, and the Jewish philanthropies paid for even more. Most of them spoke Yiddish, and I tried to teach them all English. Stan used to laugh at me because he could only speak English."

"What was Stan like?" asked Barb. "I wish I had met him."

Kitty laughed, "I suppose he was just like my father, but Stan had become a Roosevelt Democrat while my father remained a staunch Calvin Coolidge, Herbert Hoover Republican. Stan had grown to be far more tolerant than my father ever was. Did you know that Stan was only eight years younger than my father?"

"I knew something like that," said Barb.

"Yes," continued Kitty. "He was thirty years older than I was and we had a wonderful life together ... until he died."

Barb wasn't sure if she should continue down this path or not, so she sat in silence.

"Stan died in 1963; he was 74, and I was 44 with two little kids," said Kitty whose eyes began to well up with tears.

Kitty quickly changed the subject and shook her sadness off, with a little cough. "When Stan's big investment didn't pan out we moved to New Canaan.

Barb was about to say something when an orderly walked through the solarium ringing the dinner bell that Kitty could barely hear.

Its pitch was so high only dogs could hear it, thought Kitty. "I wish they'd realize that no one over fifty can hear that little tinkle of a bell," said Kitty. "They need a loud gong."

Barb laughed, "Shall I push you to dinner?"

"No," said Kitty, "I don't have the strength to be sociable tonight."

After Kitty was back in her bed, she turned to Barb and asked in a surprisingly weak voice, "Will you come again tomorrow?"

"Of course I will," said Barb. She thought the question odd. She had never seen Kitty look frail before. She had always been such a robust woman.

As Barb bent over to unlock her car door, she felt a familiar stab of pain in her hip. She had noticed it before, but this time the pain penetrated her consciousness, and she could not ignore it. *Damn, damn, damn*, she said quietly to herself. Was it the bone cancer returning, she wondered? She said little to Vince except that she wasn't feeling well and went to bed early with four Tylenol.

In the morning the pain had diminished but not disappeared, so Barb let Vince and the kids sneak out of bed and get ready for work and school, a habit they had gotten into when Barb had been bedridden the last time. *The last time*, thought Barb to herself, she felt deflated. *Did the pain mean that the cancer was returning?* As she lay in bed, she could hear Vince in the kitchen, as he closed the side door, got in his truck and drove away. The kids had gotten up, made lunch and were on their way to school already. She felt very alone. The last time Vince had worked hard at providing, at being a father, he even tried cooking, but Kitty had kept her strong. Barb tried to roll over and go back to sleep, but she was getting depressed lying there so sat up and put her feet on the floor. As soon as she stood up the pain in her right leg made her wince and she had to catch herself. *Damn*, she thought.

Barb took four more Tylenol with her coffee and waited until well after 9 a.m. to call the oncologist in New Glasgow. The receptionist said Dr. Murray could see her any afternoon that week and mornings beginning the following Monday. She wanted to see Kitty in the afternoons, so she asked for the appointment early Monday morning. She wouldn't tell Vince ... or Kitty unless she had to. In the meantime, her cane was next to the back door and her crutches, if it came to that, were in the hall closet.

Kitty was already in a wheelchair and was nibbling on raw carrots when Barb arrived. "Hello, Barb. I made some notes this morning," said Kitty. "Are you ready for story time?"

Barb had used her cane to walk from the car but had left it at the nurse's station and was feeling the pain in her hip and right leg as she walked. Kitty looked at Barb for a moment then ordered, "Barbara, sit down right now."

Barb did as she was told and sat down so quickly it hurt. The tone of Kitty's voice reminded her of the nuns she had one year in elementary school. She sat upright, folded her hands, instinctively, on her lap and looked down at her shoes and prepared herself for a lecture.

Kitty laughed, "I'm not the Mother Superior here, I remember having the same reaction when I was called on the carpet for something in my school days in Grenoble." Kitty paused and softened her voice, "You can't hide it, Barb. When did it start? Have you been to the doctor yet?"

"I'll see him Monday morning," said Barb sheepishly.

"Oh, Barb, I'm so sorry."

"He said it might not be the cancer returning. It might just be arthritis on top of the damage that's already there. You know you never really heal from cancer. The cancer may be gone, but it leaves a scar." Barb was pleading her case, but she was still scared.

"You know I had cervical cancer right after Stan died," said Kitty, "and that was some thirty-five years ago. It can go away but we do get older, and things don't work as well as they once did."

"I know that."

"... but it doesn't make it any easier, I know," said Kitty interrupting.

Barb was close to tears so Kitty pulled herself up with effort and walked the five feet over to Barb and put her arm around Barb's shoulders. She hugged her and in a squeaky little voice said, "One day at a time, one hour at a time and when it comes to it, one minute at a time. That's all you can do."

Barb nodded, but the squeakiness of Kitty's voice was a shock to her. She had heard it the night before, and it had unnerved her. She looked up into the face of a suddenly very old woman struggling for breath. "Aw, jeez Kit, let me help you sit down."

Kitty was back in her wheelchair and Barb sat back on the chair next to her. They both felt exhausted. A tear ran down Kitty's cheek; Barb turned away as a teardrop ran down hers as well.

13

Into the fire - April 1999
(November 11, 1938)

The ambulance pulled out of the Shiretown Nursing Home into the cold crisp winter air, warble-horn blaring, lights flashing — and sped off towards the causeway. Barb panicked, her adrenaline was pumping, it could be Kit, she thought, as she quickly pulled into the parking lot and walked, no ran, to Kitty's room. No one was there, not even Elizabeth which was odd, so she ran to the nurse's station fearing the worst. Where was Kitty, where was Elizabeth, demanded Barb? "Elizabeth had a small incident last night," said the nurse completely nonchalantly and without looking up, "She'll be fine."

"... and Kitty?" demanded Barb.

"Oh," said the nurse who finally looked up, "she's in the solarium, reading I expect."

Barb let out a sigh of relief and ran to the solarium where she found Kitty asleep in a wheelchair, her feet up on an empty chair. As Barb approached, she could hear Kitty snoring gently as the oxygen machine quietly hissed. Kitty's glasses had fallen off the end of her nose and were dangling from one ear. A copy of *The Rise and Fall of the Third Reich* lay open on her lap. Barb sat down quietly beside Kitty and slowly pulled the book from beneath Kitty's hands.

With a couple of snorts, Kitty woke up and grabbed the book with a surprisingly strong grip. "Oh," she exclaimed as she saw Barb, "I thought the book was falling out of my hands and I tried to grab it. If it fell to the floor, I'd lose my place, and I don't know if I could reach it down there."

Barb laughed, "I grabbed the book so that it wouldn't fall to the floor. Whatcha reading anyway?"

"It's a book about how Hitler came to power, and how he fell from grace; I never knew about most of this. Fascinating, fascinating."

"I can see that. It was so interesting it put you right to sleep," said Barb with a laugh.

"Well, it is a bit dry in places and quite voluminous," said Kitty bouncing the book in her hands. "Besides, I'm only interested in the parts that I saw myself but getting there is ... well ... boring."

"I'm guessing that you didn't like high school history either," said Barb with a laugh.

"I paid no attention at all; I was interested in opera, French literature, and boys. Nothing else. I graduated by the skin of me teeth. I've only read a smidgen of history since, but since you've been asking me to tell you my story, it behooves me to know what I'm talking about, so I'm studying. It's so much better than a sleeping pill. I got eight hours of sleep last night after I began reading this."

"Did you learn anything?" asked Barb with genuine interest.

"Why, yes. When I first met Hitler, I remember thinking that he had magnetic eyes, they penetrated you. I also remember thinking he would make a lousy boyfriend or husband. I learned I was not alone in my judgment. Everyone commented on his eyes. From the commentary, I guess he may have had some, shall we say, some deviant predilections in his personal life."

Barb gave her a quizzical look, her eyes widened. "If you say so," she said, shaking her head slightly.

Kitty laughed, "Did you know he was Stan's age?"

"You're kidding," said Barb with more focused interest. "That's almost ancient history."

"Yes, they were born the same year, 1889. If Stan were alive today, he'd be, what, let me think ... oh, my, one hundred and ten years old. Gosh, that makes me feel old. Come to think of it, I am old. What a horrible thought. I never thought I'd live to be almost eighty." Kitty was shaking her head as if her age was a new discovery.

"You've been almost eighty for a while," said Barb with a laugh, "and I expect you to be almost ninety for a while too."

That brought Kitty down to earth, "So Barb," she said with seriousness in her voice, "what did the doctor say? That is why you dropped by isn't it?"

"He couldn't tell, inconclusive he said. Told me I'd have to sit on it for a while. I told him he could sit on it for a while. I either have to wait for a month and get another x-ray or go to Halifax in three weeks for a biopsy." Barb's anger was ignited. "Why does it take so long for the medical system to do anything? If you're almost dead you get instant service; if you're not, well, take a number." Barb grumbled.

"I'm sorry," said Kitty with concern. "How are you feeling?"

Barb stopped grumbling, then smiled and said, "Actually he gave me a prescription for some new pain medication, and it works like a charm," Barb danced around Kitty's wheelchair. "I didn't need my cane this afternoon. Actually, I came in running and left my cane in the car because I saw an ambulance taking someone to hospital, and I thought for a moment it might be you; but I'm feeling okay at the moment, a little pain, not much."

Kitty straightened up. "Thank you for your concern; I wonder who they were hauling away?"

"I don't know, but what happened to your roomy, Elizabeth?"

Kitty laughed, "They carted her off to the loony bin after she faked having another stroke."

"What? What happened?"

"Well," said Kitty starting out in a matter of fact voice,

"you know she is always having tantrums with her son, who is a bit of a, hmmm, jerk?

"Anyway, he was here last night and mumbled something insulting in front of her. He thinks she's a deaf-mute, the idiot, but she can hear everything, we've established that. Anyway, she threw her bedpan at him ... again ... and the orderlies were called. I'm so glad I'm by the window and out of the line of fire." Kitty was getting worked up.

"She put up a good fight then went completely limp, rolled her eyes to the back of her head and played dead. They all thought she was having another stroke and with her 'do not resuscitate' order signed by her imbecile son, aren't children lovely, they were prepared to pull the plug which, in her case, meant removing her IV drip that did something for her, I'm not sure what.

"I knew she was faking it, at least I was pretty sure she was. When they were ready to read her the last rites I climbed out of bed, no small task I assure you, and went over and whispered in her ear, 'If you don't snap out of it, your son will pull the plug on you, and you'll just lie there and die. You don't want to give him the last laugh do you?'

"With that, she sat bolt upright, looked right at her son, and pulled the IV straight out of her arm. That's when they decided she was nuts and hauled her off to the loony bin. I'd be surprised to see her back during my tenure here."

"I've never seen anything like that."

"You're young; you've got time to see all kinds of remarkable sights."

Barb laughed, "I'm Not that young, but at my age, you saw an awful lot. I haven't seen anything, but then again, I haven't gone looking for trouble."

"I didn't really look either. It was luck, both good and bad, that found me. I was unlucky enough to see things no one should see and lucky enough to live to tell the tale," said Kitty with a shrug. "I suppose if I hadn't seen all those things no one would want to talk to me," she continued in a tiny voice.

Barb felt a sudden pang of guilt since she hadn't seen Kitty all weekend, and when she had seen her, all she did was grill her about Munich. "Oh, Kit, it's just something to talk about. I had to deal with kid stuff this past weekend, and I wasn't feeling great, so I just stayed home. I'm sorry I didn't come to see you."

"I wasn't talking about you," Kitty interrupted. "We have normal conversations, and we sometimes talk about my life in Germany. It is fun to talk about Germany but only in the context of my whole life. Talking about the Nazi era, per se tickles nothing but the prurient interest in some of these old goats here. I'm waiting for someone here to ask me if I saw anyone get killed by the Nazis. Yes, I did, and murder is not a pretty sight, thought, or experience." Kitty was getting rattled.

"Sorry," said Barb forcibly interrupting Kitty, "I came here to complain about our health care system not to talk about Germany. It's just not right." Now Barb was back to fuming.

"Oh," said Kitty with a small laugh, "I think we both need to take our blood pressure pills. Let's talk about the Hector Society or my idea for a Blueberry/Lamb festival, or how to grow pot in sandy soil."

Barb looked at Kitty with shock, then surprise, and finally burst out laughing.

"Gotcha," said Kitty.

"Okay," said Barb hesitantly. "If you didn't like history when you were a kid how did you get interested in history when you were older?"

"Well, that's simple," said Kitty, "my father was a historian, of sorts, so living through the Gr-r-reat Depression, pre-war Germany, and World War Two, I couldn't help but begin to get an appreciation for the gr-r-r-and sweep of history, even if I don't know many facts." Kitty waved her hand towards the ceiling in her magnificent gesture.

Barb laughed, "Well Kit I just dropped by on my way home from the doctor. You're the only one that will listen to my beef. I'll be back tomorrow."

But it was Wednesday before Barb could visit Kitty again, and when she did, she found her asleep in the solarium, the copy of the Rise and Fall of the Third Reich open again on her lap. Barb quickly pulled the book from Kitty's hands and laughed when Kitty woke up with a start. "Making progress I see," she chided.

"Actually, I got past Munich," said Kitty with some pride, "so I can talk about it with some authority. I believe we were last talking about the summer of 1938 were we not?"

"Hold on a sec," said Barb who was rummaging through her purse and pulled out a folded piece of paper. "Here's my list. Let's see, we were in the middle of the summer: the Jews were getting squeezed, and everyone was getting ready for war."

"Oh, that's right, and Joe and Kozie kept disappearing for weeks at a time. It turns out that they both were reconnoitering first the Czech border then the French border. I never asked if they went together or separately. We all thought they were spies, of course, just as we thought Herman the Vermin was a Nazi spying on us. Actually, I knew Herman was a Nazi spy. I saw his uniform. He was a captain in the SS.

"Joe and Kozie never said anything and we, sort of, made it a point of not asking. Well, not asking directly. We all wanted to know what they knew and how they knew it. Joe was the most forthcoming about what he did and where he went.

"About the middle of July, that's in 1938, the French and Czechs agreed to a mutual protection pact. What that meant is that the French raised the stakes for Hitler if he went to war against the Czechs. The French said they would go to war with Germany over Czechoslovakia.

"Joe wanted to see if that was an idle threat, so he went to France only to find that the French weren't doing anything besides sitting behind the Maginot Line but the Germans were fortifying their border. We all found that both interesting and ominous. The Germans took the threat seriously, and we interpreted it to mean that Hitler was serious about dismembering the Czechs. Not a good sign. We began to read all sorts of tea leaves after that and formulated our escape plans. Sam and I planned to leave via Trieste while Betty, Joe, and Kozie planned to get out via Berlin and Denmark. I began to keep my valise packed."

Barb shook her head, "I still don't know why you stayed in Germany. I mean, you must have felt threatened a bit. I would have."

"We did, but I still had lots of money to spend, and the flowers weren't dead in the consulate garden, yet."

"So you just lounged around all summer," said Barb shaking her head in disbelief.

"Hell no! When Joe came back and told us that the Germans were fortifying their border with France and then a couple of weeks later they started mobilizing the army we all decided that it was a good time to take a vacation.

"Sam and I spent August in Italy where we could spend our marks. We were about to go back to Munich when we heard from the embassy in Rome that Hitler had demanded that Czechoslovakia immediately cede the Sudetenland to Germany and both France and the Czechs began their military mobilization. We were plotting our way back to England when we heard that Neville Chamberlain was going to Munich to negotiate with Hitler. We decided that it was as good a time as any to go back to Munich, if only to pack up our apartments. When we got back, there was a great commotion because everyone, that is every German, really believed that Hitler had won without firing a shot.

"During the summer our school was closed, so we just hung out at the American Consulate and the Café Heck where Hitler and his buddies were almost every day. The next couple of months were very heady for the Germans. It was a real 'Cabaret old chum.'"

Kitty, with a big smile, pulled herself up from her wheelchair and did a little dance while singing, "Life is a cabaret old chum, life is a cabaret." When she finished singing, she threw her arms up in the air and exclaimed, "I'm feeling better."

"I can see that," said Barb with a wink. "Did they change your meds? Can I have some?"

"You have to get old first. They save the best drugs for the end."

"You don't look like you're finished quite yet."

"Hardly," said Kitty. "Not until I've told all me stories," she continued with a flourish of her hand. Kitty thought quietly for a moment before continuing, "You know, I think September and October 1938 were the most exciting times I had in Germany. I mean, there is nothing more exhilarating than cheating death, and I think that's how we all felt. We had come within an inch of war, and the world pulled back.

"We went to see all the big wigs come out of the hall after they signed the Munich Agreement and Chamberlain announced that there would be peace. It's funny, you know, potentates didn't have the same kind of protection that they do now, no armed-to-the-teeth bodyguards. So I think I told you that I walked right up to Neville Chamberlain and shook his hand." Kitty shook her head with a laugh.

"You finally explained to me why you stayed there," said Barb.

Kitty nodded, "Up until that point we all felt a war was coming, but after the Munich Pact we all felt very safe again. My opera school reopened, the American Consulate watered its flowers again, and Germany turned inward for a few months which made the rest of the world breathe a sigh of relief, but that inward look really put the screws to the Jews.

"I remember when little Sophie Goldberg was thrown out of her elementary school. After that, she would come over to my apartment with her mother for lunch almost every day. I'd leave money and food for them, and they would clean up our mess. Betty and I were not the neatest people. I think it's because we grew up with maids who picked up after us. Anyway, Joseph still tuned our pianos and would sometimes hang around for dinner if we weren't going out. Years later I realized that Joseph and his family were close to starving. I know it sounds odd to say this but being thrown in Auschwitz probably saved Sophie's life."

"What do you mean?" asked a startled Barb.

"Well," said a newly cautious Kitty, "they were having a rough time of it then, in October, but life got really desperate for them after Kristallnacht." A tear came to Kitty's eye. She took a deep breath, wiped the tear from her cheek, and said, "On Kristallnacht, November 9th, 1938, the stormtroopers — mostly SS troops in civilian clothes I think — smashed the windows of every store known to be owned by a Jew and the oldest male member of the household was arrested. The official story was that everyone arrested that night was held in 'protective custody,' then, a day or two later the Nazis decided that the Jews started the mayhem of Kristallnacht and sent every store owner a bill."

Kitty took a deep breath, "No one ever saw Joseph again...." Kitty's voice trailed off. "Sophie told me that the police said that he was killed at Dachau trying to escape, which was very unlikely."

"That's awful!" exclaimed Barb.

The two women sat in silence staring out the window of the solarium at a dull gray winter's sky before Barb asked, "So how did Sophie end up at Auschwitz and how did that save her life?"

Kitty's eyes were red and swollen, but she cleared her throat, pulled herself upright and began, "I can only tell you what I saw and what Sophie told me fifteen years later.

"After the Munich Pact was signed in October, the German Army was everywhere, some of them moved into the Sudetenland, but mostly they paraded around the city in different sized groups. Around the first of November, they disappeared. Joe told us that they had all returned to camps on the outskirts of town. I never asked how he knew. Anyway, when a supposedly Jewish kid shot a German named Von Rath in Paris, and the German media made a big deal of it, the consulate told everyone to leave or at least hide. That was on Tuesday afternoon. Sam and I were going to leave for Trieste the next day, and I had my bag already packed. That evening we all went to the Café Heck to say good bye to everyone, and that's when I met Hitler. I shook his hand, and we had a small chat.

"Everyone in the café left early except for Hitler, his buddies, and we Americans so apparently everyone knew something was up. We whispered among ourselves and decided that if something was up the safest place to be was sitting next to Hitler. I think we finally left about eleven and a German officer in attendance insisted on calling a cab. I think he even paid for the cab if I remember." Kitty had to stop and catch her breath.

"You were about to tell me about Sophie," said Barb with a laugh knowing that no story Kitty ever told was simple.

Kitty shook her finger at Barb. "I'm getting to it, but without the background, the story has no, what is the word, legs perhaps?"

"Okay, I have patience."

"The first time I was really frightened was when Joe came to our apartment and pounded on the door very early Wednesday morning, the Ninth of November, about 5 a.m. I let him in. Sam wasn't there yet, and all he said was, 'Von Rath died, and the goons are already in the street. That night became known as *Kristallnacht*, The Night of the Broken Glass.

"Who was Von Rath?" asked Barb.

"He was a petty German diplomat, I think," said an annoyed Kitty.

"The newspapers and radio were all over the story the day before blaming virtually all Jews for the Von Rath shooting, and we all agreed, then, that it would not be pleasant if Von Rath died. Sam showed up a while later with the same news and the added tidbit that the trains were not running so we couldn't leave."

"Wow, so what did you do?"

"Hunker down. What else could we do? I called the Consulate, and they said to sit tight until everything blew over." Kitty giggled. "They knew Joe was with us and told me to just listen to what he said. That's when I knew he was a spy, but I never let on. Kozie showed up later in the afternoon along with a bunch of other ex-pats that I didn't know. There were a dozen or so in our apartment and since we had plenty of booze we had a party. We could hear and see gangs roaming the streets from our window, and we could hear the sirens of the fire trucks all day and all night as well as the occasional gun shot, but it wasn't until about 3 a.m. on November 10th that we found out the magnitude of what happened. That's when Sophie and her mother pounded on our door.

"Sophie's mother, I forget her name, Jenna perhaps, had been beaten up badly and was in shock when they arrived at our doorstep soaking wet. Sophie, who was about ten at the time, was calm and I remember getting the impression that it was her idea to come to our apartment. Sophie said that gangs methodically ransacked every house on their street that was Jewish and that our friend Herman led them.

"Fortunately, they lived in a mixed neighborhood, and the bookstore had been shuttered for a while, so the gangs took their time getting to them, but when they did they broke in with extraordinary violence, and when Joseph tried to defend his family they beat him unconscious and dragged him away. Sophie's mother tried to fight them off too, and she was beaten up as well. Sophie had snuck out the back door, climbed over a fence and onto the balcony of the house next door where she hid until the gangs left the neighborhood.

"When Sophie found her mother she was curled up in a ball, crying uncontrollably amid the ruins of their apartment. The only place Sophie felt safe was with us, so she took her mother to our house at three in the morning. She was a very brave little girl.

"And ..." Kitty hesitated.

"What?" protested Barb.

"And Sophie had a gun, a pistol. Apparently, Samuel had acquired it and kept it in a drawer in the kitchen. He wasn't able to use it when the SS broke in, it wouldn't have been a good idea anyway, but Sophie knew where it was so when she was able to persuade her mother to come to our apartment in the middle of the night she brought it along. I don't know if she knew how to use it but when she handed it to me there was a cartridge in the chamber, and the safety was off. It was a .32 Spanish Paramount, a tiny pistol that packed a good punch I found out later."

"What?" cried Barb.

"Oh, yes," said Kitty, "Sophie had a loaded gun. Joe took us out to the woods where I learned to shoot it."

Kitty shook her head and took a deep breath, "Did I tell you that Sophie also told us that Herman the Vermin was in charge of the gangs that terrorized the neighborhood and beat up, and dragged her father away?"

"Yup," Barb laughed, "You just told me that."

"Oh, well that woke us up. I think we decided without saying anything to each other that we had to do something about Herman."

Barb grinned while Kitty fell silent and a tear rolled down her cheek.

After a few minutes of silence, Kitty sat back in her wheelchair and took a deep breath, "Sophie! I don't know if I would have had the same strength if I were in the same situation but I guess you do what you have to do or perish." She sighed again, "Sophie and her mother stayed with us for almost a week but after Sam, Betty and I cleaned up their apartment — with the help of their neighbors I should add — Sophie and her mom went back to the apartment. Sophie remained a clear-headed, bright-eyed, open little girl but her mother folded into herself and got smaller and smaller. In many ways, I think she was already dead by the time the Nazis took her to Auschwitz."

Kitty shook her head, "Anyway, Joseph had gotten them German passports, but they were stamped with a large purple J to indicate that they were Jewish. We took them to the American Consulate and managed to get them on some waiting list for immigration, but it was clear, to me at least, that being Jewish was an impediment. At least then, the facts of Kristallnacht had not quite sunk in.

"The morning after, on the tenth, I went out and toured the city. Every synagogue in Munich had been burned. Some were still on fire when I walked by. Near one synagogue there were a couple of corpses just lying on the ground. I don't know if they were shot or beaten to death but there they were, just lying there. No one covered them, no one seemed concerned; it was as if I was the only one who could even see them."

"Wow, you really saw that?" asked Barb feeling a bit squeamish.

"Yes, yes I did," said Kitty with sadness in her voice. "I think Germany fell into two camps after that, a few became full-blooded, foaming-at-the-mouth, Nazis while the rest fell into an unbelieving stupor. It wasn't denial really but a mental stupor. It either horrified or enthralled the German population. The Nazi propaganda machine was very proud of the way things went and gloated. It was a real turning point for Germany and the world too. Joe Medbury asked

Sam and me to write up newspaper dispatches. The AP took mine, Sam's went to Reuters, and Joe's went to UPI. My by-line was always C. Van Arnum. You should be able to look me up."

"A slightly rewritten version of my dispatch made the front page of the Chicago Tribune on Sunday, November 13th. Now I don't know for sure, but I think the Consulate smuggled our work out in diplomatic pouches thanks to Joe's contacts there. By the end of the week, the entire world knew about Kristallnacht and was pretty disgusted. The day after my story came out, November, 14th, the consulate was ordered closed for good, Roosevelt having severed diplomatic relations. Every plant in the consulate was taken out to wither on the lawn. Sam and I watched them leave." Kitty was shaking her head vigorously back and forth.

"I think Kristallnacht was the real wake-up call for the rest of Europe and America. The trouble was that everyone woke up and realized that they weren't prepared to fight Germany. From that moment on everything was just a delaying action." Kitty looked stern, "But we were in a fight, and we all knew it."

Barb gave her a look and said, "And?"

"And what?" said Kitty sounding a bit perturbed.

"Sophie, what happened to Sophie?" asked Barb.

"I'm getting to that," said Kitty with a bit of formality in her voice.

Barb rolled her eyes.

"After one of the girls got a note from Herman telling us to stop helping the Jews we decided we had to act. The Goldbergs weren't the only Jews we knew," said Kitty, "just the ones we knew the best, and we decided that it was our duty to try to get them out, the Goldbergs that is. Joe went and huffed and puffed at the police station about Joseph but got nowhere. Sam and I, with Kozie's help, determined that the safest way out for Sophie and her mom was to take a train to Holland, so we bought them a first-class open ticket. We didn't have a clue what to do with them once we got them to Holland, but at least they'd be out of Germany. There was a grand hostel just outside of Brugge, so we wired ahead and paid for two weeks in advance in our names. I gave Sophie a typewritten letter, in French, that would introduce them to the hostel owner."

"It wasn't until we heard that Joseph was dead that Sophie and her mother were finally willing to leave. That was around the first of the year, 1939. I never heard from them again until I saw Sophie on a list of refugees after the war. Stan and I helped Sophie to get into the U.S. It turned out that getting the Goldbergs on the waiting list back in 1938 did the trick. Sophie already had a permanent visa to the U. S. waiting for her." Kitty was sitting upright in her wheelchair, her head cocked at a jaunty angle, and she had the look of someone who had just decisively won a war.

Barb looked at her and laughed, "You look just like a picture I once saw of Winston Churchill. All you need is a cigar, and the picture would be perfect." Kitty turned red with embarrassment, her bubble of pride deflated.

"Well, we got them out, but we just didn't get them out far enough," said Kitty. "As far as I knew we only paid for two weeks but I later found out that Joe kept wiring money to the hostel right up until they were forced to close. That was when the phony war started after everyone declared war on Germany but nothing happened: the British, the French and the Germans, fully mobilized but refrained from shooting at each other. In September 1939, the owners of the hostel rightly figured that they were in the line of march to Paris, and they were right, so they closed it down.

"I learned from Sophie later, that when the hostel closed down, they threw themselves on the mercy of the local authorities who sent them to Amsterdam. The authorities there sent them back to Germany where they were immediately put in concentration camps. Sophie and her mother were split up as soon as they were back in Germany and she never saw her mother again. Sophie had a beautiful voice and knew a lot of operas because of her musical background, so the Nazi guards made her 'sing for her supper.' That saved her life." Kitty folded her arms, nodded her head decisively, and uttered a "harrumph."

Barb also let out a deep sigh, "Good grief, Kit. That was the longest story you've ever told me."

"It was?" asked Kitty who was now lost in thought.

"Yes," said Barb with a smile. "It was. What happened after that?"

"We cleaned out the shop and shipped the remaining books back to the states. Sam found a cute little printing press in the basement with a white rose stenciled on the side and gave it to an anti-Nazi professor at the University, and I learned to tune a piano myself of course," said Kitty who began to hum a childhood song to herself.

14

With all Deliberate Speed
May 1999 (August 1939)

It was snowing those big, almost sleet, flakes that leave a sheet of ice on unsalted roads. "Oh damn," Barb exclaimed.

Kitty laughed, "It's been doing that since you got here. I thought you knew."

"I thought the sun was out when I got here," said Barb. Kitty shrugged as Barb leaned close to the window. "It doesn't look like it's sticking."

"Well then, you don't need to run off, do you?" said Kitty, who was breathing with difficulty all of a sudden.

"Are you okay?" asked Barb.

"I think so," said Kitty. "It's odd though, every once in a while I have trouble breathing. It's not as bad as it was a few months ago but it's most disconcerting. It feels better if I get up and move a bit, but then my blood pressure goes up, and I get dizzy. This is something new."

Kitty pulled herself off the bed and walked to the door and back. "Damn," she said as she sat back down on her bed, "angina."

"I thought you didn't have it anymore." said Barb.

"This is the first I've felt it in a while," said Kitty who was breathing normally again. "It was almost like having a panic attack. I'm not sure what came over me. It was a rush of adrenalin followed by that feeling of fear you get in the pit of your stomach. Very odd! It reminded me of when Sam and I realized that we might be stuck in Munich in the middle of World War Two."

"What happened?" asked Barb who was still preoccupied with the falling snow and wondering if she should leave, or if it was too late to leave or if she shouldn't worry. Barb hadn't heard the weather report this morning and was trying to remember what the forecast was when Kitty began talking.

"I've often said that life in Munich was either hot or cold," said Kitty.

"It must be getting colder," said Barb who had decided that the snow crystals were getting smaller which made driving easier, so she didn't have to leave in haste after all.

Kitty shook her head, "Actually it was getting warmer; we were heading into spring, what my father called 'campaign season.' Apparently armies prefer not to fight during the winter months, so Hitler used the winter to prepare for war. We didn't know any better since the American Consulate had shut down and we saw Joe Medbury less. I told you we all thought Joe and Kozie were spies, didn't I?"

Barb had caught up with Kitty enough to realize that she was talking about Munich again, so she nodded vigorously. "Oh, yes, yes, Joe was a spy. I knew that."

"Well," Kitty continued, "Sam and I spent most of January through March 1939 in and out of Munich. We went to Italy to get warm in January and again in February. Sam knew people everywhere, so in March we traveled down the Adriatic to Dubrovnik and back by train through Sarajevo. We spent a week or so in Sarajevo, a beautiful city ruined in their recent civil war.

"Anyway," Kitty continued, "We were out of touch with the political scene and out of touch with an embassy and out of touch with our personal spies. So you can imagine our panic when we returned to Munich and learned that Hitler had invaded Czechoslovakia. The last thing we knew was that both France and Britain had declared that they would go to war if Hitler invaded."

"Gosh," said Barb, her eyes wide, "what did you do?"

"We got out of Germany as fast as we could," said Kitty.

A speaker above Kitty's head interrupted her, "The Shire-town will be closing in twenty minutes due to the inclement weather."

"It doesn't look that bad," said Barb to Kitty.

"You never know," said Kitty. "I suppose the weathermen know more than we do. Let's turn on the television and find out." The report was not encouraging; two feet of snow or more was predicted, and it was expected to become heavy in about an hour, and it was already snowing at the rate of three inches an hour in Yarmouth. It had already dumped nearly a foot of wet spring snow on Boston. It was a big ocean storm, "A nor'easter," said Kitty, "That means three days of heavy snow. At least that's the folklore."

Barb wrinkled her nose and said, "Humph, it doesn't look that bad to me. In fact, it looks like its turning colder so the snow will be the light, fluffy kind that the plows can keep up with."

"Well, they do have extra cots here if you need it," said Kitty with a smile. Kitty didn't believe the weatherman either. After looking at the radar, it looked, to her, that Pictou was on the colder, drier side of the storm and while Halifax, where the TV station was, might get hammered, Pictou would not.

"See," said Barb.

Kitty broke into a smile, "You're probably right, but let's keep an eye on it, in case we're wrong."

The speaker announced that the home would be closing in five minutes. Barb and Kitty looked at each other then out the window. "It doesn't look very bad now," said Kitty, "but then I'm not going anywhere."

"I'll give it another half hour," said Barb, "then decide."

Another wave of mild angina swept over Kitty. "Curses," she exclaimed. "As I was saying that last little twinge reminded me of the scariest time I had in Munich."

"Don't get me wrong," said Barb, "but I'd like to know why does everything remind you of either Munich or the Depression?"

"It's not just me," said Kitty. "The Depression and the War colored the rest of our lives, my whole generation. Prosperity and austerity are measured against the Depression, safety and security against our experiences in, or in my case, just before, the war."

"Hmmm," said Barb, "I guess I don't really have anything to compare it with. So what was the scariest moment in Munich?"

Kitty took a deep breath, "Sam and I were in Sarajevo when we heard that something was up in Germany. No one knew exactly what was up, but we met a Dutch couple that was trying to leave Germany and couldn't get home because the Dutch, as well as the French, had closed their border, so they were leaving via Greece. It was a very long way around, but Greece, at the time, was a hub of sorts for shipping. You could catch a ship from Athens to anywhere in the world. Like Heathrow airport in London today."

"And you didn't just go home?" asked an incredulous Barb.

"Well, we had left most of our belongings in Munich, and the consulate in Sarajevo said that they didn't advise Americans to travel in Germany. They wouldn't say anymore. So in spite of the warning we decided to go back to Munich and pack up whatever we could then leave. I had left most of my clothing and jewelry there.

"Sam and I took the overnight train to Zagreb and then on to Munich. We got to Munich in the middle of the afternoon of the Ides of March, which is apparently not a good time in any century ... or millennia for that matter."

"I forget," said Barb. "What's the Ides of March?"

"It's March 15th," said Kitty. "The day Julius Caesar was murdered in 44 BC, and the day Hitler invaded Czechoslovakia in 1939 AD. The next day, on the 16th, Hitler declared that Czechoslovakia no longer existed.

"Now the last we knew the British and the French had promised to go to war over Czechoslovakia, and all the Germans we knew and talked with, thought so too, so as far as we were concerned the war had already started. America was still neutral, so we were still safe, we hoped, but we figured that we better get out as fast as we could.

"Sam started calling everyone he knew. We found Kozie and Joe Medbury who were back in Munich and had dinner with them. We plotted how we were going to try to get out. Joe and Kozie were going to Berlin and planned to leave by Bremerhaven if all else failed. There was still a brisk traffic between New York and Germany, and neither thought the British would interrupt it. Sam and I were a bit more panicked and wanted to leave more quickly and get out via a more British-friendly route. The only real option open to us was to head back to Trieste and hope that we could get into Italy by train or take a boat to Athens. So that's where we headed, me and my valise, which was all I could take." Kitty was enjoying herself.

"It's only a few hours by train from Munich to Trieste," said Kitty, "and of course we traveled first class, but we were not prepared for what we found there."

"What did you find there?" interrupted an impatient Barb when Kitty stopped to catch her breath.

"Chaos, complete chaos," said Kitty as she looked out the window at the snow which was falling more heavily now. "Are you sure you want to hear this story now," asked Kitty pointing out the window.

"It could be now or never," said Barb.

"I suppose it could be," said Kitty with a shrug. "Well, as I was saying," she continued, "Trieste was chaos when we got there. Remember, Sam and I had passed through Trieste a month or so earlier, and there had been a steady stream of people, Jews mostly, exiting Europe, but this time it was a flood. You could smell the fear in the streets, and it was contagious. I remember looking at Sam and seeing something close to panic in his eyes. That didn't make me feel very good about our prospects. We tried to find a hotel room, but there were none to be had. Sam tried to rent a car but those too were gone, and we were told there was no gasoline anyway. Sam even tried to charter a boat but no one would take our German marks, and we didn't have enough of any other currency with us.

"We discovered that we couldn't go back, not that we really wanted to, and the only way out of Trieste was by steerage class on a Romanian ship bound, eventually, for Palestine with stops in Athens and Istanbul."

Just as Kitty was getting worked up again, a nurse ran into the room and said, "Miss Stevenson, your guest will have to leave now. This facility is closed to the public."

"... for the duration of the storm," Barb interrupted with a smile. "Hold that story," she said to Kitty as she grabbed her coat and was escorted to the parking lot.

Barb made it home before the storm turned into a blizzard. Vince had taken the day off, and the kids had been sent home from school almost as soon as they arrived. Just as Kitty predicted, the storm raged on for three days. Its track had gone considerably west of the predicted line, and Newfoundland was spared the brunt of the storm that was spinning itself out in northern Quebec. Pictou was buried in almost three feet of the heavy wet snow of an early spring blizzard.

Because of the weight of the snow and the deep freeze that followed the last flake, it was over a week before Barb could leave her driveway and safely drive to Pictou. She was worried. She had talked to Kitty by telephone every day during the storm, but Kitty had been quiet saying she wasn't up for a chat. As Barb drove through Poplar Hill, gusts of wind made her car fishtail on the invisible ice beneath the snow. When she got to Shiretown, a single front-end loader was digging out the parking lot, and Barb grew frustrated waiting to have a spot dug for her.

By the time Barb got inside it was just after noon, and she expected to find Kitty in the dining room. She wasn't there, and she wasn't in the solarium, so Barb rushed to her bedroom. Kitty didn't look good at all. There was an IV drip on a post on her bed, a catheter bag hanging by a hook on the side and the oxygen tube was again in her nose. Barb felt sad and, for a moment, a few tears welled up in her eyes. Kitty smiled weakly and waved her in. She was on the telephone, so Barb sat in the chair by the window.

"James, Barb just walked in," said Kitty loud enough for Barb to hear and putting her hand over the receiver whispered, "It's James."

Barb loudly whispered back, "I figured that."

Kitty smiled at Barb and nodded into the receiver. "I know James, but if I give you the stocks now, you will still have to pay taxes on my estate unless I live another five years which, at this point, seems unlikely." Kitty rolled her eyes, "Yes, I know but if I give them to you, and you spend it all, and it's not been five years then you will owe a lot of money in taxes that you could not hope to repay. It's very risky." Kitty was getting annoyed at her son and could feel her blood pressure rising dangerously. Finally, she grit her teeth and said, "James, I'm your mother and as your mother, I'm not going to give you my stocks now because to do so would be irresponsible of me."

Kitty held the phone away from her ear, sighed and looked at it disapprovingly. Barb could hear angry squawking but could not make out the words. When the angry words subsided Kitty said, "James, don't be angry. I don't think you'll have to wait very long for your legacy so please stop fighting over the corpse, she's alive and still kicking.... Okay, I will. Bye for now." Kitty hung up the receiver and let out a sigh of relief and said to Barb, "There's something to be said for drowning them at birth."

"So what is it with all this?" asked Barb pointing to the IV bag and oxygen apparatus.

"I've had a relapse," said Kitty in a voice that did not sound optimistic. "My kidneys are failing apparently. Ninety-plus percent blocked."

"I thought it was your heart that was giving you problems?"

"They call it congestive heart failure. When your heart can't pump well enough, the organs begin to fail, so I guess I'm on me last legs." Kitty was silent for a moment before continuing, "I know I'm on me last legs because Mandy Betts and her friends have taken to pestering me again. Apparently, they think I'm good for a last minute repentance." Kitty chuckled to herself. Even Barb giggled, then felt slightly ashamed at giggling at what she thought should be a more somber time.

Kitty read her thoughts and said, "Mandy Betts would be funny at her own funeral. You should have seen the wee one she dragged along this time. A Cape Bretoner who could barely speak English through his brogue."

"Did you shoo him off?" asked Barb.

"He was easy," said Kitty with a twinkle back in her eye. "I told him I wanted to take a bath in holy water, to be re-baptized as it were, but I had to get past this current situation. Everyone was pleased, and they went away apparently happy and none the wiser for it."

"You goof," exclaimed Barb with a big laugh. "You know they are going to come back. Probably with a giant bathtub and bottles of water drained from that swimming pool of hers that's probably contaminated with who knows what holy germs."

Both women giggled at that prospect. "Horrors," said Kitty, "I didn't think of that."

"Call me when they do," said Barb with a grin. "I'll bring a bottle of bleach and some penicillin for ya."

"That reminds me of the story I didn't get to finish because you left so abruptly during the storm," said Kitty.

"Oh, yeah," said Barb with renewed interest, "the story about the day you finally got out of Dodge. Do tell."

Kitty felt confused for a moment; she hadn't been in Dodge she had been in Munich – then she remembered that was just an expression. "Oh," she said and giggled. Barb looked at her with her eyes wide opened and shook her head as if to say "so tell the story...."

"We were in Trieste, I think I told you that much," said Kitty. Barb nodded. "... the only guaranteed way out was on an old Romanian ship, the SS Dacia, I think it was. It was chartered by the Jewish Agency to get refugees to Palestine. The Romanians were a bit pro-Nazi, so they happily took our German marks but every nook and cranny of the ship was filled, and the only option was third class, steerage.

"Let me tell you," said Kitty wagging her finger with authority, "there is nothing more disgusting and dangerous than steerage-class on a refugee boat. For one thing, they wouldn't let us on deck while we were underway. That privilege was reserved for first and second-class passengers, and if the ship sank, there were only enough lifeboats for, I'm guessing, 200 people, those same first and second-class passengers.

"Oh, and another thing, the food was miserable, Sam thought they scraped the leftovers from the plates of the first and second-class dishes into a pot, added some water and called it soup. It was served with stale bread. Fortunately, Sam and I purchased two fresh loaves before we boarded."

"Was it a big ocean liner?" asked Barb.

"I don't remember the ship being very big at all," said Kitty. "I think it had maybe fifteen first class-cabins, thirty or forty second-class cabins and somewhere around one hundred third-class cabins. These last were below the waterline with four bunks each and a shared bathroom every ten cabins. In our case, the holds of the ship were rebuilt to handle even more people, and that's where we were put. Our cabin — if you want to call it that — held about eighty people with wooden bunks stacked four high. Each hold had two floors, and there were two holds, so there were about 900 steerage passengers in all. We were put on the lower floor of the forward hold. The only light came from a string of bare electric lights that were run the length of each row of bunks. You could see, but you couldn't read. We were fortunate because our bunks, I had the top and Sam the bottom, were just one row and a couple of bunks away from the ventilation shaft. We could feel the gentle but tepid flow of air from the outside world.

"The toilet facilities in our 'cabin' consisted of three 'outhouses' built into a bunk space with a curtain blocking the view but not the sounds or odor, and with buckets that were hauled to the deck periodically and thrown overboard. The smell, the stench really, was overwhelming and the heat, even in March, was almost unbearable. But we were lucky, we were in the forward hold, so we got some air. I can't imagine what it must have been like in the aft hold when you add more heat, vomit, and body odors to the smell of diesel fuel.

"About four hours after we cast off people started getting sick. I suppose there was a mixture of seasickness and the stench of body odor that was retching. Sam bought some cheap brandy to counteract the seasickness, and that worked just fine, but I very nearly upchucked every time someone else did. Fortunately, a sailor would come by periodically to hose down the deck and wash it into the bilge. Unfortunately, the deck-wash from the deck above us had to pass through our deck as well on its way to the bilge."

Kitty made a face, "We spent almost four days cooped up in that hell hole, but everyone was grateful to be there. I never heard a single complaint."

"Oh, really?" interrupted Barb.

"Well, there were the usual wishes for better accommodations, but everyone was grateful to be leaving Europe. I think we were the only non-Jews on the boat, besides the crew that is, but every Jew there was celebrating. You have no idea how many times I saw someone throw up then look up, smile and say, 'Tomorrow in Jerusalem.' They were immensely happy."

Barb shook her head and said, "I'm sorry Kit, but you lost me."

"Before there was an Israel there was an old Jewish saying 'Next year in Jerusalem.' My father called it the diaspora prayer." Kitty stopped and looked away. "Hmmm," she said to herself then to Barb, "I wonder if the Dalai Lama prays 'Next year in Lhasa.'" Kitty was pleased with herself.

Barb shook her head, "Huh? What does the Dalai Lama have to do with puke on a refugee ship? I got lost somewhere."

"Oh," said Kitty apparently still lost in that thought, "I was just thinking how throughout history there have been people pushed out of their homes for one reason or another and how the memory of that home was kept alive, so the Jews used to say, 'Next year in Jerusalem,' and I was just wondering if the Tibetans will be saying 'Next year in Lhasa' two thousand years from now. I hope not." Kitty was lost in thought.

"And?" insisted Barb.

Kitty shook her head, "Anyway, in spite of the horrible conditions on board, every Jew was in ecstasy. They were going home, to Jerusalem. That's the way they saw it, and every one of them had the intention of seeing a new Israel founded. You couldn't help but wish them luck after thousands of years of pogrom after pogrom after pogrom. I really felt for them"

Kitty smiled again and after a significant pause said, "Sam and I were not quite so ecstatic. We couldn't wait to get off the boat at Athens so we could hop a more civilized ride home, or at least out of a war zone. Unfortunately, when we got to Athens, no one was allowed off the boat because the authorities feared a cholera outbreak. They also threw another hundred and fifty or so refugees onboard, so we were stuck for another two days until we arrived at Istanbul. For that leg of the trip, they let us on deck, so that's where Sam and I spent most of our time. I have some pictures of it.

"I imagined myself as Helen of Troy as we sailed up the Dardanelles." Kitty was grinning from ear to ear. "Of course, the dream did not include a thousand warships chasing after me. That, I believe, was Winston Churchill's fantasy."

There were times when Barb had to just smile and nod, and this was one of them. She was hoping that Kitty would not go off on a tangent about Winston Churchill's fantasies. The thought made her giggle though.

Kitty noticed. "Helen of Troy," she smiled and said, "Isn't it remarkable that an affair could be so celebrated three thousand years later."

That made Barb blush. She cleared her throat and asked, "So ... I take it that the boat didn't sink on the way to Istanbul, so what happened next?"

"Oh," replied Kitty, "not much. Those who could afford overland passage to Palestine got off, including us, and the rest stayed onboard for the trip to Jaffa. I assume the boat made it since I never heard otherwise.

"Sam and I checked in with the U.S. Embassy in Istanbul and learned that war had not broken out after all but that the U.S. had severed diplomatic relations with Germany entirely over Czechoslovakia. The *chargé d'affaires* suggested that we might want to go home rather than go back to Munich."

"I thought they closed the embassy after that crystal night thing," said Barb.

"They closed all the consulates," said Kitty, "but they kept the embassy open in Berlin until the final Czech crisis. After they pulled out, we didn't feel as safe. The Swiss were still there and looked after us, but things were not very comfortable."

"So is that when you finally left for good?" asked Barb.

"Heavens no," said Kitty emphatically. "There were no rumblings of war so Sam and I went back to Munich to wrap up our affairs there."

"What? Why?" Barb almost screamed.

"Well," said Kitty slowly, "I had paid rent until September, and since there was apparently no war breaking out, we explored Romania, Hungary, and Austria on our way back to Munich. All those places took our German marks. We took a lovely little steamer from Istanbul to Constanta on the Black Sea then we went by train to Bucharest, Budapest, and Vienna then on to Munich. I loved Budapest. It's my favorite European city, even more than Paris. We took our time getting back."

Kitty paused to remember the moment, "We would have gone back up the Adriatic coast like we had after the previous crisis but that idiot Mussolini invaded Albania which made the Balkans impassable. As it turns out, we took the last refugee boat, or any commercial ship for that matter, from Trieste for the duration of the war. Shipping up and down the Adriatic came to a halt."

Kitty was enjoying the story. "We took our time getting back to Munich because we thought we might not get another chance to explore the countryside. We saw a lot of preparations for war, so when we got back to Munich, I did look into booking my passage home."

"Why didn't you just leave then? I would have thought you would have been scared out of your wits," said Barb.

Kitty thought about that question for a moment then began slowly, "I was concerned, but at that point, all I had were German marks, and they were worthless outside of Germany. Except, of course, in places the Germans had absorbed or had influence. Regardless, I didn't have enough marks left to buy any useful currency on the black market, so my only comfortable option was to book passage home on a German ship or get to a friendly country and throw myself on the mercy of our ambassador."

"So why didn't you just buy a ticket right away?" asked Barb.

"Oh, I did," insisted Kitty, "As soon as I could I booked a first-class cabin on the SS Bremen. It had two sailings, one in May, but that was too soon and mostly booked, and I would have had to travel tourist-class," Kitty made a sour face, "and another in August, so I booked the August sailing in a first-class cabin."

"I can't believe you sat around waiting for a war to happen. Four months?" asked Barb shaking her head. "Four friggin' months?"

"Well," said Kitty slowly, "by June the consensus was that Hitler would wait until the spring of 1940 to make his next move because the campaign season was already half over. There was a very peaceful lull in the early summer of 1939. No one thought that 1939 would be a repeat of 1914. That is, no one except Joe and Kozie. They both agreed on a September war. Joe rightly predicted that Hitler would go after Poland next. Kozie thought he would go after Hungary and Romania for coal and oil."

Barb was about to ask a question when a nurse pushed the door open and announced that Barb would have to leave the room for a few minutes. Barb was surprised but Kitty just waved her off, "We'll just be a moment Barb. They like to measure my urine output in private for some reason."

Barb shrugged, left the room and paced nervously until a satisfied nurse came back out of Kitty's room, looked at Barb and shook her head as if to say 'I'm sorry.' Barb wasn't sure what the gesture meant when she went back into Kitty's room.

"My kidneys are failing," said Kitty in an unusually squeaky voice.

"What can they do about it?" asked a very concerned Barb.

Kitty cleared her throat. "Well, I don't know," she said, her normal voice returning. "The doctor will be here later today to inform me of my imminent demise I'm sure."

"Shall I leave?" asked Barb.

"Oh, no," said Kitty, "I haven't told you all my stories. I'm not done yet." Kitty nodded her head with finality.

Barb thought Kitty suddenly sounded very tired but leaving now, like this, at this time? Barb had to stay until Kitty was sound asleep just like she did when Kitty was first in hospital.

"Well then," said Barb trying to sound upbeat, "tell me how you made it home."

"Okay," said Kitty, "I can't remember exactly. Events began to move very quickly once we got back to Munich. I think we got back to Munich around the middle of May. Sam and I had to travel back to Munich from Istanbul by way of Romania and Hungary because of Mussolini's invasion of Albania."

"I remember," said Barb a little impatiently, "you just told me."

"Mussolini was not very bright," said Kitty shaking her head, "so the only way left to get out was to go through Switzerland to France or, because I had plenty of marks left, to leave by German ship. I chose to do the latter and booked myself a first-class cabin aboard the SS Bremen for an August sailing. The Bremen was almost the only ocean liner still making the passage since the German American Line had reduced its sailings.

"Sam went to Paris with Joe Medbury via Amsterdam after I left Munich, I'm not sure when. I went to Berlin for most of June and July. Kozie and I hung out together in Berlin. We went to the theater, the opera, and a wild collection of nightclubs. The 'Cabaret' culture really flourished more in Berlin than in Munich and, believe it or not, I wasn't the only American still there, but almost. I think the ambassador's daughter was still there even though the ambassador himself had been recalled.

"It did begin to get ominous in late July. Everyone was mobilizing — the English, the French, and most obviously the Polish. Kozie changed his mind about which direction the war was going. He was sure it was headed to Poland, but he didn't think Poland would cave in as the Czechs had. That meant, according to Kozie, a real shooting war.

"At some point in late July, Kozie received a telegram ordering him home. So he headed home via Romania and the Black Sea, and I headed to Bremen where I could get to Amsterdam easily. I heard later that Kozie went back to Berlin and stayed until 1940 or 41.

"There were half a dozen trains a day from Bremen to Amsterdam or Bremerhaven. By the time I got to Bremen, I was actually running low on marks because Berlin was, and is, an expensive city to burn money in, and I burned a lot of it." Kitty smiled, but Barb thought she suddenly looked very weak.

"I stayed in a cheap hotel on the Bahnhofstrasse, in the middle of the Red Light district," Kitty continued. "No one bothered me. I must have looked a bit forlorn by then. I was still living out of my valise because I sent my trunks on to Bremerhaven.

"When I sent my father a telegram telling him where I was and what my plans were I received a reply the next day. It said only, 'WITH ALL DELIBERATE SPEED HOME DO NOT – STOP.' From the play on words I knew my father had sent it and the phrase "WITH ALL DELIBERATE SPEED" was his code phrase for 'get the hell out of there NOW.' That frightened me a bit since I assumed that my father was privy to more information than I was so I explored other ways out, but by then the Dutch had closed their border, and I no longer had the money to get to Denmark, so I had to stick to the plan.

"Whenever Hitler was about to invade a country we would start reading stories about how oppressed the local German minority was or some such nonsense. Hitler would then start making demands. We didn't know at the time that Hitler and Stalin had already agreed to divvy up Poland, so we all hoped that this was going to be another Czech crisis, and that it would resolve itself peacefully." Kitty stopped to think, "But what we hoped for publicly and what we really believed privately were two different things. I think everyone knew, everyone, that a war was coming. When I said goodbye to my friends in Munich, it had a tone of finality and, in fact, I never saw any of them again." Kitty sighed.

"What about that little Jewish girl? What was her name? Sophie?" asked Barb.

"Oh, you're right," squeaked Kitty, "but we had said goodbye to them right after Kristallnacht, and we hoped they would make it to Israel, so I don't think any of us expected to see them again. It was a surprise to me when I found her." Kitty smiled warmly but was clearly getting exhausted.

"Well, you're looking awfully tired, girl," said Barb. "I think I better let you get some rest."

Kitty reached over and grabbed Barb's arm rather forcefully and said, "You can't leave now, at least not until I've left Germany, until I've run out of stories."

Kitty had the look of a lost puppy, Barb thought and almost laughed before the chilling thought hit her: Kitty thinks she's going to die. "I'm all ears," said Barb. "Until you fall asleep, finish the story, or send me home. I'm here." She looked deeply into Kitty's pale blue eyes and said quietly, "So, tell me another story."

Kitty cleared her throat, inched herself up in her bed, and began with her eyes closed. "As I said, we were all very nervous as the date to leave approached; by all I mean the half dozen fellow passengers, mostly Americans, I met in the week or so I was in Bremen, and the couple of days I was in Bremerhaven. In public, we were all very chipper, but in private we all had misgivings about sailing home on a German-flagged ship.

"As I remember it, I went to Bremerhaven on August 16th so I'd have a chance to explore the city before we left. It wasn't very interesting as cities go, very industrial. I think it was mostly destroyed in the war. Anyway, we boarded the SS Bremen on the morning of Friday, August 18th and sailed down the Weser that afternoon to the North Sea. We were accompanied by several warships, destroyers I think. I learned later that the entire German Navy had mobilized, and that most of Germany's submarines put to sea that day so some of the ships might have been a submarine, too. I really don't remember."

Kitty looked confused for a moment then shook her head, "It doesn't matter. Anyway, the next day, I think it was, we stopped at Southampton to take on more passengers, and I seriously considered getting off. I mean, I did not want to find myself on a German ship when England declared war. But then I didn't want to be stuck in England in the middle of a war either, so I just stayed on and hoped for the best. We went to Cherbourg next and picked up a lot of steerage and tourist-class passengers. There was a brouhaha about a crewman that was missing, and a rumor that the SS had beat him up and tossed him overboard to remind the crew who was boss, but nothing came of it. We all assumed that the SS were everywhere as they had managed to pervade everything in Germany by that point.

"I had an advantage over most of the passengers. The German crew knew I was an American and assumed that I could not understand what they said, so when they talked among themselves, I listened. I learned, for example, that on the second day out that there had been a sighting of the great French steamship the Normandie, which was also heading to New York on the same course but, contrary to custom, the captain had chosen to alter course so as not to be seen. In fact, I remember the rather dramatic course change.

"The ship changed course almost 45 degrees to the south, and we sailed in that direction for four or five hours before just as abruptly changing back to our original course. The Germans did everything without subtlety when subtlety might have been more appropriate. Everyone on the ship knew we had changed course and some poor fellow went into hysterics in the first-class lounge, demanding to know why we were heading into the tropics rather than to New York.

"But you know by keeping track of the sun, and it was a brilliantly clear day, I knew when we veered off course, and when we veered back. I had assumed that we were on a collision course with some other ship and that the captain simply wished to avoid any problems during the night. I learned later that the German Navy had ordered the change of course. Of course, it wasn't stated so blatantly, but I was able to read between the lines."

Kitty had to stop talking when she found herself suddenly short of breath and began to breathe deeply while avoiding hyperventilation. "I'll be okay in a minute," she said.

Barb said nothing.

Finally, Kitty took a deep breath and continued, "The first time I knew something big was going on was when Dr. Ferber sent all the first class passengers a note Saturday afternoon requesting our presence in the first class Hunting Salon at 9 p.m. sharp."

Barb made a face and said, "What, who?"

"Oh," said Kitty, "Dr. Ferber was the director of Passenger Services for the ship. She ran everything on board as it affected the passengers. She was Captain Ahrens's secretary.

Yes, I think that was her official title, but she ran the ship as far as the passengers were concerned. A special invitation from her was not to be ignored, so I went, and boy, what a meeting that turned out to be."

"Oh, do tell," said Barb when Kitty paused to catch her breath again.

"When we were all accounted for," Kitty continued, "Captain Ahrens informed us that he had been ordered to turn around and bring the ship home, back to Bremerhaven. Well, you can imagine what a stir that created. A number of Americans and some Brits stood up and took great umbrage at the order and pompously reminded the captain of his duty to his passengers. I asked the captain if that meant that hostilities had already commenced. He allowed that he didn't know but expected war with France and/or Great Britain any moment. We all did too which was why we were leaving Germany.

"Most of the Germans felt obliged to stand up stiffly, give the Nazi salute, and publicly announce that they felt duty bound to return to Germany, but I could feel their anxiety at the prospect. After all, they were intentionally leaving Germany too. The discussion grew quite heated and went on for a couple of hours until I had a brilliant thought. I had the impression that the captain wished to continue to New York and was looking for a good enough reason, an excuse, to continue. Heck, we were only a day and a half out of New York. So I scratched me brain for a way out, and I found it.

"I stood up and reminded the assembled crowd that our august assemblage included half a dozen German ambassadors bound for various South American countries and that whatever happened, war or peace, it would be in Germany's interest to have their ambassadors in the countries to which they had been dispatched.

"I remember the captain's eyes lit up and he seized on that idea and very soon after announced that we would, indeed, be proceeding to New York."

"WOW!" exclaimed Barb. "What happened next?"

"Well ... well, nothing really," said Kitty, "we did practice lifeboat drills every four or five hours after that but we arrived in New York two days later, and that was that for me. Apparently, the Bremen slipped out of New York harbor the next day and made it back to Germany. Anyway, that's how I finally got out of Germany." Kitty nodded her head with finality.

Barb laughed at that. "So how much money did you have left when you got home?" she asked.

"I walked off the ship with a single one thousand mark note," said Kitty proudly.

"And how much ...?" asked Barb before Kitty interrupted.

"About, oh, maybe three hundred bucks," said Kitty. "Of course that note is worthless today, tainted money." Kitty lay back in her bed satisfied. It wasn't often that she could finish a story. Most people ran out of patience when Kitty told her stories or lost interest, but Barb had been persistent, and Kitty was grateful for that. "I think I'm running out of steam," she said.

Barb thought Kitty looked very tired, and suddenly very old. "You know Kit," said Barb with a warm smile, "I think you started that story about six months ago, and I'm glad it had a happy ending."

Kitty sighed, "Yes, a happy ending." Kitty smiled as she drifted off to sleep.

15

L'appel du vide
edge of the cliff - May 1999

Barb tiptoed out of the room where Kitty lay asleep. It was early still, the light in the evening sky was a brilliant red with streaks of purple. "Sailor's delight," she repeated to herself as she got in her car for the forty-five-minute drive home. Kitty had been particularly animated today. Barb liked that. Kitty had finally told her of her story of escape from Germany all the way to its end without interruptions or detours, but with an unexpected urgency. Barb laughed to herself. She had expected Kitty to go off on a tangent about the food at the first-class table or the pedigree of the passengers or the precision of the lifeboat drills or the speculation among the passengers about how the British would attempt to stop the SS Bremen. Barb had been taking mental notes. Yes, Kitty had been particularly to the point today even if she was looking weaker and weaker.

A deer jumped across the road. It startled Barb, and she pulled to the side of the road coming to a stop long enough to catch her breath. She had been daydreaming and not paying attention. Why was Kitty in such a hurry to finish the story? Does she think she's about to ... Barb shook her head, no, don't even think like that, she told herself, but it troubled her the rest of the way home and woke her several times that night.

When the nursing home called in the morning, Barb was not surprised. The nurse said that Kitty had been unresponsive when they attempted to wake her and had been rushed to Aberdeen Hospital. They had already called Jimmy.

Barb slammed the phone down and yelled, "Damn, damn, damn," as tears welled up in her eyes.

"What happened?" asked Vince running into the kitchen.

"Kit's back in hospital," said Barb barely holding back a tear.

Vince put his arm around her and said quietly, "Well, you knew this was coming. Go down and see her. We'll keep the house."

Barb packed an overnight bag and drove to Aberdeen Hospital as fast as she could. She found Kitty unconscious in the intensive care unit, bags of blood and other liquids hanging from the post over her head. After Barb had introduced herself to the nurse, the nurse informed her that Kitty had filed a certificate giving Barb the authority to remove life support.

"I can't decide that. Have you talked to Jimmy?"

"Yes," said the nurse, "I believe they've been notified, but you are the only person listed as her health proxy."

"I can't decide that," Barb said again.

"The doctor will be here shortly to talk to you," said the nurse somewhat curtly.

Barb looked at Kitty. She had a breathing tube taped to her mouth, but she was breathing on her own. An orderly came in to add a new bag of blood to the post and remove a different bag from her feet. "She's getting a transfusion," said the orderly in answer to Barb's questioning look.

"Oh," she replied somewhat numbly.

"The doctor is keeping her knocked out until she has enough clean blood in her."

Barb sat down next to Kitty and waited. Listening to the rhythmic pulsing of the monitoring equipment and the quiet hissing of the oxygen was mesmerizing, and Barb jumped when Dr. MacKenzie walked by.

"Ah, Barbara," he said, "I'm glad you're here." Dr. MacKenzie had always felt more comfortable talking to relatives and friends of patients in serious condition than he did his patients themselves. This was especially true of Kitty Stevenson. She had been a friend for thirty years as well as his patient, and he could not look Kitty in the eye and tell her that she was dying. He could tell Barb, though, if he assumed his paternal and professional tone first.

Dr. Gavin MacKenzie took a deep breath, "As you know Kitty's health has been seriously compromised by her diabetes and her heart condition. And now it appears that she has had complete renal failure ... her kidneys have stopped working. The transfusion she is getting will stop any further progression. That is to say, her kidneys will not resume functioning, but it doesn't appear that her liver and other vital organs are involved, yet, but she will need dialysis three to four times a week for the rest of her life."

Dr. MacKenzie took a deep breath, "I should point out that even with dialysis it is very likely that her other organs will begin to shut down. Her heart is just not strong enough to keep them adequately supplied with blood. I believe that our friend Kitty has, at best, a few weeks to a month ...." He trailed off as Barb nodded.

"Well, I ... I can't," said Barb.

"I know," said Dr. MacKenzie slowly, "We'll let Kitty decide on the best course of action. I'm going to put her on dialysis for a few hours then bring her out of sedation. She should be the old Kitty again for a while." He knew his smile was artificial; he, too, wanted to cry but it would be very unprofessional.

It was early evening before a dialysis machine was available and an unconscious Kitty was connected. Dr. MacKenzie returned and carefully removed the breathing tube from

Kitty's mouth and watched her breath without it. When he was satisfied, he left the ward with a quiet nod. A moment later he came back and said to Barb, "Kitty will slowly wake up as the dialysis cleans her blood of the remaining toxins. We almost lost her you know. I had to use 10 units of blood just to get her to the point where I could put her on dialysis. Keep that in mind when you talk to her."

Barb nodded.

It was close to midnight when a nurse came in and told Barb to go home. It would be another 12 hours before Kitty would come round, she said, so, reluctantly, Barb drove the forty miles (Barb grew up on miles) back home and crawled into bed at 1 a.m. Vince let her sleep, bringing her tea when it was almost 10 a.m., and the sun brightly lit their room. "So how did it go yesterday?" asked Vince.

"They asked me to pull the plug on her," said Barb. "I wouldn't do it." Barb's eyes were still red, so she avoided looking straight at Vince.

"And why would you," asked Vince, "when there's Jimmy and Maggie?"

"Kit didn't give them permission," said Barb. "She thinks Jimmy is too eager to get his hands on her money." Barb had to laugh at that, "She may be right, but I don't think Jimmy would pull the plug on his own mother, I know Maggie wouldn't."

"But they aren't here," said Vince, "and I know Kit thinks you would do the right thing."

"And what would that be?" asked Barb hopefully.

"I don't know," said Vince, his eyes downcast. "I don't know."

It was late morning by the time Barb pulled into the parking lot at Aberdeen Hospital. Her visit with Kitty coincided with her appointment for a blood test to see if her cancer had returned. This time the tests were conclusive. The cancer was still in remission, and the pain Barb had been feeling was simply arthritis exacerbated by the chemo she had taken ten years earlier.

Kitty was still in the intensive care ward but was sitting up and eating a sandwich. She looked better but frail to Barb.

"I'm glad to see you," said Kitty.

"I'm glad to see you, too," said Barb who was feeling awkward, "My blood tests came out negative. I don't have cancer."

"Splendid altogether," said Kitty. "Dr. MacKenzie was here already."

"Oh? What did he say?"

Kitty took a deep breath, and although Kitty was determined to sound strong, her voice came out as a feeble squeak, "He says I'm dying and, with or without dialysis, I probably don't have more than a month or two. There are signs of my liver failing and, of course, my kidneys are gone."

Barb moved forward into the light so that she could see Kitty's face more clearly. "I know," she said quietly. "What do you want to do?"

Kitty took another deep breath and, with surprising force said, "Dr. MacKenzie says that without further treatment I'll be dead in about two weeks. He's promised not to let me suffer and will knock me out when the time comes, but there is not much more he can do for me and 'heroic measures' would not significantly lengthen my life nor would it improve its quality, which has been better. So ...." she took another deep breath, "I have signed a 'do not resuscitate' order and have refused all further medical treatment in writing."

"Are you sure?" asked Barb searching Kitty's eyes for an answer.

"No," said Kitty weakly, "but I can choose to go with dignity or I can choose to make a painful mess of things, but I'm going to go anyway, like it or not." Kitty shrugged, "So choosing the time and place of my passage seems preferable to any alternative." She smiled weakly, "It will be a new adventure."

Barb patted Kitty on the leg and smiled, "Did you tell Jimmy and Maggie yet?"

Kitty perked up, "Yes, I did, and they were surprisingly supportive. I realize that dying puts a strain on everyone around the soon-to-be-corpse and telling my children that there is an end to this must have come as a relief as much as a surprise to them.

"I told James that I was satisfied with my life and accomplishments and that he should be too, and that after living longer than average I had no right to protest. I'm sure they are in shock. I also told them I didn't want them here to whine and get in the way. I told them both that this was something I had to do by myself and they accepted that."

"So you don't want anyone around?" asked Barb cautiously.

"Oh," said Kitty, "I just don't want my children around. I would hope that they remember me as something more vibrant than a shriveled up old corpse. You can stay ... if you want to."

"Don't be silly," said Barb holding back a tear, "of course I'll stay here with you."

Dr. MacKenzie arranged for an ambulance to take Kitty back to the Shiretown that afternoon. As Kitty was being pushed and bumped along the corridor to the ambulance dock, Barb thought back to Kitty's triumphant exit from the hospital a year earlier. This time, she thought, the staff was not lined up in a salute. Kitty was no longer a celebrity, just a dying old woman being pushed along the corridors to be taken out to die. A tear ran down her cheek.

Kitty saw the tear trickle down Barb's chin. "It's just another part of life," she said. "So what can you do?" Kitty patted Barb on the arm. "It's time," she said, "to go quietly into that good night, to rage against what is inevitable is folly and folly is what life is mostly. To see the executioner's ax falling is a rare privilege, it gives the condemned just enough time to make peace with himself and his maker — if there is a conflict there — and just enough time to acquire the only thing worth acquiring in life and that is a little more wisdom."

"Is that Shakespeare?" asked Barb through a sniffle.

"I mixed up my references," said Kitty with a smile. "A little Shakespeare here, a little Dylan Thomas there and a little Thomas Aquinas thrown in for good measure, mixed in a stew of words that came out sounding surprisingly intelligent. They could just as easily come out differently. It sounded noble not maudlin, enlightened rather than fatalistic.

"Hmmm," said Kitty looking perplexed then grinning. "I suspect all my words from here on out should be considered fatalistic don't you think? I mean, the words of the condemned are fatalistic by definition. Wouldn't you say?"

Barb couldn't help herself, she laughed.

"What's so funny?"

"I didn't expect Shakespeare out of you."

"What then? I would hope that the realization of my imminent demise would be a source of enlightenment, of Socrr-r-r-atic inspiration, and I would expect nothing less than a Shakespearean oration from meself under the circumstances. Wouldn't you agree?"

Barb's giggle became a laugh, infecting Kitty who burst into laughter too. "I suppose I should not take myself too seriously," said Kitty, "But, if not now then when should I take myself seriously? Hmm?" Kitty looked away from Barb as the orderlies pushed her gurney into the ambulance.

"Something to ponder," said Barb with a serious tone.

When the ambulance pulled into the dock of the Shiretown Nursing Home a small crowd of employees was waiting. "Welcome back," said the director as Kitty was being wheeled in. "We'll make you as comfortable as we can, and we've taken the liberty of preparing a room large enough to accommodate your expected visitors."

Kitty looked at Barb, who had run in ahead and was breathless, and made a sour face.

"Mandy Betts?" asked Barb.

"Oy vei," said Kitty, "I hadn't even thought of her. I was thinking of 'the Ladies' of Pictou who will be calling to pay their last respects as if I can bestow some blessing on them from beyond the pale."

"Sell them a dispensation," said Barb with a wink. They both laughed.

The room was a triple that had, until recently, been occupied by a long-term patient, recently deceased, from Parkinson's disease. There was the typical hospital bed where Kitty was, in her words, unceremoniously dumped, a couch and a card table with four chairs. "Are you planning to have a séance before I've even departed?" asked Kitty to no one in particular.

"Good one," said Barb, who said she would be back in the morning. Kitty smiled and waved. Barb, who thought Kitty looked happier than she'd seen her in months, waved and smiled back.

Barb slept peacefully. Vince made it a point of sneaking out of bed and getting the kids ready for school quietly. By the time Barb woke up the house was empty and the mid-May sun pouring through the bedroom window made her squint. Kitty had put her at peace with the fact that she was about to die. Barb shook her head, she felt at ease, but a small feeling of guilt overcame her. She had no right to feel this comfortable with the idea of Kit's passing. With that thought she hurried out the door, time with Kitty was valuable.

A small pile of dirty snow melted in the shade of a maple tree at the corner of the parking lot. When Barb noticed it, she remembered how vital Kitty had been just a few months before. It brought a tear to her eye which she vigorously shook off. Must show a brave face for Kit, she thought. Barb's overnight bag was still sitting in the back seat of her car, and she thought briefly about bringing it in but decided against it. There would be time for a vigil later, not yet, she thought.

As Barb rounded the corner of Kitty's room, the massive presence of Mandy Betts filled the door frame. "Just leaving," said Mandy as Barb scowled at her. A small man in clerical garb followed Mandy out the door as Barb made the gesture of checking the room to be free of vermin before greeting Kitty.

"They mean well," said Kitty anticipating Barb's thoughts. "It's hard to fault their intentions."

"She kind of creeps me out," said Barb. "I'm not sure why but ... errrr."

Kitty smiled. "Mandy thinks she's doing God's work," said Kitty.

They sat in silence.

"I've been thinking," said Kitty in a very small voice, "there is a saying in French, *'L'appel du vide.'*"

"What's that mean?"

"It doesn't translate very well. It's that feeling you get when you are at the edge of a cliff and have the urge to jump off, so you run away."

"Oh?"

"It's being both attracted and repelled by something dangerous."

"The edge of a cliff? I think they call that vertigo," said Barb.

Kitty squeaked again and with a smile said, "Yes, I suppose it is vertigo but, of course, the French must make something more of it."

Barb laughed.

Kitty looked out the window for a minute then said, "I stayed in Germany because of *l'appel du vide.*"

"I was thinking that too."

Kitty sighed, "I am looking over the cliff again." Kitty fell quiet ... a few moments later, "And I realize that I must jump. I no longer have a choice." Kitty smiled then clenched her jaw and nodded her head as if the decision to jump only required a countdown.

Barb couldn't think of anything to say so she sat quietly while Kitty, smiling beatifically, fell asleep. Barb drifted off to sleep too.

"Sauerbraten!" exclaimed Kitty sometime later.

Barb jumped at the sound and almost fell out of the chair, "What?"

"Sauerbraten," said Kitty again, "The best thing I ever did was to make sauerbraten for four hundred people on the spur of the moment."

"What?" said Barb shaking her head.

"Sauerbraten," said Kitty for the third time. "Well, it was really a cross between sauerbraten and *boeuf aux carottes*."

"OK?" asked Barb with hesitation.

"Stan and I went to a hunting club where the members took turns doing the cooking. I just tagged along to do some bird watching. The gentleman who invited us was supposed to do the cooking that weekend, but he ran off into the woods with Stan to shoot up a storm. That left a dozen of his completely incompetent male acquaintances, who were supposed to do the cooking with him, wondering what to do. Apparently, the gentleman in question thought he could return at 4 p.m. and cook for four hundred guests in two hours, the idiot. I think he was a banker." Kitty's voice trailed off.

"And?" asked Barb quietly.

"They hadn't planned a meal or bought anything to feed the throngs. Someone had to take control, so I did. I commandeered the treasurer of the club and drove to the nearest town and bought a hundred and thirty pounds of roastable meat cut into fork-sized chunks, fifty pounds of potatoes, and another fifty of carrots, and onions, and a hundred heads of lettuce."

Kitty was out of breath, "... I made up the recipe on the spot. We bought twenty gallons of cheap red wine and as much in apple cider vinegar. Fortunately, they also had enough bay leaves, mustard, cloves, and juniper berries to make it work." Kitty stopped and smiled.

"I can smell it already," said Barb.

"You know, I don't know why they had juniper berries in a supermarket. I've never seen juniper berries in a supermarket since. Hmmm, interesting!" Kitty shook her head.

"And?" said Barb impulsively.

"Well," said Kitty with renewed energy, "I put the men to work peeling potatoes and carrots. Then I boiled the meat, wine, vinegar, and spices, for a few minutes, then put the giant pots in the walk-in icebox to marinate." Kitty had to stop and catch her breath.

Barb smiled and licked her lips, "Mmm."

"Normally you'd let them marinate for a couple of days ... but with small chunks ... I thought it would be delicious after a couple of hours and it was, surprise, surprise. We braised the meat, carrots, and potatoes just in time for dinner."

"Bravo," said Barb, clapping her hands quietly.

"I got a standing ovation," said Kitty, who paused, obviously proud and pleased with the memory. "That made me decide to become a chef. I would never have gotten my chef's license if I hadn't cooked that sauerbraten. I'm glad I did. It was a wonderful experience," Kitty's voice trailed off.

"And tasty, too, I'll bet," said Barb softly.

Kitty was thinking and talking in spurts, one minute she would be animated, and another she'd be drifting off to sleep. It was hard on Barb. It was after 4 p.m. before Barb realized that neither she nor Kitty had eaten anything. When she mentioned it to a nurse who came by to check Kitty's vital signs, Barb learned that Kitty had refused all solid food and was being fed by an IV drip of glucose. When Kitty appeared fast asleep, Barb snuck off to the cafeteria and bought a sandwich.

It was after 9 p.m., and Kitty had not woken since falling asleep that afternoon. When a nurse came by and offered Barb a cot, she realized that she should go home. "How much time does she have?" Barb asked the nurse quietly in case Kitty might hear.

The nurse nodded to Barb to follow her into the corridor, "It's hard to tell. Her vital signs are good; there is no serious sign that her liver or other organs are involved yet. Of course, it's only matter of time, and once we see liver failure, she'll go quickly. She'll be all right tonight."

Barb breathed a sigh of relief, "If she wakes in the middle of the night tell her I'll be back in the morning. Okay?" The nurse nodded.

❧

The smell of fresh coffee and the sweet smell of warm spring air drifting through the house woke Barb earlier than she planned. Vince, who heard Barb stirring, hurried upstairs with a cup of coffee. "How's she doing?" he asked.

"She's on an IV tube," said Barb, "and she's fading in and out. She'll wake up, tell me a story, then fall asleep almost as soon as she finishes it. It's hard ...."

"I know," said Vince. "Are you going back today?"

"Of course," said Barb. "I don't know how long she's got. She's not eating or drinking anything. The nurse says a week maybe." Vince nodded quietly, "I made you a lunch."

It was a beautiful sunny, and warm spring morning, the thermometer by the back door said it was 75 degrees Fahrenheit or about 24 Celsius. Barb would never get used to metric temperatures. All she could remember was that ten was bearable and 25 was warm, and it snowed at 0 or below. Every time she looked at the thermometer on her back porch, it made her think about thinking in metric. Grrr, she thought as she got in her car, which showed both miles and kilometers per hour on the speedometer. Since the road signs had been posted in metric for more than 20 years she had gotten used to them but temperature, never. She was still debating the merits of the metric vs. the English system as she pulled into the parking lot of the Shiretown nursing home.

It had been a pleasant drive. Now, as she entered the nursing home, the smell of disinfectant mixed with other, far more unpleasant, odors reminded her of her mission and a sudden wave of depression overwhelmed her springtime euphoria. As she entered Kitty's room, she had expected to find Kitty alone and unconscious. Instead, she found her sitting almost upright in bed chatting nonchalantly with a group of nearly a dozen women and several men. Barb recognized most of them: the Pictou ladies, as Kitty called them. They were the members of the various boards Kitty had been on at one time or another, the social elite of the county. Dr. MacKenzie was there as were the mayor of Pictou and his wife, and good old Harvey Veniot, former politician and a local judge. "No soft soap with Harvey A., vote him in election day." Barb always giggled at his campaign slogan and the soap dishes he handed out. His soap dish still did its job in Barb's upstairs bathroom thirty years later.

"Royalty," exclaimed Barb with a smile as she waved to Kitty from the door. Kitty waved her in.

"You all know my great friend Barbara I assume," said Kitty. There was a rumbling of acknowledgment that made Barb feel more than a little self-conscious. "Well," said Kitty, "I assume you all have places of importance to go to, so please don't let an old lady keep you from your posts."

Dr. MacKenzie was the first to step up. He put his hand on Kitty's and said, "Do let me know if you feel any discomfort. I've left explicit instructions to be sure that you are in no pain."

"I'm fine," said Kitty, "I'm feeling no pain, but I've lost my appetite, which is a little disappointing don't you think?"

Dr. MacKenzie laughed and patted Kitty on her arm as he

turned to leave. A reception line formed and one by one the gentlemen and "Pictou Ladies" said their goodbyes. When the last of them left the room, Kitty turned her head towards Barb and said, "I don't expect to see any of them again before my funeral." She laughed as she shook her head. Barb laughed too, sort of.

Behind Barb, a familiar voice boomed, "Catherine, I shall not abandon ya in yer hour of need." It was Mandy Betts.

Barb turned to look and felt an immediate urge to protect Kitty from the intrusion.

Kitty put her hand on Barb's arm to restrain her, "It's okay, Barb. Mandy was here all night."

"I'm startin' the vigil," said Mandy in her slight brogue. "I'm here for anything Kit wants, temporal or spiritual."

Kitty pulled Barb over and said in a whisper loud enough for Mandy to hear, "I'm not sure if she's here to watch me become a ghost or to prevent me from becoming a ghost."

Barb looked shocked. She couldn't talk about death, Kitty's death, so cavalierly.

Mandy laughed, "Your spirit will do as it pleases I'm sure, I'm here for your soul."

"Well you can't have it just yet," said Kitty. "I'm not done with it. Shall I put in a good word for you?" Kitty smiled without sarcasm in her voice. Mandy blushed.

"I'll be going home for a rest. Barbara can spell me for a bit," said Mandy as she packed her bag and hurriedly left the room.

When they were alone, Kitty said to Barb, "She's okay, she means well."

Barb rolled her eyes. They sat in silence.

"I had a nightmare last night. I realized then that there was nothing between me and eternity. I was at the edge of a bottomless cliff, and I couldn't look because I was being drawn into the void. *L'appel du vide.* It was frightening, but I have to face it."

Barb nodded, "So you don't mind Mandy being here? I was going to ask the nurses to shoo her away."

"I don't mind her anymore," said Kitty with a sigh as she looked away.

"I packed a bag," said Barb, "so I can stay with you, my little valise; it's in my car."

Kitty turned back, smiled, and said wistfully, "A little valise. I haven't told you all my stories yet, but then I don't think I have enough time ... but then who does?" She paused thoughtfully then said, "I don't think I regret anything I've done in my life. I only really regret the things I haven't done." She paused again, "I regret that I never sang at the Met in New York. That's the only thing I ever wanted to do was to sing at the Metropolitan Opera House. People should hold on to their dreams. Look at me, I'm almost 80 and almost dead, and the only thing I really regret is not fulfilling a dream I had when I was ten years old."

"Where did that come from?" asked Barb.

"When I was in the convent," said Kitty, "one of the nuns told me I had the voice of an angel. She played a recording of La Bohème. Opera was the only music allowed in the convent beside liturgical music. It was magic. That's all I have ever wanted to do, sing like an angel."

"Why didn't you?" asked Barb.

"Well," said Kitty wearily, "the war came along, then Stan came along, then the kids ....

"When Stan went broke we really were broke, and I suppose we might have been homeless but for the New Canaan cottage. Stan just gave up and died a year or so later, so I had to work."

"I never knew you were really that poor," said Barb. "Everyone here thinks you're rich."

"I've never thought of myself as poor," said Kitty with a look of astonishment on her face. "I've always found a way. Well, except for singing at the Met. I never found a way to do that, but then I'm not sure I really had the talent." Kitty shrugged and yawned and said, "I have always had everything I need, and I've wanted very little."

When Kitty drifted off to sleep, Barb fetched the overnight bag from her car and prepared herself for a long vigil. Nurses came and went every hour or so, checking Kitty's vital signs and fluid levels in the bottles hanging from the hook above her head. The curtains had been drawn, and the lights were off, giving the impression of gloomy twilight in the room leaving little hint of the brilliant spring day beyond. The sullen atmosphere had lulled Barb into the kind of stupor she usually experienced only during a long, boring sermon in church.

A sensor dislodged itself while Kitty was tossing and turning in the middle of a dream, sending the monitoring equipment into a paroxysm of alarms. The alarms so startled Barb that she stiffened her body and fell off the couch, hitting the floor with a loud curse just as the door swung open and a nurse came flying in to see what had happened. A disoriented Kitty woke with a start and, flailing around the bed, finally grabbed the raised sidebar with both hands. When Barb looked up, she saw Kitty, white as a sheet, staring back at her with eyes wide open and out of breath.

"Jesus, what happened?" exclaimed Barb.

Kitty relaxed her grip on the rail, took a deep breath, and said, "I don't know. I was dreaming, and all hell broke loose. Did we have an earthquake or something?"

"Kit, what you had," said the nurse laughing, "was a bad dream. You pulled your heart monitor loose, and the alarm went off."

"Perhaps we should dispense with this stuff," said Kitty holding up the wires leading away from her chest, "After all, you are not going to revive me if I drop dead this moment are you?" Kitty had a way of putting things that was both honest and sometimes overly blunt.

"Oh, I don't suppose," said the nurse whose voice trailed off before looking at Barb. "Would you like some supper? I see you haven't eaten anything today."

"Actually I am hungry," said Barb. "Kit would you like anything?"

"Perhaps a little beef consommé if they have it," said Kitty with a surprisingly strong voice.

The nurse smiled and left the room.

"Stan came for a visit last night," said Kitty in an offhand voice.

"Oh really?" asked Barb, nothing Kitty could say would surprise her now.

"Oh yes," said Kitty. "We had a lovely chat ... in French. I never knew Stan could speak such lovely French. He said you could learn anything if you put your mind to it, and I suppose he did. He said my parents were well. He said my mother was surprised that I was a master chef, and my father said I should have written a book. My father always said that."

Kitty had a faraway smile that Barb thought made her look like she was still in the middle of that dream or hallucinating. "Did Stan tell you what it's like?" asked Barb.

Kitty was swooning, "Oh, he said it was very pleasant, and that I shouldn't be worried; he said I should welcome the *l'appel du vide*. He said that I would love the flight from the edge of the cliff, that I would soar like a bird. Like an albatross, he said, but I don't think he meant it like the ancient mariner's albatross. I think he meant it metaphorically, that I would soar effortlessly. Hmmm, well, that wouldn't be metaphorical would it, if I could actually fly?"

Kitty looked confused for a moment.

"I've always loved birds and wondered what it would be like to fly. Yes, I think I would like to fly. I wonder if I can come back as a bird?" Kitty had a look of consternation. "I forgot to ask Stan which heaven was heaven, I mean is it the Buddhist, Catholic, or Protestant heaven? Maybe it's an Islamic heaven. No, it can't be that, I don't think Stan would like that, I know my father wouldn't put up with it. ... Whatever it is."

Barb was laughing at her.

"What?" protested Kitty.

"It sounds to me," said Barb with a teasing grin, "that a religious war is going on inside that noggin of yours. Who's winning?"

A fully awake Kitty smiled, "It's more of an artistic battle based on the aesthetics of what the hereafter might be." She paused, "Atheism doesn't offer much esthetically, a blank wall I suppose. I am much too simplistic to think that one has to pass through Dante's Hell before arriving at bliss. Dante's Hell always sounded too close to this." She waved a hand in the air, "and purgatory always sounded like the waiting room at Penn Station — no fun being there, just nearly eternal boredom and not much better than the atheist's void." She looked off dreamily, "If there's a heaven, and Stan says there is, I always pictured it as a garden in late spring, like now." Kitty looked around and for the first time noticed that the curtains were drawn. "Throw open the window, will ya Barb?"

Barb jumped up and pulled the curtains back. The bright afternoon light flooded the room, and both Kitty and Barb had to squint. "Open the window too, if you can," said Kitty. Barb obliged but the rush of air was cooler than both of them expected, and Barb quickly closed the window again. "That smelled great," said Kitty. "It's still early I guess."

"We've had frosts later than this," said Barb.

Kitty nodded and fell back in her bed, smiled and drifted back to sleep.

By the time an orderly arrived with a cup of beef consommé for Kitty and a plate of poutine for Barb, they were both sound asleep, Barb on the couch, Kitty in her bed. The orderly left the food on the card table, closed the curtains and turned off the light.

Kitty woke first. It was dark out, no light was seeping from behind the curtains, and the room was darkened enough to prevent Kitty from reading the clock on the wall. Kitty's mouth was dry, and she remembered the consommé she had asked for and wondered where it was. "Barb," she called in a voice just above a whisper.

"She's asleep, let's not wake 'er," said a quiet voice Kitty did not immediately recognize without turning up her hearing aids. "I'll help ya." It was Mandy Betts.

"Oh," said Kitty, "How long have you been here?"

"An hour or two," said Mandy.

"Where's Barb?" asked Kitty.

"Shhh, she's sleeping on the couch," said Mandy in a very quiet voice. "Let her sleep. What can I do for you?"

"I asked for some beef broth to wet me whistle," said Kitty. "I wonder if you could track it down."

Mandy moved closer to Kitty. "It's right here, it's cold, and there is a plate of cold poutine here, too. Did ya want that, too?"

"No, no," said Kitty, "just the broth."

"That's good," said Mandy, "because I ate the poutine. It was cold, too."

"That was for Barb," said Kitty a bit curtly.

"But it was cold; cold poutine is not very tasty," said Mandy a bit defensively.

"I suppose we can always ask for more," said Kitty in a resigned voice.

"I've been praying for you," said Mandy.

"Well, that's nice," said Kitty. "I suppose it can't hurt and you never know when it might be helpful."

Barb was awake now and had heard the last exchange. "Oh, great," she mumbled under her breath but loud enough for Mandy to hear.

"Ah, the dead have arisen," said Mandy with relish.

"What," said Kitty, "I'm not dead yet, and I don't need to get up.... I can't get up. Oh, but call the nurse, I do need my diaper changed."

Barb heard the exchange and burst into laughter. "Kit," she said between laughs, "You're not dead yet, but you are as deaf as a stone."

"I know that," said Kitty who had turned up the volume on her hearing aids. "What did I miss?"

"Nothing serious," said Mandy who was now standing next to Kitty stroking her hair gently and feeding her the cold consommé. "Barb," she continued, "I'll gladly stand watch overnight if you'd like to go home and get a good night's rest."

Barb was about to protest, but Kitty intervened, "Go ahead, Barb, get a good night's sleep. I plan to, and I'm not great company whilst snoring. ... And I don't think I'm ready to kick the bucket tonight," she added as an afterthought.

Barb thought about leaving Kitty in the hands of Mandy Betts and would have protested, but Kitty's smile put her at ease. "Get some rest," said Kitty in a squeaky voice. "I don't think you need to keep a vigil quite yet and ...." Her voice trailed off.

"Okay," said Barb reluctantly, "I'll be back early."

"I'll take good care of her," said Mandy, "really ... I will."

The drive home was uneventful, and Barb remembered none of it by the time she fell into bed. Her sleep was dreamless but deep, and Barb was surprised to wake up to the mid-spring sun burning its way into her bedroom at such an early hour. The clock said 5:12. Vince was still asleep. A sense of urgency drove Barb to the kitchen for a quick cup of coffee, then back on the road. It was approaching 7 a.m. when Barb pulled into the parking lot of the Shiretown Nursing Home. Mandy Betts' gaudy truck with its exclamations of Christian piety accompanied by dimly flashing Christmas lights was still sitting right where it had been the night before, in the most prominent parking place next to the main entrance. Somehow, Mandy had acquired a handicap parking permit and always parked in handicap zones with her Christmas lights flashing. The flashing lights were very dim, and Barb laughed at the thought of Mandy's soon-to-be-dead battery.

The door to Kitty's room was closed, so Barb went to the nurses' station first to ask if everything was all right. It was. The nurse laughed and described how Kitty had politely thrown Mandy out when she woke up to find Mandy holding what Kitty described to the nurse as a séance with some Pentecostal preacher. Kitty had pressed the nurses' call button and had announced very publicly that she had "soiled herself" and asked to be excused while the nurses cleaned her up. That had ended the séance and chased Mandy and her preacher out of the room. Kitty then told the nurse that she was not receiving visitors today.

"Oh, I'm sure she'll see me," said Barb a little hesitantly.

"I'm sure she will, but let's follow protocol, shall we? But before we go in, I should warn you that Kitty has taken a turn for the worst."

"Whatcha mean?" said Barb sounding more chipper than she felt.

The nurse said nothing as she led the way into Kitty's room.

Kitty assured Barb that the order against visitors only applied to Pentecostal missionaries holding séances. Then in a serious voice Kitty looked at Barb and said, "Look at me, Barb, I'm getting jaundiced. I'm turning yellow; that means that me liver is failing, and I cannot live long without me liver."

Barb had to stifle a laugh at Kitty's mock Scottish accent.

"Call the nurse in for me, would you Barb," said Kitty authoritatively.

When the nurse and Barb were standing in front of Kitty

she began, "I can tell from the way I feel that I'm only a day or so away from my ... my death. I guess there isn't a way to sugar coat it is there?"

Barb and the nurse stood in stunned silence, Barb nodded.

"I don't know how much longer I can stay conscious. I felt exactly like this just before I was hauled off to New Glasgow the last time." Kitty paused. "But I won't be going to New Glasgow this time, so I want to make my final arrangements. Is that okay?" Kitty looked at the nurse, she nodded. So did Barb. Kitty was still in command.

"Fine," said Kitty. "As soon as you think I might be ready to kick the bucket, I want you to call Dalhousie Medical School. In fact, I think you should call them now and tell them about the expected delivery of a fresh corpse." Everyone nodded. Kitty continued, "Barb, you know my desire to be delivered to Dalhousie and so does James, so please inform him of the status of my request as soon it's known."

"Yes ma'am," said the nurse. "Is there anything else?"

"Ordinarily I'd say 'that's all for now,'" said Kitty with a sigh, "but this time I think I'll have to say that's all period." Kitty punctuated her statement with a firm nod of her head and a coy satisfied smile.

"You sound like you're enjoying this," said Barb who was feeling a bit confused.

"Well, I suppose I am, in a way," squeaked Kitty. "This is a very new experience for me, and I am looking forward to being with Stan again, if that's possible. That would be splendid altogether." A dreamy smile came over Kitty's face, and she closed her eyes. "Make lemonade," she said in a whisper, "make lemonade."

The nurse motioned for Barb to come out to the hall.

"Once the liver begins to fail, death normally comes in less than 48 hours. I just thought you should know," said the nurse, and a few minutes later, "You can tell Kitty that I called Dalhousie; they'll be here with an ambulance the day after tomorrow which is about the right time frame, or sooner if the situation calls for it."

Over the next few hours, Kitty began to look worse. Her pallor moved from yellowed jaundice to an ashen light brown. She slept fitfully, but the slow decay of her body did not appear to affect her mind. At one point when Barb had her feet up reading a book and sipping tea, Kitty suddenly sat up and delivered a thoughtful monologue about Plato's description of the death of Socrates and how she could suddenly relate to Socrates because her legs were becoming numb. Barb didn't really know what Kitty was talking about, but she nodded furiously and made a mental note to tell Jimmy when he called, as he always did at almost exactly 6 p.m.

Kitty had drifted off to sleep, but seconds before the telephone rang she woke up and announced that 'James' would be calling. When the phone rang, she motioned to Barb to answer it. It was Jimmy, but before Barb held the phone up to Kitty's ear, she turned the volume on the amplified handset to maximum loudness because Kitty had taken her hearing aids out.

"Hello," said Kitty in a loud but very squeaky voice.

"How are you, Mom?" asked Jimmy.

"Well ... I'm dying," said Kitty emphatically.

"I know, Mom, I know," said Jimmy. Not knowing what to say he added quickly, "Shall we start a vigil?"

"I suppose it is appropriate," said Kitty, "but I don't want any maudlin presence at me death bed."

Barb could almost hear Jimmy laugh.

"No, Mom," said Jimmy quietly, "I'm sure the spirits would much prefer to dance on your grave than hold a somber vigil."

"It's the least I can do for my legacy," said Kitty growing obviously tired. "I need to go to sleep now."

"Okay Mom," said Jimmy with a tear in his voice, "Bon voyage then Mom, bon voyage."

"Bye, for now," said Kitty holding back a tear herself. "Bye, for now," she said again after Barb had hung up the phone. Kitty took a deep breath then said to Barb with surprising force, "I'm ready now."

Barb sat quietly next to Kitty who was crying softly. Kitty had been looking at the two photographs she had saved from the valise. She kissed the photograph of Sam Anderson and said, "Good night Sam, old buddy." She picked up the other photograph and waved it in the air as tears welled up in her eyes. It was Herman the vermin.

"I have one last story to tell you," said Kitty with a tired energy. "I've never told this to anyone, not even Stan, and I'm not sure I shouldn't take it to my grave." She paused.

"Then I don't need to hear it," said Barb quietly.

Kitty took a deep breath, "No, I think I need to tell it. It's part of my legacy, and that's all I have left.

"About a week after *Kristallnacht,* Herman showed up with tickets to the opera in Stuttgart. Sam didn't want to go so just Joe, Herman, and I got on the train. We had lots of time, so Joe bought us tickets on the slow train, not the express that we usually took. When the train pulled off on a siding for twenty minutes, as it always did, to let a freight train go past, I hopped off the train to walk back to the station to buy a pack of cigarettes. Herman came with me. When the freight train rumbled past us, I took Sophie's pistol from my purse and shot Herman in the chest. He fell under the freight train and ... oh, it was horrible."

Barb gasped quietly under her breath and put her hand on Kitty's.

Kitty shook her head, "I got back on the train and never said a word to Joe, and he didn't ask. No one ever asked about Herman. I've never told anyone."

Kitty began to cry, "It was war., damn it, it was war."

"I know," said Barb, not really knowing what to think, a tear rolled down Barbs cheek too.

They sat in silence for, what seemed like hours to Barb.

Finally, Kitty said, "Barb, tell the nurse that my back is aching, and I'd like some relief."

The nurse came in and injected something into the IV line running into Kitty's hand. Kitty smiled and thanked the nurse who smiled back and stroked Kitty's hair. When the nurse left, Kitty turned to Barb and managed to say "I think ...." before closing her eyes and falling into a deep unconsciousness. An hour later a different nurse came in and reattached the monitoring equipment Kitty had ordered removed several days before. Barb began to ask "why, " but the nurse interrupted her to say simply, "So we know." That left Barb speechless.

Night and day became a blur to Barb as she sat next to Kitty watching the monitor's hypnotic rhythm. Occasionally, Kitty would put up a fight. Then the heart and breathing monitor would come to life, but after a few minutes the effort would subside, and Kitty's breathing would become shallow again, and her heart rhythm would slow and occasionally skip a beat or two. Kitty was dying.

Periodically someone would bring Barb a sandwich, a cup of coffee, a pastry or a cup of tea. With equal predictability, Mandy Betts would pop in and offer to "spell" Barb, but she would have none of it. Barb was feeling stretched to her limit, even dozing on the couch next to Kitty was no longer refreshing. She was in the bathroom changing her clothing when she heard the rumble of male voices in Kitty's room. For days the voices had been female. Fearing the worst, she rushed from the bathroom still buttoning her shirt to see two burly emergency medical technicians with Dalhousie Medical School emblazoned on their uniforms.

"You can't have her yet," said Barb.

"I know," said the older of the two EMT's, "but we just wanted to assure the family that Dalhousie will be honored." Barb later couldn't remember exactly what they had said, but she was surprised at the formality.

Twelve hours later Barb was on the edge of total exhaustion. The nurses had continually offered Barb a bed in the neighboring room promising to wake her up if anything changed, but Barb had continually refused. Even Vince, who stopped by on his way home from work, was unable to convince Barb to sleep. Oddly, it was Mandy Betts who finally talked Barb into sleeping in the room next door. Mandy promised to keep watch and to wake Barb if anything happened. As much as Barb disliked Mandy, she believed in her kindness and trusted her word. Barb was sound asleep almost before her head nestled into the pillow. Mandy put her feet up on the couch next to Kitty, and within minutes the rhythmic pulse of the heart monitor put her to sleep, too.

The official time of death was put at 6:47 a.m., when the heart monitor recorded Kitty's last heartbeat, but it wasn't until almost 7:30 when a nurse entered Kitty's room and woke Mandy. Barb woke on her own when she heard the sound of male voices again next door. This time there was no rush. Barb knew what the sounds meant, and she was both sad and angry that she was not by Kitty's side as she took her last breath. Still, she had been there for her, and she didn't think Kitty would have minded her exhausted sleep.

As Barb walked in, the EMTs were already preparing to lift the corpse into a body bag, a task delayed only by the exchange of formal documentation and the arrival of the doctor on duty to sign the death certificate. Barb looked at the peaceful face of her friend, and when she brushed hair away from Kitty's face, she noticed that the body had already lost much of its warmth. The coolness of the corpse made her recoil.

Barb asked the nurse, "Have you phoned Maggie and Jimmy yet?"

"It's early still in Alberta, but I'll call Boston as soon as we're done here."

Barb nodded.

After the remains were placed in the body bag, zipped

up, placed on a gurney and covered with a thin blanket, the EMTs pushed and pulled the gurney to the loading dock. There were no ceremonies; the gurney was placed in the ambulance, the two technicians got in and drove off. Barb watched the ambulance as it drove down the driveway, turned onto the highway and disappeared as it crossed over the causeway.

Barb returned to the nurse's station in time to hear the call to Jimmy:

"Hello, is this James?" asked the nurse.

"Yes," came the disembodied voice.

"This is Margaret MacKenzie from the Shiretown home. Catherine asked me to tell you that she's on her way."

"Okay," said the voice after a long pause.

After a still longer pause, the nurse said, "Oh, good heavens, I mean your mother wanted me to tell you that after she passed on; the people from Dalhousie Medical School came and took her. She's on her way to Halifax right now."

"Okay, I got it, thank you," said the voice.

"And thank you," said Barb to the nurse when she had hung up.

"Will there be a service?" asked the nurse.

"I don't know," said Barb shaking her head. "I don't know."

The sun was hot but there was still a chill in the late spring air. The tulips were in bloom around the main entrance to the Shiretown nursing home, and an apple tree beyond the edge of the parking lot filled the spring air with its sweet smell. Barb shook her head as a tear ran down her cheek. Yes, she thought, it was a war, dam it, it was a war, and you won it Kit. You finally won.

Epilogue

Never Rest in Peace - June 1999

Mandy was beside herself. "No funeral? No chance to say goodbye? How can they be so ... so thoughtless?"

Barb was tired. She had been on the phone with both Maggie and Jimmy, and neither one of them wanted to have a funeral in Nova Scotia. Jimmy had even said, "She had a wake, isn't that enough?" Barb felt stuck in the middle between a family that wanted to get on with their lives, and Mandy who wanted something just short of a state funeral.

"They haven't even bothered to put a notice in The Pictou Advocate," said Mandy who felt very put out.

Mandy couldn't see Barb shrug on the other end of the phone line, but Barb felt a little cheated too so she said, "Well Mandy, Jimmy, and Maggie don't know that Kit had so many friends here that might like a memorial service so why don't you arrange it. I'll get an obituary together and send it in. OK?"

That mollified Mandy and after a loud "Humph," she agreed and hung up.

Barb called Jimmy back and told him that Mandy was going to arrange a memorial service for Kitty anyway.

"That's fine with me," said Jimmy. "Let me know when and I'll try to make it. By the way, I'm mailing you the obituary that was just printed in the New York Times; could you send it to the local papers?"

Mandy would have preferred to have a memorial service at the Pentecostal Church in Stellarton, but she knew better, she knew that few of Kitty's friends would attend. She also knew that Kitty occasionally attended the United Church in Scotsburn so when she called the rector and asked permission to hold a service for Kitty, she was pleased to be received warmly. The memorial service was scheduled for a Saturday two weeks hence.

A few days later the obituary arrived in the mail. Barb stopped at the library to make copies and drove to Pictou to drop one off at The Pictou Advocate, then off across the causeway to drop off another copy at the New Glasgow Evening News. She mailed a copy to the Halifax Chronicle Herald and, of course, to Mandy Betts. Mandy, in the mean time, had called the newspapers to add the date and location of the memorial service, should anyone wish to attend.

When the day arrived, Jimmy flew in early, rented a car, and arrived at the church a full two hours before the service. Maggie arrived twenty minutes later about the same time Barb, Vince, and the kids pulled into the parking lot. After saying hello to each other, they wondered privately if Mandy had indeed made the arrangements. A few minutes later Mandy arrived with her truck freshly strung with Christmas lights and a big sign that read "Kitty's memorial" hung from the side. Mandy parked where the sign would be most visible from the road.

As they waited for the expected crowd to arrive, Jimmie and Maggie sat in stony silence in the front row of the church with Barb, Vince, and the kids right behind. The altar was unadorned save for a small picture of Kitty that Maggie had taken when the two of them were in Budapest during some festival where confetti had covered the onlookers like a fresh blanket of snow. Mandy served as the usher, greeting everyone who entered. Neither Jimmy nor Maggie turned to face the parishioners but kept their attention on the small smiling face on the altar.

Finally, after what felt like hours, the rector of the United church rose to the lectern and greeted those in attendance. He admitted that he was new to the parish and had not known Kitty very well. However, he had been assured by his parishioners that she had indeed been an upstanding member of the church and that, as far as he knew, she was the only member of his church to be made a lifetime member of the national United Church Women's Association, a high honor indeed.

Both Jimmy and his sister Maggie snickered audibly at the mention of their mother's alleged religious piety. Barb, who heard the snicker, gently poked Jimmy in the back and quietly hissed, "shhh."

After the greeting and invocation, Mandy assumed the role of master of ceremonies introducing one cleric after another, each of whom agreed what a fine Christian woman Catherine Stevenson had been and what a pity it had been that they had not had the chance to get to know her fully. Barb only remembered seeing a few of the characters that claimed to have known Kitty but then again, Mandy had been sneaking in to see Kitty whenever Barb left. That angered Barb, but Kitty had never said anything. Still, she felt annoyed.

Barb was getting bored and could tell that Jimmy was too because he kept nodding off. Barb poked him more than once after which he would half turn to her and nod. Maggie stayed awake. Finally, Mandy announced that the benediction would be read by the Reverend Angus MacDougall, senior pastor of the Shelburne Pentecostal Baptist Church of the New Covenant.

Angus MacDougall was a tall wisp of a man, slightly bent over as might be expected of a man who had spent most of a lifetime inside a coal mine before being born again in the Spirit and becoming a full-time preacher. His eloquence was tempered only by a limited vocabulary and by a Cape Breton accent so thick it would give a Highland Scot pause. Before he began the benediction, he confessed his own experience of the magnificent Christian spirit of Catherine Stevenson. He said, "I think I was the last one here to see Catherine alive, and I asked her, 'Catherine do you have any religious stirrings?' and she said to me, 'Yes reverend I do. I consider myself a lapsed Unitarian'."

Postscript

Ashes to Ashes - July 2006

On most days Jimmy didn't think about his mother. After all, it had been, what, six, no seven years since she had been "on her way to Halifax." He still giggled over that whenever he thought of her. "Halifax" was his new code name for purgatory, a joke he shared only with his family. If he had to stay late at work he had to stay in "Halifax," or if a client complained, he had a "problem in Halifax." If his kids were annoying, he'd threaten to "send them to Halifax." He even yelled at a co-worker once to "go to Halifax."

Now he stood dumbfounded, holding a piece of mail he had just retrieved from his mailbox: a plastic bag addressed to him and marked "For Postal Use Only." The bag contained a mangled letter with the return address "Dalhousie Medical School" clearly visible through the plastic. The Canadian postal indicia, also visible through the plastic displayed a date almost three years in the past.

Nearly one third of the letter was missing but Jimmy was able to reconstruct its message: It thanked the family for its donation and announced that the school was finished with the remains, and should the family wish to reclaim said remains it should get in touch with the school within three months otherwise said remains would be cremated and the ashes disbursed in a Potters field within the medical school courtyard.

Jimmy thought about calling Dalhousie Medical School but never did. What would he have said anyway?

DALHOUSIE
UNIVERSITY

"HERE LIE THE MORTAL REMAINS OF THOSE WHO DONATED THEIR BODIES
TO THE FURTHERANCE OF MEDICAL SCIENCES AT DALHOUSIE UNIVERSITY.
BEYOND THE SPHERE OF EARTHLY LIFE, THEY HAVE GIVEN
OF THEMSELVES FOR THE GOOD OF OTHERS."